I0615809

After The Dance

Lindy Larsen, Volume 2

Gayle Siebert

Published by Idyllbeck Opportunities, 2021.

After The Dance – ©Gayle Siebert 2021

This book is a work of fiction. Names, places, characters and incidents are either products of the author's imagination or are used fictitiously. Any resemblance to actual persons, either living or dead, events or locales is entirely coincidental.

Gayle Siebert

www.gaylesiebert.com[1]

https://www.facebook.com/gaylescaprice/

Cover by Miblart.

Author's photo by www.ckellyphoto.com[2]

Idyllbeck Opportunities

Nanaimo, British Columbia, Canada

---

1. http://www.gaylesiebert.com

2. http://www.ckellyphoto.com

To Lorna, Patricia and Brian.

Thank you.

Also by Gayle Siebert:

Novels
The Pillerton Secret
The Dark River Secret
The Bear Mountain Secret
The Spirit Bear Secret
Silver Buckles
Wembly
Call Me Lisa
The Feeder

NOVELLAS
Astrid
Where The Mule Grazed

One

I SLOW THE bus and turn into the pick-up lane, pulling to a halt at the curb where there's a queue of raucous, jostling students. As usual, the biggest boys are at the front of the line. Why is getting on the bus first such a big deal? Just so they can get the seats at the back? The smaller kids don't want to be back there anyway so the seats would be theirs even if they were the last to get on.

I pull the lever and the door opens with a hiss. The boys vault up the stairs without glancing my way and thunder down the aisle, pushing and shoving and squawking. The smaller kids climb on, only slightly more orderly. The teacher follows the last student to the door and says, "Hi, Lindy. John Henry will be a couple more minutes. He's having a chat with Bob."

"Thanks, Marg." I nod and settle back to wait. John Henry had to go to the principal's office again. I know he's a problem, but why can't they deal with it during school hours so the rest of the kids don't have to wait? I've got a schedule and would like to keep to it. Well, if nothing else, filling in until they find a permanent driver has given me a new appreciation for all that Red had to deal with when she was driving.

The kids are screaming. Something hits the floor with a thump. A girl shrieks, "Get off me!" I look down the aisle. The offender is immediately obvious. "Terry," I call out, "can't you see that seat's taken?"

Terry smiles and shrugs. "Sorry, Ms. Larsen," he says, and goes back to the empty seat across the aisle.

A white pickup truck pulls to the curb in front of the bus just as I turn around. The driver gets out and comes up beside my window. I slide it open and say, "Hi Jake. What's up?"

"Saw the bus was still sittin' here so I thought I'd swing in and say hi," he says, giving me the wide grin that always reminds me of Nick. "Someone late?"

"Yeah. I don't know how Red managed to keep to a schedule. Some of these kids have chores to do at home, and here we sit."

"How's she doin', anyway? Red, I mean. She gonna be back drivin' soon?"

"She's doing okay, not on crutches anymore, but she's decided to give up driving. I was only filling in while Red was away so that'll be it for me, too. The new guy can't start for a couple weeks." I spot John Henry coming out of the school and strolling toward the bus. "Look at that kid! He's kept us all waiting. You'd think he could hustle, wouldn't you?"

"Ay-yuh. You'd think. But then he wouldn't be such a cool dude." He lifts his cowboy hat and scratches the top of his head, then smooths his hair and resettles the hat. "I, um, you goin' to the dance over at the community center tomorrow night?"

"I, er..."

"Would you though? Go to the dance, I mean? With me? Please? I know you don't like the drive-in movies but I thought you might like to dance. It wouldn't have to be like a date. Just a couple friends goin' out together. No pressure."

Just then John Henry comes clattering up the steps and past me, stirring squawks and hisses from everyone as he goes by. More chaos erupts from the back of the bus. I know without looking that he's bullying his way into a seat instead of taking one closer to the front, causing a mass reshuffling. That's John Henry. I sigh, pull the lever to close the door, then turn back to Jake. "Okay."

"Oh yeah?" He stands taller and takes a step closer. Grinning, he says, "good! Starts at eight. I'll pick you up at seven?"

"How about I meet you there?"

"Oh. Sure, I guess. If you'd rather."

"Saves you a bunch of driving."

"I don't mind."

"No, it's all right."

"Okay. If you're sure?"

"I'm sure."

He backs away a couple of steps, shrugs and says, "See you there, then."

"See you there." I smile, close the window, put the bus in gear and steer it away from the curb. When I check the mirrors, I see him standing in the middle of the lane watching the bus leave.

Jake came to town a few years before I did but like me, he's still considered a newcomer and people would tell you he lives on the old Prentice place, as if everyone knows where that is. Maple Creek isn't big, just a couple thousand including the sparsely-populated ranches surrounding it, so newcomers stand out. Unlike myself, though, he's well known because of his businesses: he raises and sells hay, and buys and sells second-hand implements. Nothing new or big, just mowers and manure spreaders, stuff like that.

Jake is so much like Nick: tall, fair-haired, a rancher and he is—or was—a rodeo rider, too. I'm both put off and drawn to him because of it. I tell myself I agreed to go to the dance to get to know him better and see if I'm only attracted to him because he reminds me of my first love. It's only one date, and not really a date at that. I don't want to rush into anything. Things went too far too fast with Brett and fell apart just as fast. I won't let that happen again.

I first saw Jake shortly after I started working at the bank last fall. I happened to look up over my typewriter just as he walked through the door and for a heartbeat I thought it was Nick. It hit me like a punch in the stomach. How is it even possible to have a reaction like after all this time? It's not like I don't know he's dead. I was at his funeral, after all.

Josie had turned away from her teller station for a moment, happened to see me, and came to my desk to ask what was wrong. I couldn't tell her. I escaped to the ladies room and had a little cry before I could calm myself enough to get back to work.

Well-meaning people tell me grief lasts a year, the implication being there's something wrong with me because I still grieve for Nick. Not all the time, of course, and it doesn't always sabotage me like that. It's just that once in a while it blindsides me. Marriage did nothing to banish it. If anyone was to ask, I'd tell them grief lasts as long as it lasts.

After that I started noticing Jake around town. At the feed store. At the rodeo. And of course when he comes to do his banking. I'm not a teller, though, so I'm not at the counter but at a desk in back, and we never actually come face to face. The first words we spoke to each other were when he was coming out of the bank just as I was going back in after lunch. We made eye contact as he held the door for me. I said thank you. He said you're welcome. That's it.

A few weeks later I was at the check-out in the Field's store buying underwear for the boys when he came up beside me, pack of T-shirts in hand. We paid for our purchases and walked back to our vehicles together, talking about what a cold spring it had been and how late the pastures were greening up. That's right. My first chance to talk to this beautiful man and I wasted it talking about the weather. Such a cliché! But I had just gotten together with Brett and we were still in the can't-keep-our-hands-off-each-other stage. Sure, I thought Jake was drop-dead gorgeous, but I never would have done more than look.

At the rodeo in the summer, he came and sat in the bleachers with me. Well, not really with me but with our group. Stu knew him slightly from back in his rodeo days, and introduced him to every-one. I talked to him a little, just joined in the conversations of the group really, but didn't pay much attention. I was mostly watching Brett, who was all over Diane of the Double D's and that's not the name of her ranch. Poor Diane, she can't get shirts to fit. That snap in the middle of those fun jugs just will not stay closed. Shortly after that Brett and I split up. In retrospect, it would've been a good time to hook up with Jake and give Brett a dose of his own medicine.

Anyway, within a week of Brett and me splitting up, Jake was waiting for me outside the bank and asked me to go to the drive-in with him. That's the thing about small towns, everyone knows every-one else's business, especially who's sleeping with who. If you believe the gossip there's always been wife swapping, but in The Eighties it's gone wild. Or maybe it's just more out in the open now. Seems risky because husbands don't always get their wives back. Maybe that's the point.

I imagine Jake suggested a drive-in instead of lunch or at least coffee because he was anxious to see a re-run of Smoky and the Ban-dit, or maybe he just wanted to patronize the drive-in so it wouldn't close down like so many have thanks to everyone having a VCR you can rent movies for right at the Safeway, or maybe just because there's isn't much to do in a small town. But a drive-in movie with a man I barely knew? I tried unsuccessfully not to be offended, and declined. Besides, after Brett, I promised myself a year of being on my own.

Some inner part of me must have decided that although it hasn't been a year and in fact it's only been a few months, it's time. Meeting Jake at the hall instead of having him pick me up eliminates the pos-sibility of anything going too far too after the dance. Sexual revolu-tion be damned.

Two

"**F**OR GOD'S SAKE, Red, would you sit down? You didn't come to clean my kitchen, did you? Relax and enjoy your coffee." I'm perched on a stool at the island with a steaming mug warming my hands.

Red turns to look at me and says, "you know I like to be busy."

"Well, I'm starting to think you have a low opinion of my housekeeping. Although I'll be the first to admit you're right. For some reason, I don't think it's all that important anymore. There's days I don't even make the bed."

"Nor do the laundry, from the look of yer jeans." She points at my legs.

"What's the point of washing them when they'll just get dirty again the next day? Besides. You guys are always telling me this part of the country is considered desert. I'm conserving water."

"We got a good well. You can run yer damn washing machine."

"Yes, mother."

Red snorts, gives the counter next to the sink one last swipe, then wrings out the dishrag, pulls out the under-sink towel rack and puts it away. She pours a fresh mug of coffee and comes to sit on the stool across from me.

"It's good you won't have to drive the school bus no more, but asking fer more hours at the bank? If they give 'em to you, how will you have time, what with the ranch and you doin' so much with your mom's business 'n' the winery 'n' the farm store yer tryin' to start up? And the days you spend up in Calgary workin' fer your mom—would the bank give you time off every month for that?"

"I'd keep doing that weekends. I'm worried about that mad cow thing. You know they've been testing for it for a few years now. There's talk of quarantines, and that herd south of the border was euthanized."

"It's a worry, I admit."

"That's why I want more hours at the bank. And it would be good to diversify, in case we lose our herd like that."

"We got diversity. We got them little spuds 'n' we got wine 'n' we got rhubarb jam 'n' saskatoon jam to git made up fer the fairs 'n' we got the pies fer Marie's store. You got plenty on yer plate. We're not doin' bad or I wouldn't of gave up drivin' the school bus." She tucks a stray lock of salt-and-pepper hair behind her ear.

"I know."

For a moment the only sounds are us quietly sipping our coffee, and the odd whinny from the horses in the near pasture. Finally Red says, "Sittin' havin' coffee's when I miss smokin' the most. 'S why I got up to do somethin'." She shrugs, takes a sip of coffee and leans forward on her elbows. "How was the bus run yesterday? You never said nuthin' about it."

"It was a little busy around here when I saw you last night so we never had chit-chat time. At least Diamond's okay this morning. Damned colic, always such a worry. That horse! Gonna be another fat vet bill. Next time, I think we'll just shoot him."

"You know you won't do that! Yer father's horse? You couldn't pull the trigger 'n' I doubt Stu could neither."

"I know. Why can't he be more like Petey? Ten Peteys are less trouble than one Diamond. If a horse gets out on the road, it's Diamond. If a horse gets its foot stuck in the fence, it's him. If a horse gets a foxtail abscess in his mouth, it's him. If anything goes wrong with a horse around here, why is it always him?"

"Attracts trouble, just like his previous owner," Red says, and chuckles. "Don't look at me like that! You know very well what yer father was like."

"I know. Still wish I could've had more time with him though."

"Well..."

"I know what you're going to say, Stu's right, if he'd lived any longer he likely would've lost this place in a poker game."

Red shrugs. We sit in silence as a couple of minutes tick by, each lost in bittersweet memories. I'm musing about how different my life would be if that happened.

Then Red says, "Anyway, much as the paycheque was nice, I sure don't miss driving that bus! And you never did answer me about how it went yesterday."

"Morning was okay. Afternoon too. Had to wait on John Henry, that's all. He was in the principal's office after school again." I drain my mug, then spot a dying leaf on the aspidistras next to the pepper-mill and pull it off.

"That thing's gittin' a little shy on leaves," Red says, indicating the potted plant with a lift of her chin. "Only you could kill one a them."

"My brown thumb. Good thing I do office work instead of tending the rhubarb patch," I agree. "But there's something else I wanted to tell you, Red. Jake Jordan came up to the bus while I was waiting for John Henry and asked me to the dance at the community center tonight."

"He asked you out again? He must have a hide like a rhinoceros, askin' you out after pissin' you off about the drive-in. So damn stupid he'd ask you to go to a drive-in movie on yer first date 'n' you barely knowin' each other?"

"Maybe it wasn't so bad. Maybe he's just, er, a social klutz. Uncle Stu would've said something if there was something sketchy about him. They've known each other for so long Jake still calls him Porky."

"Well, that sure don't endear him to Stu. 'N' I don't think he knew him all that good. I was around then, remember, 'n' I didn't know him good."

I dig around in the plant a bit more, pull off another yellowing leaf, then lock eyes with Red and say, "I said I'd meet him there."

"What? You said you'd go? Well," Red says. She takes a sip of coffee and then asks, "How come he ain't pickin' you up?"

"He offered."

Red's brow puckers for a moment, then she says, "Oh, I see."

"Yeah. So. What do you think? Would you and Stu come along? Your leg's good enough now you can dance." I continue before Red can voice objections: "That way, we can leave early. You know, you can say your leg's bothering you. If it turns out I like him, you know, *that way,* and wouldn't mind spending some alone time with him after the dance, you guys can leave without me."

"So we'd be doin' you a favour."

"But it's not just for me. I think you guys would have fun, too. Probably be lots of other people we know there, and when's the last time you were off the ranch other than to get groceries?"

"Hmmm," Red says, squeezing her eyes shut. Then she shrugs.

"So you see? You need to get out. I need an excuse to leave early. It's a win-win."

"Makes sense I guess. When d'ya wanna leave?"

"Not too late. Starts at eight. So, seven-thirty?"

"Okay." Red finishes her coffee and gets up. "More coffee?"

"Ahh, no, I'm coffee'd out. Besides, the boys are going to ride out to the community pasture to check on the pairs. I said I'd go with them, just for the ride, so they're bringing Chica in for me. I'm looking forward to the ride, but I also don't like them going out there on their own in case they decide to practice sorting pairs or think they can train those green horses to be cutting horses and keep the calves away from their moms. Last time they did that they got the whole herd riled up."

"What? My boys?"

"Naw, not your boys. The boys they turn into when the devil gets in 'em," I say, and chuckle. "They're good kids, you know I love 'em. Anyhow, we're leaving pretty quick so I should get a move on."

"Great weather right now, but I don't like the looks of the sky up north. Dunno if you should go all the way to the community pasture."

"We might not get that far. Don't worry, we'll keep an eye on the sky. Anyhow, a little rain never hurt anyone. We're not made of sugar, you know."

"They're sayin' on the radio we're in for snow, though." Red takes her mug and mine to the dishwasher and finds a spot for them inside, then turns, leans against the cupboards and looks back at me. "You know, Lindy," she says, "you may be playin' with fire, startin' somethin' with Jake."

"It's just a date, Red, it's not starting something. And I'm taking it slow this time. I know you and Uncle Stu never really took to Brett, and you were right about him. Anyhow, despite what you think, I'm smarter now."

"It's nuthin' to do with bein' smart. Smart people can have low self-esteem. A person needs to be okay alone before they're any damn good in a relationship..."

"I don't have low self esteem and I *am* okay."

"There I go, preachin' at you again!" Red studies me for a moment, then pushes away from the counter and heads to the door. "You need to get off the ranch worse'n I do 'n' I guess we all deserve some fun. I hope this dance tonight ain't too highfalutin. You know I got nuthin' to wear but jeans."

"Well, it's a country band at the community center, Red. All you need is polished boots and a clean shirt."

"Clean jeans wouldn't hurt neither."

"I'll be back in time to do laundry.

Three

WE MOVE PAST the corrals, heading up the trail to the windmill, our horses marching along in a purposeful, ground-covering walk, the dogs trotting one ahead and two beside us. I'm on my Paint mare. Charlie and Johnny are on geldings that Stu outbid the meat buyer for at the auction over in Weyburn a couple of months ago.

The boys are putting miles on the horses to get them ready for adoption. Thank heavens for those two! They're just boys, but decent riders already, having ridden Nick's horse Petey everywhere practically since they were old enough to walk. Nothing fazes them, not even being piled off in rattlesnake country. Without them it would be difficult to find homes for rescue horses and we'd end up with more horses than cattle on the ranch. Stu and his big heart. Besides Petey and Diamond, we have a couple of other retired rodeo horses, and it never fails, he takes cattle to the auction and comes home with horses any time there's a meat buyer bidding on them.

The boys don't remember much about their lives before they came to live on the ranch, and are cowboy through and through. They've both been in the sheep riding at the Maple Creek rodeo. Charlie even got in on the steer riding this year, and stayed on to the horn. Can't wait until he's old enough for the bull riding. They got Stu's old rigging cleaned up, and as soon as they get a chute built Charlie will get his chance, on cows, anyway. It's a sure thing Johnny won't want to be left out of that. Thinking about them riding cows was bad enough, then one day Stu came home from the auction with an emaciated humpy-backed bull. He said when he spotted a Brahman in the kill pen he thought, *what's a bucking bull doing here?* One look at the glimmer of fire in the old bull's eyes told him he hadn't given up. He couldn't let him go on the meat truck.

The kids were ecstatic, dreaming of all the practice they'll get once Stu decides they're old enough to ride that bull. My guts clench every time I think about it. In my mind, bull riding is the worst rodeo event there is. I don't understand how the crowds are so crazy for it. Maybe it's the danger. A sort of gladiator sport. Thankfully progress on the bucking chute is slow and it won't be finished until next spring after work on the new farmgate store building is done. Cows are bad enough, but the bull? It's got to be ten years before the boys are old enough. The bull might be dead by then and with luck, the boys will have gone on to other interests.

Not likely, Stu said when I voiced that hope. He assured Red and me that the bull is as tame as a kitten, far better for them to ride him than one of our herd bulls. He claims he must be a lousy bucker or he wouldn't have been at the auction. He was careful not to say that within earshot of the kids, of course.

Damn you men! You're nothing but adrenalin junkies, I told him. *And that's why you love us,* he had replied. I can't deny I've never been drawn to any guy as I was to the cowboy I met that long-ago summer.

The tall grass along the corral fence is parched and pale as it was at the end of the few brief months I had with him. As so often happens when I'm riding out, my thoughts turn to that summer, and Nick. Our emotions had the intensity of youth: the highs so high, the lows, in the basement. It feels like another lifetime. Everything since, even my marriage. My divorce. Brett. Barely touched me. Everything seems bland and colorless, as dull and beige as the bucking bull and the prairie in the fall.

A north breeze springs up, its chill edge breaking into my thoughts. I put my reins in my teeth and zip up my jacket.

We pass the last corral and are heading east toward the low hills that mark the start of the Badlands, when Charlie says, "Wonder what's raising that." He points to a cloud of dust billowing up over the brow of the hill half a mile ahead.

As if in answer there's a bellow and half a dozen cows with calves comes charging over the hill toward us, followed by the old beige, tame-as-a-kitten Brahman bull. We rein our horses to a stop. They watch the approaching herd intently, heads high and ears pricked.

"Someone leave a gate open?" I ask. "We can't let them run into the yard or they'll end up out in the road. We have to turn them before they get to the lane. Johnny, go open the corral gate so we can drive them in and stay there so you can turn them if they try to go around you."

Johnny turns his horse and digs him with his heels, setting off at a gallop to the gate two hundred meters away.

The little herd slows as it nears us and starts to turn away from the corrals. "Charlie!" I yell, "Go head them back toward me. I'll stop them getting into the lane and head them toward Johnny."

Charlie pulls his lasso off the saddle and gallops away, circling back up beside the herd, swinging his coiled rope, hazing them back toward me and the corral. I dig my heels into Chica's sides and she leaps up beside the bull to block the lane and keep him heading in the right direction while Charlie rides back and forth behind them. With the help of the dogs, we manage to herd them toward Johnny.

Johnny has opened the gate and is back on his horse a dozen meters to the side of it, ready to turn the small group into the corral. The first cow reaches the gate, stops and eyes Johnny. She starts to go to his right but he reins his horse over. The horse responds quickly to cut the cow off. She tries to go between Johnny and the gate, but the horse spins and leaps back in front of her again. Now the cow spots the open gate and hurries through, her calf right beside her. The rest of the cow-calf pairs follow her into the corral.

The bull stops, looks around, and bellows. Charlie whistles and one of the dogs darts in to nip at his heel. He paws, and charges off a dozen meters or so, then bellows and paws some more. Seeing the three riders and the dogs closing in, he turns and bolts through the gate into the corral. Johnny pushes his horse up against the gate to close it, then leans over to secure it.

"Good work, guys!" I exclaim. "Johnny, that horse of yours has some cow!"

"Yeah," Johnny agrees, "It was like he knew what I wanted him to do. I didn't hardly have to do nuthin'. Maybe I can keep him."

"Anything."

"Anything?"

"You didn't have to do anything."

"No, I never," Johnny agrees.

"No, you *didn't*." Johnny looks at me and tilts his head. I click my tongue and shrug. They're going to speak the way all the cowboys they idolize do no matter how often I correct them. Maybe it's a lost cause. I study Johnny's earnest little face, the joy shining in his eyes as he rubs the horse's withers, and tell him, "Maybe you can keep him. You work that out with your Dad."

He looks up and says, "Maybe you could, um, tell Dad you think it's a good idea?"

"I'll do that."

Johnny's grin splits his face and he's practically squirming with excitement. He says, "Great! I'll turn on the water to top up the trough." He wheels his horse and heads up to the windmill at a lope.

Charlie and I wait by the fence, watching the cattle milling around. The bull stands apart, throwing his head from side to side, spewing strings of saliva. He paws, lifts his tail and squirts feces as he whirls around. Blood drips from wounds on his legs and chest.

Charlie brings his horse up beside me and says, "Domino shouldn't of been out here, should he, Auntie?"

"No. He should be with the other bulls in the bachelor herd."

"Somethin's got him riled. I never seen him like this."

"Looks like he tangled with some barbwire. Nothing too serious from what I can see, though."

Johnny rides up beside us just as water starts spewing from the spout into the tank. "I'll go turn the pump off on our way back," he says.

"Good idea, John, but I think our ride's over," I tell him.

"Domino shouldn't of been out," Charlie tells his brother. "We gotta figure out how he got out 'n' make sure he can't git out again."

The cattle begin to quiet, and finally Domino, although still wary, goes to the trough for a drink. A yearling-size steer is in the mix, and draws my attention. I say, "See that steer on the far side there? The one with the heart-shaped spot on his flank? I don't remember any of ours with a marking like that."

"Me neither," Johnny says.

"Me neither," Charlie agrees.

"Pretty unusual marking. Can't see his brand."

"I'll go in and have a closer look," Charlie offers.

"Well, okay. But keep an eye on Domino."

"I will."

"I'll get the gate." I dismount to open the gate far enough to let Charlie through, then push it shut behind him, waiting there to let him out again.

Charlie's horse, not as comfortable around cattle as Johnny's, has white-ringed eyes and skitters around, lifting up off his front feet as if to rear. A race horse in his former life, he's still wound up from the gallop and nervous about the cattle. I have a moment of panic visualizing Charlie being bucked off in the corral with the still-agitated bull. But Charlie sits quiet and nudges the horse toward the cattle. The cattle part to get out of the horse's way, and the horse seems emboldened. The target steer turns and canters off, but he broke out of the herd long enough for Charlie to get a look at his brand. He comes back to the gate and when I let him out, tells us, "You're right, he ain't ours."

"Whose is he, then?"

"Dunno, Auntie. Don't know the brand. I think it might be new. Looks raw, like it just got done."

"That's odd," I say. No one brands at this time of year. Although maybe they hadn't planned on putting them in the community pasture and had to brand now. But people are bringing their cattle in now, not turning new ones out. I blow out a long breath. "Okay, guys, we need to go back in and tell your Dad about this. He'll need to go see what kind of a mess Domino made of the fence. You guys go with him and you can turn off the pump then."

"What if there's other bulls out? We should take the horses instead of going with him in the truck."

"You're right," I agree. "Could be we got cattle from the community pasture in with our bachelor herd or our bulls out there. You can chase 'em back in. But it could be a bigger mess than that, in which case we're going to have to get a crew organized to set things right."

"Yahoo!" Johnny yells.

"It's too late today," I caution, "but maybe we'll make a day of it tomorrow. Haven't had a barbeque for a while. Could be our last one before the snow flies."

"Double yahoo!" Johnny yells. The boys put their heels to their horses and gallop back along the trail for home.

Chica bobbles around, tugging at the reins in hopes I'll let her run with them. "Settle down, Chica," I tell her, "we're not going to gallop home. And those little twits know better than that, too."

They do know better, but it's thrilling to watch the boys race along the lane. Johnny had a head start but in a heartbeat Charlie's ex-race horse hits his stride and easily catches the smaller Quarter Horse. They run close until they get to the turn, when Johnny's horse falls behind. They're within view of the barn now and I cross my fingers they can stop their horses. I'm sure they know if Stu catches them they'll get extra chores.

Maybe they think the thrill of the race was worth it.

I'll never admit it, but in my mind I'm running with them.

Four

STU GUIDES THE pickup into the parking lot at the Community Center and heads for the open parking spot between two other trucks at the edge of the lot. "Looks like a pretty good crowd here already," he observes.

As soon as the truck is still, I push the door open and get out. Red slides along the seat and gets out right after me, bouncing on her good foot as she favours her still-not-completely-healed leg. We go around the truck to join Stu and together make our way through the parked vehicles to the building entrance. As soon as we step into the lighted area under the canopy, Jake materializes in the doorway, grins, and comes to greet us.

"Oh, there you are," he says. "Hey, Red! Porky! Didn't know you were comin'." The two men shake hands as they exchange greetings.

"Wouldn't miss it," Red says.

Jake turns to me and says, "I paid fer you."

"Thanks," I say, and walk in beside him. At a table near the door, two women in frilly western shirts are taking money, stamping hands and selling drink tickets.

"Here she is," Jake says as we come up in front of them. I stick out my hand to be stamped.

"Ladies," Stu addresses the ticket sellers as he pulls his wallet out of his hip pocket. "What's the club raisin' money fer now?"

"New warm-up ring," the dark-haired woman responds. "There's folks that want to use the rodeo grounds for other things besides rodeo."

"What else is there?"

"You old cowboys think there's nuthin' else in the world," she says, and shakes her head.

"Old?" Stu snorts. "I ain't old, I'm experienced. 'N' anyhow, may I remind you there's still lotsa good tunes to be played on an old fiddle."

"I guess your wife will be the judge of whether you got good tunes or not."

"Be nice if he had more'n one, 'n' I mean jokes, too," Red says.

"Well, all jokin' aside," Stu says as he hands her a twenty dollar bill, "I'd like to see more stuff goin' on there. More horse shows and so on. Two please."

"Club thinks it'll be good, too." She takes his money and puts it in the cash box, then gets set to stamp their hands. She tilts her head at the woman sitting next to her and says, "Marnie has the drink tickets."

"I'll take twenty bucks worth," Stu tells Marnie, and she tears tickets off a roll. As he folds the tickets, he turns to us and says, "You go git a table. I'll git drinks. Beer, Jake?"

"I'll go with you," Jake replies. "What's yer pleasure, Lindy?"

"White wine if they have it. Otherwise, beer's fine, thanks."

The two men head for the pass-through to the kitchen where the volunteers wait to serve drinks, while Red and I scan the tables. We select one close enough to the stage to see the band but far enough from the speakers we'll be able to have a conversation once the band starts, and take chairs at the end next to the wall.

Stu and Jake come with the drinks and once they're settled, Stu says, "Say Jake, you know of any new cattle bein' turned out in the community pasture?"

"No. Why?"

"We had a bull bust out today 'n' he come back up to the corrals with half a dozen of our pairs, 'n' a steer that ain't ours in the mix. Brand looks fresh. Don't know whose it is."

"That's odd," Jake says, his eye narrowing. "He come off the community pasture?"

"Yep. That's where they was comin' from, although our bull wasn't supposed to be out there. Him 'n' a couple others. Found 'em when we went out to fix the fence, but nowhere near the numbers of cows that should of been in that herd, by my reckoning. I called Ernie but his wife said he was over in the other community pasture he manages. He ain't called me back yet."

"Don't he usually keep the herd together?"

"As a rule, yeah. Dunno why but they've scattered into small herds. I patched up the fence all right but we gotta get folks who run cattle out there to come 'n' make sure none have gone missin'. Unless we find more of ours, we got some missin' so no doubt others will, too."

"Dunno where they'd go from there," Jake says. He lifts his hat, scratches the back of his head, and resettles it. "If they git out into the Badlands, it'll be hell to round 'em up. Bad enough just in the hilly part of the community pasture. Not easy to do a head count, neither."

"As if 20,000 acres ain't enough of a challenge, hell, if they're out in the Badlands, might never find them. That's why we need more people, enough riders to cover it all off in one day before they have a chance to git that far. Couple other groups goin' out from different ranches but yer on my list fer ours. Good yer here since I got no answer when I called yer house earlier. Far as I know you ain't got cows out there but we can use all the help we can get. Can you make it? You 'n' Leo?"

"Yer right, I got no cows out there. I got pasture enough for what I got. But I'll come fer sure. Leo might be workin'."

"Leo's got a job? Where's he work?" Red asks.

"Nuthin' steady. He picks up a few days' work here 'n' there," Jake replies.

"Doin' what?"

"This 'n' that. Ranch work, mostly," Jake tells her, then looks off toward the door and says, "There's Jonesy and Arlette!" He waves. Arlette spots him and they come to join us. Jonesy folds his 6'6" frame into the chair next to Stu.

"What's this?" Arlette asks. "Why don't you let me sit by Stu and you go sit beside Lindy. Boy-girl-boy-girl like it's supposed to be."

"This ain't the high school prom," Jonesy says.

"What would you know about high school proms?"

"I may not of took you to the prom but you weren't the only gal in town who was sweet on me back then any more'n you are now," Jonesy tells her. He hands her some drink tickets and says, "Don't sit down. You know what I want." Ignoring his wife's frown, he turns to Stu and says, "Hey, Stu, Arlette said you called. 'Bout tomorrow, I'll come fer sure but I got no license on my trailer so I can't bring my horse."

"You can ride one of our rescues. We got one big enough fer you needs miles put on him. Just bring yer saddle."

"If you'd rather ride yer own horse," Jake says, "I can swing by yer place. There's room in my trailer."

"What's it about, anyhow?" Jonesy asks. "As usual what Arlette said didn't make no sense."

By the time Stu has explained, the musicians are on stage fussing with their instruments and Arlette is back with a red Solo cup of beer in each hand. She slides one across the table to her husband and takes the chair beside me. The house lights go down, the stage lights come on, and the banjo intro to the Stampeders' *Sweet City Woman* issues from the speakers.

Jonesy says, "Whaddaya know, they sound okay 'n' I ain't even drunk yet." We all laugh and agree. At the end of the song, the front man greets the crowd and introduces the other band members, then they launch into the first set. A few couples venture out onto the dance floor, but it isn't until everyone has had a beer or two and the band strikes up *Crazy Little Thing Called Love* that the dance floor fills. Stu, Red, Arlette and Jonesy get up and go to join the couples on the dance floor, leaving Jake and me sitting by ourselves.

After an awkward moment, Jake asks, "You wanna dance?"

"Yes!" I reply. I stand up. Maybe I actually jumped to my feet.

Jake gets up but doesn't start toward the floor; instead, he leans in close to my ear so I can hear him, and confides, "I ain't much of a dancer, Lindy."

I take his hand and tell him, "you don't have to be. It's a line dance. Anyone can do it." I tow him out onto the dance floor, remembering my first line dance. It was at a rodeo and Nick showed me how. Later that night we slept together, another first. I push the bittersweet memory away and focus on the dance.

To his credit, Jake does his best to follow along. When the song ends and the band plays a waltz, I put my hand on his shoulder and we clasp hands, my right to his left. I say, "For a guy who claims he ain't much of a dancer, you did good."

"Thanks. Just tried to follow the other guys. I ain't much good at waltzing neither but I sure like it a lot better." He drops both hands to my hips and pulls me in close.

I stiffen, take his hand again and put some space between us. "Friends, remember?"

He grins good naturedly and agrees, "friends."

When the waltz is over and the band segues into a two-step, Jake says, "Now *that* I definitely ain't gonna manage. I see Walter 'n' Leanne are sittin' this one out too. You know them?"

I look in the direction he indicates and see a couple I don't recognize. "Umm, no, I guess I don't."

"They live over on the road to Avonlea. Buy hay from me. Come on, I'll introduce you."

We get our drinks and join the other couple. The men waste no time in getting into discussions about the quality of the hay in Jake's barns, what it costs this year, the price of fertilizer, and problems with machinery.

After small talk establishing the number and ages of Leanne's children, that she's a stay-at-home mom, the fact I have no kids but claim Red and Stu's fosters as my nephews and that I work part time at the bank, Leanne asks, "How long have you and Jake been together?"

"Together? We're not together."

"Oh? Didn't I see you with him at the rodeo?"

"Nope. Well, I was at the rodeo, but not with him."

Leanne frowns and says, "I was so sure. Hmm. You say you work at the bank?"

"Yeah. Three days a week."

"I thought you were starting up that wine business. What's the name?"

"Wacasko-wâti."

"Wacasko what?"

"Wacasko-wâti. It's Cree for rat hole. More or less."

"I knew it was something a little, er, unusual. How'd you come up with that?"

"Well, we thought it should describe the ranch, so we tossed around a few ideas, like *Rusty Old Truck In The Ditch On The Corner* or *Fifty Miles of Bad Road*, but in the end decided to just name it after the ranch. Rat Hole is what my ex called the place so at first it was a joke, then it just stuck. But it sounds better in Cree, and Red has roots with the Nekaneet—"

"I actually know where that truck is!" Leanne interjects. "Your ex wasn't a country boy, I guess."

"Nope. Not by a long shot. Liked what he called the finer things in life, which didn't include fifty miles of bad road."

Stu and Red appear at the table, followed by Jonesy and Arlette. The topic of conversation becomes tomorrow's cook-out at Wacasko-Wâti, particularly what each will contribute to the potluck.

I notice a tall woman in the knot of people just coming in. It's my friend Carole, and when she scans the crowd, I get her attention with a wave. She and her husband join our table just as the discussion turns to who would have turned a freshly-branded steer out onto the community pasture community pasture just a few weeks ahead of all the cattle being moved off. The men have switched chairs and are now engrossed in their own conversation, leaving the women to visit.

"Jonesy!" Arlette calls across the table to get her husband's attention. "I love this song! I wanna dance!"

"We already danced," he replies.

Arlette gives him the middle finger salute, but he's turned his back. She hisses, "To hell with him! I didn't come here to sit and gab with a bunch of old hens." She gets up, scans the dancers and the other tables, and when she spots a group of young men at the back of the hall, heads off in their direction.

"Jeez, not even thirty and already I'm an old hen," I say.

"I definitely feel like an old hen some days," Carol says.

"I been called worse," Red says.

I watch the dancers for a couple of songs, then Carol and I go to the ladies' room. I get more drinks on my way back, set the beer in front of Jake and go to sit beside Red again.

"You okay? Havin' fun?" Red asks.

"Well, sure, I like people watching, but I wouldn't mind dancing more," I tell her.

"You could always go haul one of them young guys out onto the floor like Arlette done," she suggests.

"I don't want to dance that bad. I'll settle for the line dances. How're you doin'?"

"Well, see I got my leg up on the chair? It's really startin' to ache."

"Oh no! We should go, then."

"Don't be crazy, we just barely got here! I'm okay. Stu brought me another drink and I'm havin' a good time people watchin', just like you."

The music is good, the front man has a decent voice, and I find I'm enjoying myself, visiting with friends and at times, singing along. Carol says none of our guys are much interested in dancing so let them visit, and we'll consider it a concert where you don't have to wait for intermission to drink. We all agree, and get another round.

I notice Jake watching me from his position on the other side of the table and several chairs down. I smile and give him a little wave. The band starts into a slow song and Jake nods his head in the direction of the floor. I get up and skinny through the chairs to meet him there. As we're dancing, I say, "You guys are deep in conversation."

"Yeah. About the cattle, Lindy. Walter says he heard twelve cows went through the auction at Swift Current last week that were suspicious. A guy had thirteen stole. They think they might of been his." He steps on my foot. "Oops! Sorry!"

"It's okay." The waltz ends and when the band starts in on *Guitars and Cadillacs*, a line forms for another line dance. "You up for this?" she asks.

"I am," he agrees.

After *Guitars and Cadillacs* comes another two-step and Jake says, "I don't think..."

I take his hand and say, "Let's get a drink."

He blows out a long breath, relieved, and takes my hand. When we get back to the others, he sits next to me, looping his arm around my shoulders, and pulls me, chair and all, close. "Thank you," he breathes into my ear, and plants a kiss on my neck.

"What for?"

"Fer not makin' me stay up there lookin' like a clown. And fer comin' tonight."

A surge of arousal floods through me. At that moment Red comes up behind me, leans in close and says, "We're takin' off."

"I'll come with you," I tell her.

"Oh? I thought the two of you were gittin' along good." She nods to Jake's arm, still around my shoulders.

"We are. That's why I want to go."

I lean in close to Jake's ear and tell him, "We're taking off."

"Oh? Already?"

"Yeah. Red's leg is bothering her." I squirm, he pulls his arm away, I push my chair back and stand.

Jake gets up and faces me, cupping my shoulders. "Stay a little longer, Lindy? Please? I'll give you a ride home."

"I'm tired, Jake, and I've had more'n enough to drink. Early morning tomorrow and anyway, I'm ready to go."

He pulls me closer and says, "I know you 'n' me didn't dance much, 'n' I'm sorry 'bout that. I wisht I was a better dancer. I don't mind leavin' now." He drops his voice and whispers, "I'd feel like the luckiest guy alive if you'd let me take you home."

At the nearness of him the manly scent of aftershave and tobacco fills my senses. "Thanks, Jake, it's tempting, but—"

"Aww, Lindy, come on," he coaxes, and nuzzles my hair.

I've had enough to drink that my inhibitions are almost MIA. I'm attracted to him. Too attracted. My resolve falters. With a jolt I remember my post-divorce relationships that went too far too fast. I give him a quick kiss on the cheek and pull away.

"I had a good time, Jake. Thanks for inviting me. See you tomorrow. Don't forget, there's a pancake breakfast at my house."

"I ain't fergot."

I say goodbye to everyone and give a little wave as I hurry through the dancers to catch up with Red and Stu, breathing a sigh and telling myself leaving now is the right move.

Damn it.

Five

FROST ON THE grass glistens in the weak rays of late autumn sun bursting over the horizon. The sky is an amazing display of red, gold and fuchsia. Although the skies are mostly clear and the temperature is hovering above freezing, a bank of clouds to the north makes the forecast of snow later in the day credible. We hope to finish the count by mid-afternoon, just in case.

I was up early and drank half a carafe of coffee before getting busy outside, wiping down the picnic table in the covered area of my patio and setting up folding tables and chairs. I got Stu to help drag the microwave, cart and all, out of my kitchen. I'm setting up the big coffee percolator when Red comes along with two baskets of muffins: one with rhubarb, one with saskatoons.

"Good morning! You must've been up super early." Being up first to get everything ready for everyone is how Red operates. She's a little dynamo. I don't know how she does it. I grab one of the still-warm rhubarb muffins before she sets the baskets down.

"Not really. Made the batter fer the muffins last night. I gave you that overnight muffin recipe, didn't I?"

"You're the cook in this outfit," I remind her.

"I know. I'm just damn glad you help with pies."

"Least I can do," I say. "Boys still in bed?"

"Are you kidding? They're so excited, you'd of thought it was Christmas. They're out doing barn chores now. They'll bring Chica in along with their horses, a'course."

"Great! Thanks." I lift the muffin to indicate I'm thanking her for it, not for the boys bringing my horse in although I'm glad about that, too. I peel the paper, break off about half of it, and take a bite. "Mmmm. You've outdone yourself."

"Thanks." She stands hands on hips and looks around, then says, "We need a garbage bin. You take care of that while I start the barbeque."

She goes to the barbeque and opens the lid while I head into the garage to get the garbage can and extra bags. When I'm back on the patio, the barbeque with its griddle in place is heating up and Red is heading over to her house to get groceries.

The sun is beginning to float above the horizon and fade the sunrise away when the first truck and horse trailer rolls in. Soon half a dozen similar rigs are in the yard. Horses, most already saddled, have been unloaded and tied to the sides of the trailers along with nets full of hay that's their breakfast. There's no sign of Jake and Jonesy yet.

Cowboys and wives have congregated on the patio and there's a run on coffee and muffins. Red is at the barbeque turning out bacon and pancakes. Bud's wife is frying eggs on the electric griddle.

Fred Laker pulls in. Carol is with him, and there are two horses in the trailer. They unload their horses and tie them to the side of the trailer with a net full of hay like the others, and join everyone on the patio.

"You gals that's ridin' today, git yer breakfast. I got plenty of help here," Red says.

"Don't have to ask twice," Carol agrees. We load up plates and join her husband and a couple of other cowboys at the picnic table.

A white pickup I recognize as Jake's and towing a trailer rolls in. The yard is crowded so it pulls out of view on the far side of the barn. Minutes later Jake and Jonesy come to the patio, greet everyone and get Styrofoam cups from the stacks next to the percolator.

"Where's yer wife, Jonesy?" Red asks.

"Still in bed, most likely," he replies, filling his cup with coffee and topping it up with cream and sugar. "She ain't feelin' too good this mornin'. My head ain't too good neither."

"Well, I guess there's more'n a few sore heads this mornin," Red says. "Good thing we got lots of coffee. Grab a plate, you two."

Jake loads a plate and brings it and his coffee to sit next to me.

"How's your head this morning?" I ask. "You were so late getting here I was beginning to think you weren't going to show."

"I'm fine. I'd of been here sooner but Jonesy wasn't ready when I got to his place."

"Hmmm. Late night?"

"I left soon after you but Jonesy 'n' Arlette stayed to the end."

From the other side of the table, Fred says, "No surprise Arlette ain't feeling good this morning. She was partyin' pretty hard already when we left 'n' I heard it went until two. They got up a collection and paid the band to stay late. Might've gone longer 'cept they ran outta booze."

Jake stabs a chunk of bacon, puts it in his mouth, chews and swallows. "This sure hits the spot," he says. "You ridin' out with us, Lindy?"

"Yeah. Carol brought her horse too." I drain my third or forth coffee and stand up. "In fact, soon as I get rid of some of this coffee, I'm gonna go tack up."

"I'll go with you," Carol says.

As we leave the table with our plates, Jake tells us, "I'll just be a few minutes. See you over there."

WE ALL HEAD OUT ALONG the lane next to the corrals with Stu leading the way. The three dogs stay beside us or trot a short distance ahead. When we reach the farthest corral, Stu reins in, turns in the saddle and points, calling out, "Anyone recognize that steer there? The one with the heart-shaped white spot?"

"That the one you say has a fresh brand?" Bud asks. He scratches his grizzled whiskers. "Can't make out his brand."

"It'd hafta cover his whole damn side for you to read it without your glasses, Bud," Carol says.

"Whatever his brand, I'm pretty sure he's mine," Bud says. "Can't be though, if you say his brand's fresh. Mine were all branded months ago."

"Like everyone else's," Stu says. He turns his horse to face all the riders. "Two possibilities, like I said on the phone. Someone just got approved to turn their cattle in here so they hadda brand 'em first. But gettin' the okay to turn 'em out this time of year is odd. 'Course bein' the weekend I couldn't reach no one at the community pasture office 'n' Ernie ain't called me back yet. The alternative, 'n' I don't like to think about this, someone put their brand over someone else's. Which besides ol' Domino bustin' out and makin' a big mess we have to sort out, is why we're here. We might have rustlers operatin' in this area."

"Hope the hell yer wrong," Larry says.

"Me too," Stu agrees, "me too. So, let's fan out. Make sure we cover all the ravines. Any cows you find, head 'em back in this direction like we talked about. See if we can git the herd back together. 'N' mostly, let's hope we git a head count that proves me wrong." He wheels his horse and sets off at a lope. Our dogs follow him.

We split up and head out into the rolling hills.

"See you back at the barbeque this afternoon," Carol says.

"For sure," I nod, and put Chica into a comfortable ground-covering lope to follow Stu out to the north. I rein off so I'm just within view of him, keeping to his left. He soon drops out of view over the brow of a low hill. I slow Chica to a jog and turn her onto a cow path that goes left and down to the bottom of a ravine. It's a well-worn trail, and I follow it through the stand of aspen, over the dry slough bed and along the bottom until it swings up again on the far side of the ravine. As I come up over the ridge, I'm surprised to see Jake just a few hundred meters off. He spots me, too, and lopes over to ride beside me.

"Hey," he says, "any sign?"

"No. Plenty of tracks and manure, nothing fresh," I reply.

"Yeah, same here. But look there. Cattle." He points to pale beige dots off in the distance and we both rein our horses toward them.

The dots turn out to be a cow laying down, surrounded by seven calves. The cow gets up and eyes us warily as we approach. "It's the baby sitter," I say. "Larry's got those pale blonde Simmentals, I think."

"Well they sure are well camouflaged, this time of year anyhow," Jake says. "I think yer right, they're Simmentals. They must be Larry's then."

I pull pencil and paper out of my jacket pocket and mark the count, the location, and once we're close enough to confirm it, sketch their brand.

"The rest of these babies' mommas must be close. Surprised we can't see 'em. Must be down there on the other side of the bush," Jake says, and points to a stand of dwarf birch down the ravine. "Let's find 'em 'n' git 'em headin' back toward yer place. Say, Lindy..." He's interrupted by a shout from another rider behind us. We look turn to see Jonesy loping toward us.

"What you got?" he shouts as he pulls up.

"Some of Larry's, we figger," Jake says.

"Well, I got nuthin' over my way. Might as well ride with you. My head's poundin' so bad I can't hardly see nuthin' anyhow," Jonesy says.

Jake frowns, turns his horse and jogs ahead with Jonesy and me right behind. As expected, we find a half dozen cows on the far side of the bush and turn them back toward the others. When we have them back with their calves and heading toward Wacasko-Wâti, we aim our horses east again, fanning out to cover more territory.

Half an hour or so later, I hear a shrill whistle and see Jake waving his arm over his head. I nudge Chica into a lope and pull up beside him. "What is it?" I ask.

"Come look," he says, and leads the way down into a wide gully where Jonesy waits next to an area of trampled grass. The turf is torn as if by many hooves and in places, nothing but dirt. Where the gully opens out, there are tire tracks.

"Judgin' by them tire tracks, it's a bull hauler. I think we're pretty close to the road here," Jonesy says.

"We must be, if they could git a semi in here. I think we're gonna find we're missin' quite a few cows," Jake says. "And I think I know what happened to them."

AFTER I UNTACK, I STICK Chica in a stall with a flake of hay and head up to the patio where I find Carol with a glass of wine. I get my own and since Red and the other ladies have everything ready for the barbeque, join Carol at the firepit. The temperature has dropped along with the sun, so the warmth of the fire is very welcome. Other riders start coming in once they've taken care of their horses.

Red is at the barbeque. Stu, beer in hand, comes to take over the grilling.

"Everyone!" Red calls out. "We got Carol to thank fer this box of Riesling here on the table 'n' she says everyone's welcome to it. Just come outta the freezer so it should be good 'n' cold. Anyone who didn't bring a beer's welcome to one out of the ice chest."

"Steaks'll be ready soon," Stu declares. "Best git your plates ready, everyone."

"How'd it go, Stu?" Red asks. "Find anything?"

"Ay-yuh, I was just at the house callin' it in to the cops," Stu replies. "Didn't find no more with fresh brands, but we got a dozen missing. Larry 'n' Bud both have some missing too. Even though the herd is usually all together, they might've just thought they were in a ravine somewhere. That ain't unusual. But Jake found a spot where someone had a lot of cattle bunched up. Pretty sophisticated operation from the looks of it. Temporary corral, remains of a fire, prob'ly over-branded 'em. All they had to do was herd 'em up the ramp into the hauler."

"So it's rustlers, then. Pretty organized, too."

"Ay-yuh," he says, "these guys ain't small time. Bold, too, doin' that so damn close to our place. I guess they figured it would be easy to git away with it. 'N' they were right, goddammit. No one hardly ever goes out there 'n' wouldn't think twice about seein' a stock trailer bein' loaded with cattle if they did."

"Unless they saw my Simmentals, realized they're my damn breedin' herd 'n' knew they shouldn't be goin' nowhere," Larry adds. Beer in hand, he moves closer to Stu to get a look at the steaks. "I might not of noticed any missin' fer weeks but fer that ol' bull of yers, Stu."

"If the calves were bleating like they were scared, he might've went out thinkin' to protect 'em," Stu suggests. "It ain't the first time he busted out. We have to git better fences."

"Maybe you should start breedin' bucking bulls."

"That's the last thing we need!" I exclaim.

"Lucky you guys found him when you did."

"Lucky," I agree, "but we didn't find him, he found us. Might've brought his little herd right up into the yard if we hadn't been there to turn them into a corral."

"Imagine what them guys must've thought, seein' him come blastin' at them, no doubt bellowin' his head off. Prob'ly had to go clean out their pants," Larry says.

"He was still bellowing when he got to us," Charlie tells the group. He goes to the cooler and pulls out a can of Coke.

"The rustlers, they wouldn't of been expectin' a bull, 'specially one as big 'n' pissed off as that one," Fred says as he leans over the cooler and sorts through the beer cans.

"Well, let's hope the cops find some evidence. Maybe take plaster casts of the tire tracks or somethin'. Plus they should get word out to all the auctions to be on the lookout for anyone consigning cattle with fresh brands," Stu says.

"Could be someone we know," Bud suggests, and wipes his moustache with the back of his hand.

"Hope the hell you're wrong 'bout that, Bud," Larry says. "Bad enough we got rustlers, but it's guys we know?"

A chorus of subdued agreement goes up, and with it comes a mounting sense of unease as everyone looks around.

"That's the damn trouble with open range," Larry says. "Partly my own fault. I don't go check on 'em near often enough. But if I did, 'n' if I noticed a few missin', I'd just figure they were in the bush in a ravine somewhere. Last thing you think of is someone would steal 'em."

"It's gonna be the first thing any of us thinks of now, though," Bud says. "Wonder when's the last time Ernie was in this part of the pasture."

"He's stretched pretty thin, what with this 'n' the other big community pasture to manage," Stu says. "He needs more'n a couple dogs to help him. Last time I talked to him he said he's hopin' the Feds'll give out a contract fer another manager. Anyhow, even if he noticed cows missing he might not of realized it wasn't just one of us takin' our own stock back home ahead of the round-up. Unless he caught 'em in the act."

"They must've been at it when Lindy 'n' the boys run into Domino."

"They were almost at our corrals then, though," I tell them. "A long way from where they were working. They must've started early. We didn't see or hear anything and we didn't think anything of it, just got them into the corral and then went to get Stu so he could go fix the fence."

"Well, it must of took some time to get set up," Jake says. "Just about as much time to put everything away."

"We didn't see nuthin', but then we didn't really go lookin', neither," Stu says. "We weren't thinkin' about rustlers. Didn't see no bull haulers goin' by on the road, neither, now that I think back."

"They must of headed west into Alberta. Maybe they come from Alberta, too," Red says.

"Well whatever, just hope the cops catch 'em," Stu says. "Steaks are ready. Who's first?"

IT'S FULL DARK AND there are tiny wet snowflakes beginning to fall when everyone starts to leave. I've said my goodbyes and I'm heading down to the barn for night check when I walk past Jake's truck. Jonesy is in the passenger seat and Jake is just settling into the driver's seat. He looks my way, changes his mind about closing the door and slides out. He comes around the front of the cab and falls in beside me.

"Hey," he says, "hold up a sec?"

I stop and face him. People scurry around, busy stowing gear and checking latches; he takes my arm and guides me out of view around the corner of the barn.

"What's up?" I ask.

"I was, uhh, hopin' to get a chance to, er, git you alone, but every time I got near you some other yahoo come along. I wanted to ask you fer a date, no dancin' this time, but maybe I could buy you supper?"

The scent of his aftershave mingled with sweat and horse is masculine and pleasant. "That would be nice," I agree.

"Okay? Saturday?"

"Oh, no, I'm going to Mom's for the weekend. I do her payroll."

"How about Friday then?"

"Friday would be great."

"I'll pick you up about six?"

"Six," I agree. Our eyes meet and I feel a rush of arousal.

He hesitates for a second, then as if reading my thoughts, cups my shoulders and tugs me close. His kiss is soft and gentle, but grows more insistent as his tongue seeks mine. He drops his hands to my waist and slides them inside my jacket, backing me up against the wall, pressing his body against me. I'm nearly overcome by desire. If this was a True Confessions magazine, here's where it would read 'her body betrayed her'. Alarm bells chime in my head. If I really want to take this slow I need to back off now, but the comforting warmth of him enfolding me and the hard maleness of his body is stirring. I don't want it to end. Thankfully, the decision is made for me. A couple of short toots of his truck's horn startles us and he releases me.

"This is awful nice," he murmurs, his voice husky.

He's leaning in for another kiss when Jonesy hollers, "Git yer pants on, you two! Let's go!" He punctuates his demand by leaning on the horn and flashing the headlights.

"I guess anyone who ain't left yet heard that. Asshole!" Jake hisses. He draws a deep breath and with a small grin, says, "I'm gonna need a cold shower!" He backs the few steps to the corner of the barn. "See you Friday, beautiful," he says, and turns away.

I follow him around the corner and as he crosses the pool of light from the lamp over the barn door, admire his narrow hips in those tight jeans as he strides back to his truck. He gives a little wave before he slides behind the wheel and puts the truck in gear, then pilots the truck and trailer around the yard and down the driveway toward the road, giving the horn two short toots as he drives past.

My face feels warm. I'm going to have whisker burns tomorrow and Jake's not the only one who needs a cold shower! How quickly we've gone past 'just friends'.

The snowflakes are becoming larger. I turn my face to the sky, welcoming the cooling snow on my cheeks.

"IT'S FUCKIN' STUPID! No, it's beyond stupid, it's fuckin' *insane*, grabbin' cows so close to home. And off a community pasture? Wanna have every rancher for a hundred miles after you?"

"That's the beauty of it. Them cows is free for the takin'. No one worries about 'em until it's time to bring 'em in."

"I got news fer you. They already know they're gone 'n' how that happened." He shakes his head, leans forward in his recliner to grab his boot and pull it off. When both boots are off, he tosses them in the direction of the kitchen, leans back and says, "Goddamn bold, takin' 'em close enough to the road anyone drivin' by could see you."

"Nobody thinks nuthin' of some guys loadin' cattle out on the community pasture. No one drivin' by would say, hey, them cows don't belong to that guy. And no one knows whose cattle're whose out there. If anyone saw a strange rig out there they'd just think it was a buyer, or someone hired to haul 'em. Anyhow, it ain't my call. The boss..."

"Yeah, the shithead boss. Is he tryin' to git caught? He'll wind up in jail 'n' yer gonna be right beside him. Or more likely, you git caught, you go down 'n' he skates."

"Don't worry, he ain't stupid. He ain't gonna sell 'em around here. They're already over on his place near Cardston. Same as the bunch we brought there from Watrous last week. He's gonna run 'em through the Lethbridge auction."

"Does he really think takin' them to another province is gonna save his ass? It's barely a four hour drive. Idiots!"

"No one's gonna notice. They're all mixed in with the boss's other cattle. What's a few hundred extra cows in a herd that size?"

"Someone might notice the Simmentals."

"They ain't all Simmentals. There's everything in there. And I don't really know how many. There's other crews. That's just what our crew done so far."

"So far? You ain't quittin'?"

"Why would I? Pay's good. When's the last time you made two hundred bucks fer a few hours work? It's more'n I make in a week humpin' feed."

"Humpin' feed won't land you in jail though. Anyhow, I hope the hell that's the last time you hit around here."

"Like I said, it ain't my call.

Six

"WELL THAT FRIES it as far as the cops gittin' anything from tire tracks," Stu says, shaking his head in frustration and disgust. "Goddamn! When's the last time it snowed this early?"

"Snows in August sometimes so after Labour Day ain't that unusual," Red says.

"Well, it couldn't of held off another day?" He stands with his mug of coffee looking out the kitchen window toward Lindy's house, five hundred meters off and on the other side of the cottonwood grove. The snow is already a foot deep and there's more coming down. More than enough to obliterate the tire tracks they found the day before.

"Uh-huh. It could've," Red agrees. "By the way, the last of the eggs went into the cookies." She opens the oven door, releasing a cloud of steam, and checks the meat thermometer. "Alf was supposed to bring a couple dozen today but who knows when he'll get out now. Lindy called to say the roads were bad everywhere and white-out conditions on the road to the Jacksons which of course always gets plowed last. They brought the kids out to the highway on snow-mobiles but they ain't gonna deliver eggs that way."

"Nope."

"I think we should git chickens again."

"After the last ones did nuthin' much but feed the cougars 'n' eagles?" He strolls over to look out the front window and says, "They're home."

The school bus is just pulling into the yard and backing into its parking spot beside the equipment shed. The dogs went out to wait there before the bus arrived and now leap around, tails wagging frantically as they greet Lindy and the two boys. The boys scurry up toward the mobile and Lindy heads for her house. She looks up and waves.

Charlie and Johnny shout hello as they shed their jackets and boots in the porch. They jostle for position as they come through the doorway into the kitchen, pile their books and lunch kits on the counter and start rummaging through the pantry.

"There's cookies in the cookie jar," Red tells them.

They wrestle for possession of the cookie jar, with Charlie coming out the winner. He puts the lid on the counter and reaches in to grab two before letting his brother put his hand in. When they both have a couple more, they go into the living room and park in front of the T.V.

"The minute they're in the door, all hell breaks loose," Stu says.

"It's too quiet when they ain't here," Red says. "They're exactly how boys their age ought to be. Never took you for a guy who thought kids should be seen 'n' not heard."

"A little bit of *not heard* would be okay. Just give 'em a minute, Once they're done stuffin' their faces, they'll be fightin' over the Nintendo."

"Little bulls findin' their place in the herd," Red says. She goes to get the carafe from the coffeemaker, fills a mug, and takes a sip. "Ugg. I should make a fresh pot. Will you have another cup if I do?"

"Might as well. I got time before chores. Wouldn't mind a couple of them cookies neither."

Red sets about getting fresh grounds and water in the coffeemaker, and says, "about the chickens..."

"I guess it's a good idea," Stu agrees. "Why don't you call around 'n' see if anyone has a few layin' hens they'll part with. The boys 'n' me'll git the henhouse cleaned out on the weekend."

"Good," Red says, and looks out the window over the sink. "Still snowin' to beat hell. Wonder if they'll close schools tomorrow. I don't envy Lindy havin' to drive. I sure don't miss it."

"That bus contract's the reason our road gets plowed first thing. Gonna miss that when the new driver takes over." Stu joins Red at the kitchen window and as they're watching the snow coming down, an RCMP cruiser drives in and parks next to the hedge. "Dwight's here. Just in time for coffee."

"Tell him there's a fresh pot, 'n' if he gets in here quick, there might still be cookies."

"Ay-yuh," Stu replies, and goes out to meet him. He's back inside after just a few minutes.

"That was quick," Red observes. "He didn't want to come in?"

"Yeah, he said thanks but he got a called to an accident up on the highway. Anyhow, he said when they got the call yesterday, they put the wheels in motion, contactin' auction marts 'n' so on. Even sent someone by the stockyards in Brooks. That's about all they can do anyhow now that any sign of what them bastards was up to is under a foot of snow. Might not be anything to see when the snow melts, neither. They're gonna have a marked car drive around the community pasture at a different time every day, but that's closin' the barn door after the horse is gone. He agrees we should reschedule the round-up, though. Git everyone's cows back home sooner rather than later, just in case they ain't done here."

"Yeah. What else can we do? Unless the cops git a tip from someone. Maybe the Cattleman's Association ought to offer a reward for information. We should set up regular patrols, too. Everyone who runs cattle out there should have to take a turn."

"Now, them's two real good ideas. You always was the brains in this outfit." Stu comes to where his wife stands, pulls her to a chair and sits down with her in his lap. "Yer ass is awful goddamn boney, darlin'." He gives her breast a gentle squeeze and whispers, "no tits, neither. Good thing I married you fer yer brains 'n' not fer yer body."

"Hsst! I'm exactly the way I always was 'n' you never could keep your hands off me."

"Still can't. Oh, my!" He slides her off his lap and pulls her hand to his crotch. "See what you done to me? How 'bout we go for a quickie while the boys're busy playin' Space Invaders?"

"How 'bout you go do yer chores? Don't bother puttin' on a jacket. The cold'll help you out with that li'l problem of yers. I'm gonna make some calls to see about gittin' some hens."

Seven

WHEN I ARRIVE at work Wednesday there's a stack of files in the middle of my desk. Thanks to the second blizzard that blew in overnight, I'm half an hour late owing to the poor road conditions. On top of the slow going I had to hoof it through the snowbanks from the school because what on-street parking there is in downtown that wasn't taken up by piles of snow from road clearing was already full. And now two days' work waiting for me? I must not be living right if I deserve a morning like this.

At least I made it here. Everett's office is still dark. It's not surprising he's not in yet—he lives an hour and a half away on a good day—but Irene's chair is empty too and she only has a few blocks to walk. She misses work every chance she gets, so even a small amount of snow and she's housebound. Might as well let the person that has to brave the lousy road conditions to get here do her work. She didn't come in yesterday, either, so much of the work in the pile should be on her desk.

I wouldn't mind so much if she left the key to the stationery supplies cabinet but it stays with her. It's like in Grade Two when Miss Massey guarded the pencil sharpener to make sure no one took more than three turns of the handle and judged whether your old pencil was truly short enough to warrant your getting a new one. Now that I think of it, Irene even looks like Miss Massey. You have to feel sorry for her. Being the secretary to the manager of a dinky little branch like this is quite a come-down. She was the General Manager's secretary when she worked in Regional Office, don't forget. Maybe being the Stationery Nazi makes up for her reduced position. She never leaves the key laying around. I wouldn't be surprised if she sleeps with it. It's comical how worked up she gets when I request something she doesn't think I need, such as pink Liquid Paper for corrections on the loan applications. In her view, I should just overstrike or X out, or better, be more careful so I don't make so many mistakes. In her day, they had no Liquid Paper and somehow managed. I took that request as far as I could before switching it up and asking for a red pen.

I stuff my purse in the bottom desk drawer, take the cover off my typewriter, fold it and put it in the drawer with my purse, then check through the files. There's an unusual number with pink forms clipped to them. Loan applications. Everett worked late last night. He'll want these typed and put in the clearing for the courier so they get to Regional Office tomorrow, but without Irene, it might not be possible.

As usual Everett has non-urgent correspondence mixed in with the loan applications, which means transcribing the entire tape, typing everything to get to the loan applications. There's so much work in the pile I'm sure I won't be able to get it all done by the time I have to leave to pick up the kids. It can't be helped. I wonder how I thought I'd like to do this job full time.

I tell myself this pile of typing is job security, shove the tape cassette into the Dictaphone and pull out the first loan application. When I have carbon papers between the sheets I feed the packet into the typewriter, roll the platen until the paper is at the appropriate space on the form, stick the headphones in my ears, step on the pedal and begin.

"Knock, knock!"

I turn to see Josie at my desk. I take the headphones out of my ears and ask, "what's up?"

"I know you just got in," she says, "but the Baxters are here. They had an appointment with Everett and of course he's not here yet and they can't wait, they just want to know... um... something about their line of credit application. Can you talk to them?"

"Me?"

"Unless you want me to send them away, you're it."

I draw a deep breath and say, "Okay, I guess I can give it a try. Can you get me their file?"

"I already put it on Everett's desk. I'll bring them in." She turns and heads back through the desks to the public area beyond the tellers' counter.

As I head to Everett's office I watch her approach a tall man in a sheepskin jacket and a ball cap, and a woman almost as tall wearing a toque and a ski jacket. When they look my way, I smile and wave them in.

I wait near the doorway to greet them as they come through. I introduce myself to Judy and Dan, and go behind the desk while they take the chairs across from me.

"Someone could've called us to save us the trouble of coming," Judy says.

"Sorry 'bout that," I reply. "I was late getting here myself and we haven't heard from Everett. I hope he's not in a ditch somewhere, with the roads so bad."

"Yeah, we know the roads are bad, we just drove in on 'em. Some-one should've phoned us."

"It's okay, Judy," Dan says, "I needed to go to the feed store any-how. And we left before the bank was even open." He makes eye con-tact with me and smiles, the corners of his eyes crinkling. He's cute and seems charming. How do guys like that always wind up with cranky women?

"Okay, then," I say, "I don't know if I can help, but I'll give it a try. What did you want to see Everett about?"

"He was going to see about an increase in our line of credit. Supposedly had an answer and we were going to discuss it today," Dan explains.

"Which probably means they turned you down again," Judy scowls, frowning at the man in the chair next to her. "If it was good news, he would of told you over the phone."

"Give me a minute to have a look." I open the folder and locate the pink loan application with Regional Office's reply tacked to it. I read through it quickly, then compose my thoughts and look up at the couple.

"Yeah, I can tell from her face they turned it down again," Judy says. "You should change banks."

"No, it's not all bad," I assure them. "They've agreed to an increase, just not for the full amount you wanted. And they've got suggestions for restructuring that they think will help, with a promise to take another look at it when your accountant has the financial statements for your fiscal year end done. So it's not a denial." I study the scowl on Judy's face and quickly add: "Everett knows more about this than I do, of course, so he can go over the restructuring suggestions with you. I hope he comes in soon. Would you like to go to Tim Horton's for a coffee while you wait...or, umm, check back after you've got your feed?"

"We can't hang around town all day just to find out what excuse they've come up with now." Judy jumps to her feet and nearly climbs over Dan to get to the office door. Dan pushes his chair back, stands and looks at me.

"Thanks, Lindy," he says. "I have animals to look after and other stuff to do at home so I can't be in town too long, but I'll check back in before we head out." He reaches his hand out to shake mine. I stand up and come around the desk to take his hand.

"Sorry."

"It's not your fault." He smiles and a tiny dimple forms in his cheek as he gives my hand a gentle squeeze. His eyes are a clear deep blue. He's standing so close I can smell peppermint on his breath, and notice a small scar near his ear. Then he drops my hand and turns to follow his wife, who is already halfway out the door.

Nice tight little butt. He was definitely inside my personal space. Does he do that to everyone? And was that little squeeze suggestive of something or was he just being nice, trying to assure me everything's okay despite his wife's hostility?

What's this? Lustful thoughts about a married man? At least he wouldn't want to move in with me. I've often thought that might be a good reason to have an affair with a married man. Am I actually considering it? No. Maybe.

I return to my desk and get back to work. I've just finished transcribing the first tape when my phone rings. It's the school secretary calling to say the storm is getting worse so they're closing and sending the students home. It was bad enough this morning. I mentally curse whoever made the call not to close the school then.

I get my purse, go and put my coat and boots on. On my way through the office, I stop to explain to Josie why I have to leave. "If the Baxters come back, I hope they'll understand. If Everett makes it in, I hope he's not too mad that I didn't get anything done."

"I hope so too, on both," Josie says. "If the storm is really that bad maybe we should close early, too. I'm sure Regional Office wouldn't want to risk anyone getting stuck in a blizzard on their way home."

"Why don't you phone Regional Office and ask?"

"I was hoping you would."

"Ha ha ha. Nice try."

Eight

THE NEXT DAY there's a full staff when I arrive at work. Irene has her headphones stuck in her ears and is typing away, a black expression on her face. She doesn't look up when I greet her, just snarls, "Everett wants to see you."

"Nice to see you, too," I mutter. "Feeling better?" I say this under my breath, even knowing she can't hear me with her headphones on because if she did, she would never let me have another new pencil. She's already turned me down for a red pen, because in her estimation I don't need it. I'll keep requesting it, though, until I think of something else.

I go to the cloak room, shed my coat and trade my boots for heels. I go back to my desk, stash my purse, and go to Everett's office. I avoid another look at Irene but feel her glare boring holes in the back of my head.

Everett's door is open; he looks up when I tap on the doorframe. "Good morning. You wanted to see me?"

"Good morning."

"If it's about me being late, it's just, you know I've been driving the school bus. The roads..."

"You're hourly anyway so no big deal. It's not about that. Come in and close the door."

When the door is closed, he indicates the chair across the desk from him.

"Is it about the Baxters? I, er, Irene called in sick and you weren't here yet when they came in so I talked to them."

"I know."

"I don't think I said anything I shouldn't have. Mrs. Baxter was upset at their loan being denied again. She was talking about changing banks..."

"Mrs. Baxter? No, I don't think you said anything wrong. In fact, I think you must have handled it well. Dan seemed impressed, anyway."

"Oh, good! You saw them?"

"Yeah, I was here when they came back."

"You know, I was thinking about their loan, wondering why Regional Office didn't suggest that Mrs. Baxter co-sign. It would bring their jointly-registered real estate behind the loan. That would help, wouldn't it?"

"You're right, it would."

"So why—?"

"The reason he has such a big loan in the first place is because he needed the money to buy Mrs. Baxter out of the ranch."

"Oh. But then why was she here with him?"

"You mean Judy? She's his sister. I don't know why she was with him. Maybe she just didn't want to wait in the truck." He chuckles, then pulls a file off the credenza behind him and opens it on his desk. "The reason I wanted to talk to you is, Regional Office authorized a new position, lending officer. I recommended you for the job, and they agreed."

"What? Oh....!"

"It would be full time, of course, but it's a pretty significant increase in salary," he tells me, takes a letter out of the file and pushes it across the desk.

When I see the salary range, I nearly gasp. It would sure help pay off some bills! But all I do is type Everett's loan applications. How can I be a lending officer? "But I...I mean, don't they have someone that already knows the job they could transfer?"

"If they give you the job, they don't have to pay moving costs for someone to transfer here. And you know, we're a small branch with a low lending limit so they'd send a rookie anyway. Might as well be you."

He leans back in his chair, gives it a little swivel, studies me as he clicks his pen. Click. Click. Click. "Of course you need training. You'll have to spend time at Regional Office shadowing one of the senior loans officers, and then you come back here and dive right in. What do you think?"

"I'm, er, this is awesome!"

"This is just the starting salary, too, Lindy. There'll be bump-ups over time. And the usual cost of living allowance increases everyone gets. Of course a percentage of a higher salary means a bigger COLA increase. Opportunity for advancement, too. There is one other thing you should be aware of, though. You have to agree to be mobile in Saskatchewan."

My spirits plummet. "I might be transferred?"

"Yeah, but not for a while. You'll need a couple of years here at least. They might send you to do a stint up north. And you can always turn the transfer down."

"I guess I have to think about it."

"Well, don't think too long. That stack of work on your desk? I've been putting in long hours as it is, taking files home too, and we're going to get busier as folks start wanting to get their financing organized for next year. Our branch is growing. You wouldn't believe the targets Regional Office has come up with for us. Personally I think we'll be lucky to meet them but they seem confident. And you know, I'm not going to be here forever, either."

"You?"

"I'm mobile, too. I've already been here two years and I'm expecting, well, *hoping* would be more accurate, to get transferred back to Swift Current, this time as manager, before much longer. That's why I never moved here."

"Oh. I hope it's not for a while. Although I imagine your commute is getting old."

"It is. So? What do you say? Do I sense some hesitation?"

"I'm just so surprised. And, full time? I've thought about it. My, er, partners think I have enough to do as it is. Can you give me until Monday to decide?"

"Sure," he says. "Meanwhile, can you get on top of that typing? Those credit apps can't wait. With you leaving early yesterday and Irene being away two days, we're already behind."

"I know." I get up and take a couple of steps toward the door, then turn and say, "but if I take the lending officer job..."

"We'll have to hire another steno," he says, completing my thought. "Easier than filling the lending officer position. Don't worry." He pulls another file off the pile and opens it. When he looks up again and I'm still standing here he asks, "something else?"

"Umm, no, just..." I sigh and bite my lower lip. "Just—thank you."

Nine

I PACE AROUND the kitchen, into the living room and back again, watching out the windows for Jake. This must be the tenth time I've made the circuit. He was supposed to be here at six. Now it's ten to seven, I've had my jacket and boots on for half an hour and my stomach is growling. I know if I go to the bathroom one more time, he'll show up while my pants are down. I do it anyway. Predictably, the doorbell rings.

"Coming!" I call out. I tuck in my shirt and zip my jeans as I scurry to the door and open it on Jake.

"Hey," he says, and takes a step inside, leaning toward me for a kiss.

I'm in no mood for that after waiting so long, so I dodge it and go past him out onto the porch. He follows, pulling the door shut. "Sorry I'm late. Family issues," he says.

"Family issues?"

"Yeah. You know how that goes. Or maybe you don't since you ain't got family."

"What do you mean, I ain't got family?"

"Nuthin'. Anyhow, looks like yer ready to go."

Since I had my winter coat and boots on when I opened the door, that's obvious. I don't point that out, though, just say, "more than ready. I'm starving." I hurry to the truck, pull the door open and climb in. He comes up behind me and gives the door, which I'm already closing, an extra little shove, then goes around and gets into the driver's seat.

"Lindy, I know yer pissed but I couldn't git here any sooner. My kid got stuck. I had to give him a hand. I'm sorry."

"Okay," I say. I breathe out and settle my purse on my lap. "Where are we going?"

"I thought The Jasper."

"How about we go to Billie's instead of going all the way into town? Or the café at the Husky station."

"Umm, but the Jasper is a lot nicer," he says.

"If we go to there it'll be at least two hours before we eat and I can't be out late tonight. I have to be on the road to Calgary by five tomorrow morning."

Jake studies me for a moment. "Okay, not the truck stop, though. Billie's it is," he agrees, and puts the truck in gear.

Once we're out on the road and underway, I ask, "how's your week been?"

"Fine."

He's staring at the road and seems lost in thought. Or maybe he's mad because I didn't want to go into town. Or maybe he's just being super careful because the snow is rutted and it's not easy to see where the road ends and the ditch starts.

We ride along in silence. I wish he'd ask about my week because I'm pretty stoked about my new job offer, and don't want to just bust out with it. Finally I go ahead and blurt, "Well, I had a good week. They offered me a promotion."

"Oh yeah? Congratulations."

"It'll mean full time, though."

"You want full time?"

"I think so."

"Good, then."

I lean against the door and check my watch, and try to think of something to interest him in talking about. I come up with nothing.

We arrive at Billie's to find the parking lot nearly full and once inside, the tables all taken. We perch on stools at the bar.

"Hey, Jake," the bartender greets us. "I see you picked up a passenger. This one's a lot prettier than the last one."

"Fer chrissake, Justin," Jake says, "I hope you don't expect a tip, runnin' your mouth like that."

"The way you tip, it's no loss," Justin says. He locks eyes with me and says, "I'm just teasin'. What can I get for you?"

"I'll have a glass of house white, please."

"I'll have a pint of Labatt's," Jake says. "We'll need menus, too. And we'll move to a table when one opens up."

"You got it," Justin says, and moves off.

Naturally, I'm wondering who Justin was talking about, and Jake is smart enough to realize it. He turns to me and explains, "I was here this afternoon with Jonesy. He wants me to hire him to do hay deliveries."

"Well, that's nice, if you want to contract it out. Do you?"

"Dunno. Right now I can handle it myself. But if I expand the equipment business," he shrugs, "maybe."

Another lengthy pause in conversation. I watch Justin working behind the bar and the reflections of the crowd behind us in the mirrors that back the liquor bottles. Finally, I ask, "So what was your family emergency?"

Justin returns with our drinks. When he has moved on again, Jake blows out a breath and says, "another argument with my kid. He storms off. Half an hour later he phones from the neighbour's to say he put his truck in the ditch."

"Oh no! Was he hurt?"

"No. But he wanted me to pull him out even though it's obvious the truck ain't driveable. 'Pears there was a telephone pole involved. Prob'ly a write off. Left it where it was 'n' he can deal with it." He takes a long draft of his beer. "I can't leave him at the side of the road but does he want to go home? Of course not. Another argument 'bout that. To shut him up I take him into town 'n' drop him off at Fast Eddy's so he can hook up with his buddies. Was gonna call you from Eddy's but the payphone was tore off the wall so I came straight from there to yer place."

Okay so maybe I shouldn't have been quite so bitchy about him being late. To make up for it, I ask, "what's Leo doing these days, anyway? I know you said he's working here and there. Has he quit school all together, then?"

"Says it ain't fer him. I tell him workin' a few days here 'n' there he ain't gonna git ahead 'n' he needs to finish high school. He says 'oh yeah, like you done?' And he wishes it was me who was gone instead of his mother so he didn't have to wait for me to croak before he could take over the ranch."

That's harsh. "Sorry," I say, sip my wine, study his profile, then tell him, "Charlie and Johnny are still pretty young. Charlie actually likes school, so far, although Johnny... Well, I suppose we have stuff like that to look forward to but I can't imagine..."

"No, you can't imagine. And even if you could, they ain't yer kids. Wait till yer arguin' with someone as big as you are 'n' you'll find out." He takes a long draft of his beer then seems to notice something of interest in the mirror, slides off his stool, and says, "There's someone I gotta talk to."

Off he goes, beer in hand. It's just as well he leaves now before I can respond, because I'm still miffed about him saying I have no family, and now this remark about the boys not being my kids? They aren't, of course, but that comment was snotty. I watch him go through the doorway to the adjoining room, but can't see where he goes from there. I finish my wine and when Justin asks if I'd like another, I agree. When Jake still isn't back and I'm halfway through this glass, I put the coaster on top of it and ask Justin to keep an eye on it while I go to the ladies room.

I'm in no hurry to get back. All week I've been mentally replaying that Sunday night kiss and fantasizing about more. I was even thinking sex on a third date, or a second date if you don't count the cookout as a date, is taking it slow enough. Now Jake is so distant I can't believe he's the same man. He leaves me sitting at the bar alone for half an hour? I've had enough. Forget dinner! I look at my watch for the hundredth time. It's not too late. Red will still be up. I can call her to come and get me.

When I go back out my wine glass is still where I left it. Justin comes to pull a pitcher of beer from the taps near where I sit. "Could I get change for the phone, please Justin?" I ask.

"You can use the bar phone if it's not long distance. Over there," he says, and points to the wall phone next to the door into the kitchen. "If you're looking for Jake, he's got your table." With a lift of his chin he indicates the raised area at the back where Jake is sitting. I wasn't expecting this. Instead of calling Red, I'll ask him to take me home. I pick up my glass and make my way through the tables. He doesn't look up from the menu as I approach him.

"Jake, I—"

Before I can complete my sentence, he looks up and says, "I'm sorry, Lindy. That was rude."

"I think I'll call it a night."

"No, don't do that. Please, sit down."

I draw a deep breath, then pull the chair out and perch on it. He reaches across the table and takes my hand as he looks me in the eye. "This has been a shitty week but that's no excuse fer me to take it out on you. I'm sorry."

I take a deep breath, nod and say, "Okay. But I did ask about your week, and you said it was fine."

"You know, Lindy, I don't want to talk about it. I don't even want to think about it. I'm happy to be here with you." He punctuates that statement with a quick nod, releases my hand and gives my forearm a rub. "I'm gonna have the Billie Burger. What do you want?"

I pick up the menu and begin reading as I say, "I, er, usually have the Cajun Chicken Caesar..."

"I'll go order," he says. He gets up and goes to the corner of the bar where there's a passthrough under a sign reading "Order Food Here".

Okay, I guess Cajun Chicken Caesar it is. I look around the crowded, smoky room. Some faces are familiar—people I recognize as customers at the bank or that frequent Billie's and other places around town—but no one I know well enough to ask them to join us. Damn!

Jake comes back to his seat, puts the plastic sign with the number 34 on it on the table and says, "it won't be long."

Behind me, a woman's voice says, "Hey, Jake."

He looks up. Expressions of surprise, then shock, then anger play across his face. A pretty thirty-something brunette slides in between the tables to sit on the bench next to Jake. Very close. She looks at me, eyes narrowed, and says, "Hi. You been dating Jake long?"

"Umm, no, not long..."

"Well, me and Jake go way back."

Jake squirms in his seat, then he glares at her and says, "Don't do this now, Martine."

"Oh, not now?"

"No, not now."

"Fine!" She gives me a long look before getting to her feet and saying, "Good luck."

Before I can think of anything to say to that, she is out of earshot; I turn to watch her as she pushes through the crowd around the pub tables and heads for the door.

I turn back to look at Jake. He's holding his beer in one hand and pushing the coaster around in circles with the other, his forehead creased in a frown.

"So, who is she?" I ask.

"Nobody," Jake shrugs and doesn't look up.

"Nobody?"

He looks me in the eye and says, "Nobody important. She's a friend of my wife's, that's all."

"Seems like she's mad at you."

"That's her problem." Jake takes a deep breath and says, "Truth is, she's been hittin' on me for years. I guess she thought once my wife was outta the way I'd pick up with her."

"And did you? Pick up with her, I mean."

"We went out a couple of times. It ended there. That's the god's honest truth." His gaze shifts as if something behind me has drawn his attention, and he says, "She was here this afternoon. I told her then we needed to talk. This ain't the time or place fer it, though, not now no more'n it was then." He raps the table with his knuckles, gets up and says, "I'll go see what's keeping our food."

If I thought things were on an upswing after his promise to act happy, I was wrong. It was a promise he couldn't keep. I watch as he goes to the passthrough. There's tension in the set of his shoulders as he stands with his back to me, hands shoved deep into his front pockets.

I feel as tense as he looks. Too late to cancel the food. We're stuck together until after we eat. I finish my wine and when the server comes by, order a carafe.

FROM MY KITCHEN WINDOW, I watch Jake's truck drive off. Lights are still on at Red and Stu's so I don't take my coat and boots off; instead I go back outside and trot along the well-worn path through the snow to their porch, open the door and step inside. I take off my boots, tap on the door, open it and go into the kitchen. "Hello!" I sing out.

The boys have set up their slot car track on the floor next to the kitchen table; they look up and say hello in unison.

"How come you guys are still up?"

"Come on, Auntie," Charlie says with a *tsk* and a shake of his head, "tomorrow ain't a school day 'n' I ain't a baby."

"I guess you aren't at that," I reply.

Red calls from the front room, "In here!"

I shuck my coat onto a hook by the door and carefully navigate the slot car track. In the living room, I find Stu in his recliner and Red curled up in an armchair, watching *All In The Family*. I cross in front of Red and flop down onto the couch.

"Don't mean to interrupt you in the middle of your show," I tell them.

"It's okay, Princess," Stu says, "we seen this episode before."

"About a dozen times," Red says. "What's up? How come yer home so early?"

"That was the most miserable date I've ever had," I tell them. "Well, except for date nights with my ex before he was my ex."

"What? You finally go out with Jake and it's a miserable date? After that steamy hot smooch after the cookout?"

"Allrighty, then, I got chores to do," Stu declares. He rights his recliner and gets to his feet with speed that's impressive for a middle-aged man his size. "You need a glass of wine. You want a top-up, darlin'?" Red drains what's left in her glass and passes it to him. When he's delivered our wine, he goes back into the kitchen and says to the boys, "Come on, you meatheads, time you put your Hot Wheels away 'til tomorrow. Come 'n' help me with night check."

I hear Charlie say, "But we already done night check."

"Well, we're gonna do it again."

There's grumbling but in minutes they're gone, leaving Red and me alone.

"He doesn't want to hear any girl talk," Red says.

"He's good about leaving us to talk, although at times it might be nice to have a man's opinion."

"The older I get, the less I value a man's opinion," Red says. "Anyway, what was so bad about yer date?"

"Well, for starters, he was an hour late. I was really hungry by the time he showed up. He didn't explain why he was late, seemed to think he could just say he was sorry, give me a hello kiss, and that would make everything right. But I was in no mood for a damn kiss, so I ducked it. Might've gone better if I hadn't, I suppose."

"You should of ate a cookie. You know you git grouchy when yer blood sugar's low."

"I don't get grouchy," I exclaim. "Well, even if I do, you're not really going to make it my fault, are you?"

"Naw, just pointed that out. But anyway, didn't he say why he was so late?"

"Family issues, he said. When we got to Billie's, he was more like his old self, very sorry and so on. Said Leo drove in the ditch and he had to go help him."

"You sure that was the issue? That kid's been in trouble with the law since he was in high school."

"Oh? Well, it sounded reasonable, roads the way they are. But beyond that, we had nothing to talk about. Strange! I guess I expected more, although when I think back to the dance, we didn't really talk much then, either."

"Maybe he don't know how to talk to women," Red suggests.

"He's asked me out half a dozen times and now he can't talk to me? I told him about my promotion, but he was so disinterested I'm not sure it even registered." I take a swallow of my wine, exhale a long breath, and say, "I really thought after that kiss... But of course I was pissed off when he was late. If I'd given him a little warmer greeting, maybe that would've set things off on the right foot, so that part of it's on me. It never did get right, though. At the bar, he told me about an argument with his kid over school, and I started to tell him about Charlie and Johnny and he snarled at me, then buggered off to talk to someone. Left me sitting alone for half an hour. I was thinking of calling you to come and pick me up. Then he apologized and things should've improved, but this woman came and sat next to him. He was surprised to see her, and not in a happy way. She said she and Jake go back a long time. He said something like he didn't want her to "do this" just then, and she took off. He didn't want to talk about her, but he finally said she'd been a friend of his wife's and admitted they'd dated but it was over. But she sure wasn't acting like an ex-girl-friend. I bet the times he's asked me out, they were still a couple. So I guzzled a carafe of wine and neither of us could get the date over with soon enough."

"Aww, that's too bad! He seems nice. Handsome, too. 'N' you were looking forward to seein' him."

"Yeah, I really was. Just proves once again that I'm a poor judge of people in general and men in particular. And he probably thinks I'm a lush."

"Aww, well, he ain't the only fish in the sea."

"Well, I'm done fishing. Goddammit Red, men are more trouble than they're worth. Uncle Stu excepted, of course."

"And Reggie."

"Yeah, Uncle Stu and Reggie excepted. And Arnie too, I guess."

"Well, I wouldn't be so quick to say Arnie's no trouble."

"Probably right." I take another sip of wine, then set the glass on the coffee table. "I really don't need this. You want it?"

Red shrugs and says, "sure."

"Speaking of Reggie, this is my Calgary weekend. Are the pies ready to go?"

"Yup, they're boxed up 'n' we loaded 'em into yer truck already as I imagine you're gonna want to get away bright and early."

"Yeah, earlier than bright, actually. Goddamn! I'm gonna have a hangover and I can't sleep in. Mom says customers have been asking about the pies and she's promised they'll be out by noon. She wants us to up the production and make more than two deliveries a month."

"You don't want to make the trip every weekend, I'm sure."

"No. And as far as upping production, I'm not sure we have enough rhubarb or saskatoons frozen to make more. Right?"

"Right."

"Well," I reply, "not this year, anyway. Next year we could plant more rhubarb and until it's producing, buy rhubarb locally, buy more saskatoons from pickers or maybe even start our own berry patch now that a domestic variety is available, and we can expand little by little with very little expense. Maybe hire someone to help with the baking and a driver to make the Calgary run. We should think about it."

Red sips her wine and leans back, then shrugs and says, "I guess we should."

I bite my bottom lip as I think. "Maybe tomorrow when I'm not drunk it'll seem like a stupid idea. Anyway, I'll do payroll Sunday and should be able to leave Calgary early in the afternoon, so home by supper time. Wish the roads were better."

"The Trans Canada will be okay. Some black ice though. So take it easy."

"Always." I wobble slightly as I get up and go to the doorway. I turn and say, "Thanks for listening. See you Sunday afternoon."

Ten

I ARRIVE AT the Mall, drive through the parked cars and around the back to the lane that runs behind the shops. The door at the end is open. I stop next to it, put the truck in park, and get out.

"Good morning, Reggie," I call to the fifty-something balding man in jeans and cowboy boots standing in the doorway, dolly at the ready. "Hope you have coffee on!"

"Ay-yuh, it's been on fer a hour. We were expectin' you 'bout that long ago. Startin' to worry."

"Yeah, I was late getting away, and the roads aren't great so I took it real easy."

"Wall, you go ahead 'n' try the coffee, but you'll prob'ly want to make a fresh pot. I'll take care of offloading the pies 'n' move yer truck back out to the lot when I'm done. Just gimme yer keys." He holds out his hand and I drop the keys into it, then go past him through the stock room to the tiny staff room. I use the washroom then get a cup and fill it with the strong-smelling brew in the carafe. One sip and I decide that although I'll drink it for the caffeine fix, I don't want a second cup. I empty the carafe and make a fresh pot.

A short, pleasantly plump woman comes through the door from the sales floor and exclaims, "finally!"

"Hi, Mom," I respond. "I overslept. Didn't get away until six. Reggie said you were worried. I've had lots of experience driving in these conditions, you know."

"I wasn't worried about your driving, I was worried about the pies getting here." She slips a marker into her apron pocket.

"Good to know you have your priorities straight."

"There's already someone waiting for them."

"Well, your hubby's unloading them as we speak."

"Okay, I'll go get them and start putting them out. You know they'll be gone by close of business today. You guys have to start making more." She shakes her head and clicks her tongue. "Anyway, I'll see to the customer. Meantime, you can start on the new window signs."

"Can we go for lunch pretty soon? I'm about ready to eat right now."

"Too busy! Have a muffin." She indicates the Tim Horton's box on the table and hurries off. A second later, she comes back to the door and says, "Oh, by the way, we're going to the Keg for dinner. Arnie's joining us." She turns away, closing the door behind her.

The Keg's great, and Arnie joining us is great, as long as he doesn't bring some random man to introduce me to. I select a carrot muffin from the Timmie's box and as I peel the paper off, think about the last guy. He was a contractor Arnie knew through his plumbing company. He claimed the guy was "a catch" and thought he was doing me a favour. Other than both knowing Arnie, we had nothing in common and he had such bad halitosis our one and only kiss nearly gagged me. I can only assume Arnie was never close enough to him to get a whiff.

When the coffee's ready, I dump the old stuff out of my mug and refill it with fresh before setting it on the table. I go to the closet housing office supplies and get the pack of paper sheets with "SPE-CIAL" printed in a banner across the top and the bin of felt markers, and sit at the table. Mom's notes on the whiteboard list the specials so I start making posters.

I BREATHE A SIGH OF relief when Arnie shows up at The Keg alone. He joins the three of us and after greetings, tells the server what he wants to drink. When we're waiting for Arnie's drink we pick at our shared appetizers and I tell Arnie about my job offer.

"I worry about you going full time," Mom says. "You still need to help Red with the pies, and I still need your help with the payroll. But I'm being selfish. I'll push the payroll over to the accountant. Actually, when I think about it, I should've done it before now. I hate bookkeeping, so why didn't I?"

"Because it was an added expense you didn't need when you were just starting out, Mom," I tell her. "Now that you're established and have the cash flow it doesn't make sense. But you don't need the accountant to do most things, just a bookkeeper. Send your books to an accountant once a year, to do your financial statements. But you should talk to someone who knows more about business than I do."

"Sez the gal with a degree in business admin," Arnie says.

"You do a great job, honey, but I know you'll be busy with the farm store business pretty soon, too. I need to let you go," Mom nods, gives me a little smile, and sips her wine. "That doesn't solve the pie thing though. And what about that *mobile in Saskatchewan* requirement for your new job? What if they transfer you?"

"Everett says that won't happen for a few years at least, and I don't have to accept the transfer."

"If you wanna be *upwardly* mobile, you do," Arnie says.

"Do you want to be, um, upwardly mobile, Lindy?" Mom asks.

"Not if I'd have to live somewhere else."

"Well, I git that! If I had a place like Wacasko-Wâti, I'd never move neither," Reggie declares. "You ain't been out there fer a while, Melon, but you 'member our weddin' in the grove? A lot's been done since then so the yard 'n' so on's even nicer now."

"I been there since that. I was with you guys at Lindy's twenty-fifth, remember?"

"Oh yeah. Anyhow, there's gonna be enough work fer Lindy once the farmgate store's runnin', if you ever git the damn plumbin' done. If she gits tired of drivin' to town fer her bankin' job she can just quit 'n' git serious 'bout makin' pies 'n' runnin' the ranch. What could be better'n that?"

"Nuthin," Arnie agrees, and wipes a hand across his bushy moustache. I'm struck by the fact there's quite a bit of grey in it. When did that happen? Arnie continues: "And fer yer information I'll git the rest of the plumbin' rough-in done as soon as they tell me they're ready. When I show up with my crew, it'll be done in a day. Unlike some others I don't waste time fartin' around. Done quick 'n' done right's my motto."

"He's just yanking your chain, Arnie," Mom assures him.

The servers arrive with our meals and we all lean back in our seats to allow them room to set the dishes in front of us. Once it's determined all we need is more drinks and the servers scurry off, Arnie says, "I have news, too."

"Oh yeah?" Reggie says as he saws off a piece of prime rib. "What?"

"So, you know I was in Kamloops scoutin' out warehouses, thinkin' to expand my business there?"

"Actually, no," I say, "I didn't know. Well, I knew you were talking about opening up in another city but I thought you meant Regina or Vancouver."

"Yeah, I was, but construction kind of took a nosedive with the mini-recession, so I'm not sure about branching out. It's kinda on a back burner fer now. But I thought instead of another big distribution center I might do something smaller, 'n' if I could git a good deal on a lease in the depressed market, I might lock up a property now even if I don't do nuthin' with it until the economy turns around. Maybe even buy somethin'. So I was drivin' to Vancouver 'n' as I was goin' through Kamloops, I thought, why not have a look there? I booked into a motel 'n' called a realtor to set up a couple appointments."

"Jesus, Melon! Is this gonna be one of yer great big long-winded stories that takes ten minutes to git all the unimportant details right before you git to the actual news?" Reggie asks.

"Oh, are we goin' back to usin' our old nicknames now?" Arnie asks. "Well, you still live up to yers, Wiggles. Quit squirmin' 'n' lemme tell the story."

"Don't mind him, Arnie," Mom says, and gives her husband a dig with her elbow. "Did you find something?"

"Yeah, but not a warehouse. Or a property."

"*Wallll*," Reggie drawls, "Christ on a bicycle, would you spit it out?"

"So, who should I run into, but a gal I dated back in high school. She's livin' in Kamloops now. Went out fer dinner with her 'n' her husband 'n' met up with a couple friends of theirs. They joined us fer drinks. It's what they call a brew pub, you heard of those? They got their own brewery right on site. I hafta say, I really enjoyed their lager."

"Oh, so what did everyone have to drink, then? 'N' don't you remember what they had to eat? Goddammit, Melon!" Reggie hisses.

Arnie laughs. "That's what you git if you accuse me of tellin' too many unimportant details!"

Reggie blows out a loud breath; Mom and I chuckle. "Go on," I encourage him.

"Well, one of 'em really caught my eye. Divorced, got a couple of teenaged girls. We been dating."

"Oh, that's great!" I exclaim.

"What lies did you tell her to git her to go out with you?" Wiggles asks.

"Never have to lie, Wiggles. She was hooked the second she cast her eyes upon me."

"Jesus, yer head's still as big as a melon."

"Reggie!" Mom exclaims. "Don't pay attention to him, Arnie."

"You know I don't," Arnie replies. "I ain't changed since we rodeoed together 'n' neither has he. He never could git the girl. How he managed to rope a woman as gorgeous 'n' as smart as you is still a mystery."

"Aw, thanks, Arnie," Mom says, and reaches across the table to give Arnie's forearm a rub. "So. When do we meet this new girl of yours?"

"She's coming to Calgary at Christmas. I'm hopin' you guys can meet her then. I'd like to invite you all for the big dinner but she has family in these parts, so our schedule's gonna be tight."

"We'll try, for sure," I assure him. "Call and let us know. Even if it's just for coffee. Whatever works for you. I'm happy for you, Arnie."

"Thanks, Lindy," Arnie says.

"You sure you wanna go meetin' her whole family, Melon?" Reggie asks. "Might not be the best idea if you wanna keep this gal."

"Reggie!" Mom scolds.

"It's okay, Marie," Arnie assures her, "I'll be on my best behaviour."

"Her family will love you," I say.

"Not necessarily," Reggie says. "If they're city slickers they might not take to the horse shit on yer boots."

"Wouldn't I love to have horse shit on my boots again! But anyhow, her folks ain't city slickers. They got a ranch east of here. But I'll shine my boots just in case."

"East of here? Out my way or further north?" I ask.

"Not sure exactly where, Lindy. I know her parents live near Brooks, but her brother's place is a ways into Saskatchewan."

"Maybe you'll go to his place, then," I suggest. "If it's not far from Wacasko-Wâti, maybe something will work out there."

"Maybe."

"I hope so. Red wouldn't want to miss meeting your new girl-friend. I wouldn't either."

"I'll make sure somethin' works out."

"Just don't do nuthin' to piss the lady off so she dumps you before then," Reggie says.

"Come on, Wiggles, you're usually more romantic than that!" I scold. "Arnie's a catch. That won't happen. But if it does, you come anyway, okay, Arnie? You know you've got an open invitation to stay at my place."

"I know, 'n' it's a nice offer," Arnie says. "What about you, Princess? Anyone new in your life?"

"Nope, and I'm gonna keep it that way."

"Naw, don't say that," Reggie says. "You been too long on yer own already."

"There's nothing wrong with being on my own. For your infor-mation, I had a miserable date last night," I tell them. "Men are more trouble than they're worth. Present company excepted of course."

"Aww, sweetie," Reggie says, "If a ornery ol' coot like Melon can find someone, there's someone fer everyone. Someone'll come along."

"In that case, I might change my mind. But I don't really care and I'm not going to go looking. End of discussion!"

"You know Reggie just wants the best for you, Lindy," Mom says.

"We all do," Arnie chimes in.

"I know. And right now, being on my own is what's best for me. Just ask Red." I spear some salmon and push it around in the sauce before popping it in my mouth. As I chew, I remember I haven't told them the other big news. I swallow, and say, "hey, I didn't tell you guys... We got hit by rustlers."

"Rustlers?" Arnie asks. "Seriously? Goddamn!"

"Yeah. You know our land borders the community pasture. It's the Wild West out there only now they ride ATVs, herd them into a squeeze chute to brand them, and haul them away in a semi. We lost a dozen."

"Holy shit, that's worth..." Reggie gazes off while he mentally does the math.

"A lot," I finish for him. "We were weeks away from shipping them. They were supposed to be our semi-annual payment on our line of credit."

"That's tough," Arnie says with a slow shake of his head.

"Yeah. Bank's not happy about it either. Anyway, we weren't alone. Pretty well everyone that has a herd out there lost at least a few and twenty of Larry Ford's breeding stock Simmentals are gone. He got hit the worst."

Arnie utters a low whistle and says, "Jesus! That's a big loss."

"Bastards," Reggie growls. "Whatcha gonna do about it?"

"Well, for now the manager of the pasture is on alert, for all the good that does. He's only one guy, and he's got Lone Tree and Big Stick both to look after."

"Which is where?" Arnie asks.

"Sorry, I guess you wouldn't know. Lone Tree is south west but Big Stick is the one that's adjacent to our property. Probably 50,000 acres between the two of them for one guy to manage. Mounties are driving around our end of it once a day. I don't know how long they'll keep that up or if it'll do any good. Red is bribing them with coffee and cookies in hopes they'll do it more often."

"Maybe she oughta start makin' donuts," Reggie suggests. "She'd never git rid of them then."

Everyone gets a chuckle out of that.

"Ain't that nice," Arnie says. "But drivin' around once a day—they'd hafta be pretty damn lucky to spot anything. And if the bastards know where the manager is, they got plenty of time to make sure they hit when he's at the other one, right?"

"I never thought of that, Arnie," I say. "But that means it would have to be someone familiar..."

"Yeah. Someone either inside or who if he's askin' questions, it ain't suspicious. Jesus! I wisht you 'n' me, Wiggles, could git on a couple of Porky's rescue horses 'n' patrol it proper. And Porky too."

"You guys," Mom chides, "you think you're going to get up a posse? You do realize you're not thirty-something anymore?"

"We still got what it takes," Reggie assures her. "Ain't all that long ago we were bronc riders, remember."

"Stu does fine," I tell them. "Of course he rides pretty much every day. When's the last time either of you put a leg over a horse?"

"Don't worry, Wiggles is right, we still got what it takes. I still got my saddle," Arnie says, then shrugs and sighs. "But it's a dream. We got businesses to take care of. I can't git away right now."

"Well, it's late in the year. Stu thinks that's the end of rustler season," I tell them. "For now, let's be sure we all get together sometime over Christmas."

"He thinks they'll quit just because it's getting cold?"

"I guess that's it. Also, the days are so short unless they can work in the dark, they'll be active when folks are up and around."

"I wouldn't be so sure that they can't work in the dark," Arnie says. "With enough moonlight? 'N' they got headlights on them ATV's. Hope he's right, though. Meanwhile, what're you gonna do about that new job?"

"Yer gonna take it, ain't ya?" Reggie asks.

"I'm going to take it."

I GET HOME LATE SUNDAY afternoon. It's already gathering dusk. Too late to go for a ride, which is unfortunate since the temperature is mild and it had been a lovely sunny afternoon. I was looking forward to it but had trouble balancing the payroll account so I left Calgary later than usual.

Red comes out on her porch when she sees me drive in and when I'm walking from the garage to my porch, calls out, "Come over fer supper, Lindy!"

"I sure will, just give me a minute," I call back. Thank you, Red! I go into my house to use the bathroom, then head over.

"Looks like I'm just in time," I observe. The boys are setting the table and Stu is already in his chair at the far end, beer in hand.

"You go sit," Red instructs, so I take the chair at Stu's elbow. I've barely sat down when Charlie puts a glass of wine in front of me.

"Thank you, Charlie," I say. "How'd you guess I'd be wanting this?"

"Tsk," he clicks his tongue. "Auntie!"

Okay, so apparently I have a reputation. "You know I love you, right?"

He grins and I think he's blushing. He goes off to fetch the bowl of mashed potatoes Red is handing him.

"How was yer weekend?" Stu asks.

"Arnie met us for dinner at the Keg," I tell him. "He's got a new girlfriend."

"That right?" Stu says.

"I told them about our rustler problem. Arnie pointed out something I don't know if we've considered before."

"What's that?" Red asks as she sets the platter of roast pork and a gravy boat full to the brim on the table. The boys pile into chairs and she takes her usual seat nearest the kitchen.

"Maybe you guys thought of it, but I hadn't. Arnie said maybe the rustlers have someone on the inside who's tipping them off to which community pasture Ernie's working on any given day. So when Big Stick got hit, he was over at Lone Tree. Coincidence?"

"Hmmm," Stu says as he scoops potatoes onto his plate and passes me the bowl. "No, don't believe we talked about that, other than to say the rustlers could be one of us."

"Well, I was thinking about it on the drive home. It could be someone at the community pasture office."

"Could be," Stu agrees. "But it ain't just the community pasture that's got hit."

"Oh?" I pass the potatoes to Charlie.

"Was talkin' to Jonesy at the Legion yesterday. Jonesy's neighbour Walter, him 'n' his missus made one of them senior's bus trips down to Reno this past week. Jonesy was feedin' fer 'em, showed up one afternoon to find the corral empty."

"Don't mean it ain't someone on the inside," Red says.

"Maybe we should make a list of all the ranchers around here and eliminate those who had cattle stolen," I suggest.

"I don't think you could eliminate them just 'cause they had cattle stole," Red says.

"What? No one would steal... Oh, I see what you're getting at. It would be perfect, wouldn't it? No one would suspect someone who was also a victim. Then all he has to do is sell his own cattle."

"Ay-yuh," Stu agrees.

"Maybe even Jonesy."

"I just won't believe that," Red says.

"Me neither," Stu says. "But if we're plannin' on goin' somewhere, best not tell him, just in case."

"As if we're likely to go anywhere."

I think of Jonesy sitting there at our cook-out, eating, drinking, laughing with everyone and all the while knowing he'd stolen from them! But we don't know it's Jonesy. It could be anyone. "No, we never go anywhere. But until they catch the guys, I'll never look at our friends without wondering if it's them."

"Bad news all around," Red says.

That about sums it up.

Eleven

I T'S NINE O'CLOCK and I just got home from another week at Regional Office. I've changed into my nightgown, put on my fuzzy robe, and I'm pouring a glass of wine when headlights alert me to a vehicle turning off the road and into the yard. Although it's late I don't pay attention because anyone coming here always wants to see Stu. Then the lights shine into my living room window. Whoever it is, is coming to my place. Before I get to a window to look out and see who it is, the doorbell rings. I open the door on Jake. He's got his hat in one hand and flowers in the other.

"Hi, Lindy," he says. "These are for you." He pokes the bouquet at me.

Surprised, I take the flowers.

"I know I should of called and I have called, lotsa times, but you ain't been answering your phone."

"I, um, haven't been home much."

"I ain't seen you at the bank, neither, 'n' there's a new gal at yer desk. I dropped by here but yer truck was gone 'n' no one around to ask. I thought you might of moved. But then I seen Stu at the auction 'n' he told me you come home every other weekend 'n' he expected you home tonight."

"Oh." I'm holding the door open, processing what he just said. If this is true, he's been trying to get in touch with me for a few weeks at least. Why?

"I, er... Can I come in?"

The blast of cold from the open door hits the thermostat and I hear the furnace kick in. I stand back to let him in and shut the door behind him.

"Thanks, Lindy," he says. He shuffles his weight from one foot to the other while I wait for him to say something.

Finally I ask, "What's up, Jake?"

"Er, can we talk?"

Did I think he was just going to give me flowers and then leave? But showing up unexpectedly after that miserable date and not hearing from him for weeks has put me back on my heels. I blow out a breath and say, "I guess so. I was just going to have a glass of wine. Would you like one? Or a beer?"

"A beer would be great."

"Come in, then. I think all I've got is Bud Light," I tell him.

"Bud Light's okay."

I put the flowers in the sink and go to the fridge for the beer. When I turn back, he's pulling his boots off. He stands them on the boot tray by the door and puts his hat on top. I hand him the beer.

"Come ahead," I tell him. I lead the way into the living room and sit in the armchair.

Jake sits on the near end of the couch kitty corner from me and holds his beer out toward me as he says, "To good horses."

"Good horses," I reply, and reach over to tap his bottle with my wine glass.

He takes a long swallow of his beer, glances around the room and takes another, before saying, "Stu said you been away. In Calgary. Can I, er, ask why?"

"I'm in training for that new job I told you about. Learning all there is to know about consumer credit and hopefully getting at least a working understanding of commercial and farm credit." From his expression it's obvious he has no recollection of me telling him about my promotion.

He says, "Oh, so yer gonna come back 'n' work at the bank again, then?"

"Yes." It's just as well he forgot details of that miserable date. I pretty much had, before he showed up on my doorstep five minutes ago. After an awkward pause, I add, "I'll be the person you talk to when you need a loan."

"That right? Well, I guess I better be nice to you, then."

I frown.

"Just kidding, Lindy."

"Sure," I agree. I take a long swallow of wine and then ask, "So, what's going on, Jake? Why are you here?"

"Um, well, I been thinkin' 'bout you a lot. We didn't part on good terms. I don't want to leave it like that. I, er, well, I want to apologise."

"Okay. Apology accepted."

He leans toward me, elbows on knees, scratching at the label on the bottle as he looks me in the eye and says, "I really am sorry. I had a lot of bad shit going on. No excuse, but I got things sorted out now 'n' I'm hopin' you believe me when I say I'm sorry. I was a jerk. A total jerk." He peels a strip of the label off while maintaining eye contact.

He looks so much like Nick I have to guard against forgiving him too easily. I focus on his eyes—blue, while Nick's were somewhere between hazel and green—just to remind myself he's not Nick.

"What bad shit?" I ask.

He draws a breath, balls up the strip of paper between thumb and forefinger before replying. "Business stuff. I got in with some bad people."

"How?"

"Trust me, Lindy, yer better off not knowin'. It's nuthin' to worry about. It's solved now."

"Good," I say. I look at my watch, drain my wine, and stand up. "Let's leave it at that, then. I'm tired. Worked all day, then a four hour drive. I'm ready for bed."

He gives me a look as if to say something more, but doesn't. He stands, takes one last long pull on his beer to empty it, sticks the paper ball into the bottle and puts it on the coffee table. He follows me to the door. He plops his hat on and as he hunches over to pull his boots on, says, "Thanks fer the beer, Lindy."

"Thanks for the flowers."

"Yer welcome." He puts his hand on the door knob, then turns back to face me and asks, "I don't suppose you'd give me another chance? Go out with me again? Fer supper? I won't be late this time, that's a promise. Maybe I could take you to Jasper's like I wanted to last time?"

I hesitate, remembering that painful time at Billie's. I exhale and study his face. He looks so sincere, his brows nearly joining as they rise in the middle just like Nick's did when he was worried. I focus on the colour of his eyes again to remind myself that's where the resemblance ends. The problem is that it's been years since I saw Nick and now when I think of him, I'm not sure it isn't Jake's face I see.

"Please?" he pleads.

"All right," I concede.

"Good! Great! Tomorrow night?"

"Um, all right."

"You won't be sorry! You just say what time 'n' I'll be here."

"So, if we're going to Jasper's, how about you come here at five-thirty? So we'd eat before seven then? I'm always too hungry to eat later."

"Five-thirty it is." He releases the doorknob, takes a step toward me and cups my shoulders. "See you tomorrow," he says, and I think he might try to kiss me. I kind of want him to, but at the same time,

I don't. I stiffen and take a step back. He grins, opens the door and says quietly, "Bye."

The door clicks shut behind him and I stand looking at the closed door, wondering what just happened. Weeks ago I made up my mind I didn't need or want a man in my life. Tonight he shows up out of the blue and I agree to go out with him again. Worse, I'm pleased about it.

Although I told Jake I was going to bed, I pour another glass of wine and try and puzzle out if I'm an idiot or if another date is the right thing to do. I think about talking to Red, but it's probably too late to bother that early riser. I look out through the bare cottonwoods to her house but see no lights. It'll have to wait until our morning coffee.

I find a vase for the flowers and push the aspidistras aside to set the bouquet on the island. My glass refilled, I pull up a stool and study the ailing plant. It has only a few green leaves left and they're drooping right along with the yellow ones. It's been trying to die for quite a while and now appears to be succeeding. Suddenly it reminds me of myself. Was the best part of my life that summer with Nick? Have I been drooping ever since, just putting in time until I die? Am I so desperate for attention I agree to another date despite the first one being a flop?

Suddenly I hate the miserable plant. If it wants to die so badly, I'll put it outside where it can freeze to death and get it over with. I pick it up and take it to the door. Then I change my mind and set it on the boot tray. I'll figure out what to do with it, and Jake, tomorrow.

I'm in bed trying to fall asleep, mentally replaying my conversation with Jake, when I realize I didn't give his statement about bad shit and bad people the attention I should have. Maybe he'll tell me more tomorrow.

It dawns on me he has an account at the bank. When I'm back at the branch again I could check it out. Would it be unethical or violate any of the bank's rules? Doesn't matter. Even if it's a hanging offence it I'm going to do it.

Twelve

I HAVEN'T HAD a chance to talk to Red about Jake. Will she think I'm an idiot for agreeing to go out with him again? I have to choose the right time and the right words before I tell her.

Red isn't my mother or even a relative, just the wife of a man my father grew up with and thought of as a brother, but still, I don't like being on the receiving end of her disapproval. Maybe it's because growing up, there was no path to my mother's approval. She was too busy making the best of her marriage of convenience and finding solace in the bottom of a bottle. In her husband's view his daughter Jillian, a few years older than me, could do no wrong and I could do no right, so approval was hard to come by. Me running off with the rodeo people when I was supposed to be leaving for university sealed the deal.

Fortunately Mom turned her life around, got a divorce, and we're good now but I still resent her claiming my biological father wanted nothing to do with me when it wasn't true. I had to run away from home to connect with him. I met Nick, Red and the rest of his rodeo buddies that summer. Because of her, my father and I had less than a year together. Maybe on some level I still hold that against her and it could be why I value Red's opinion more than my mother's.

Until now we haven't had time to gab because we've been busy getting the pies in the oven. This usually goes smoothly but today the flour bag ripped when Stu was emptying it into the bin. Flour everywhere! While we were cleaning that up, the custard for the filling boiled over and caught fire. Fortunately I was right next to the stove, turned off the burner and threw all the towels at hand over it. No fire damage, all it did was set the smoke detector to screeching and ruin a bunch of towels. And of course we had to make another batch of custard. No small task when you're making gallons at a time. End result: we're running behind.

At last Stu and the boys are off doing chores and Red and I are at the island over mugs of coffee, taking a break now that the ovens in both our houses are filled and there's another dozen waiting to go in. Since I've been away week days, Red's been left to bake pies all on her own with no help from me except weekends. And now Mom wants even more and I'm working full time so me not helping will be chronic.

Packing the fifty-pound sacks of flour around is difficult for me and impossible for Red since it's half her body weight. Not that she doesn't try. Stu does it when he's around so she's not completely without a helper. Now she's even got him on the assembly line rolling out crusts. I told him he looks cute in his baker's hat. He frowned. I guess he thought I was putting him down. I told him the world's top chefs and probably bakers, too, are men. He thought about it for a second, shrugged, and grinned.

Red is so organized that with what she and Stu made this week and what we're working on today, there will be dozens of pies ready to go with me when I go back to Calgary Sunday night. I'm hoping we can have a day off tomorrow. I haven't suggested that yet either.

"I know your mom wants more pies, and it's good we got two stoves," she says, "but it's damned inconvenient they're in two houses. I'm thinkin' we could put a second one in my porch, next to the big freezer."

"You'd have to run 220 out to it, and there might not be room on your panel. Have you asked Stu?"

"I did. He said the same thing, somethin' 'bout we only have a 60 amp panel. I figgered it was just Stu bein' a man, always comin' up with excuses fer why my ideas don't work."

"Yeah, I've run into that myself. Which is one reason why I swore off men." Since I have a date tonight, why did I say that? Red has already admired the bouquet of flowers and said it was nice Jake came and apologized. Why didn't I tell her about our date then? I'm about to tell her when what might be a brilliant idea comes to me. "Red! What about switching my stove out for a double wall oven? My furnace is propane, not oil like yours, and the furnace is next to the kitchen so there's already a gas line right there. I could have a propane cooktop dropped into the counter, and then there would be two ovens, you know, the stacking type, where the stove is now. I've got a 200 amp panel, which is likely enough anyway but switching from electric stovetop to propane will make sure."

Her forehead creases and her eyes narrow as she thinks about this. "Goddamn, Lindy, that might work. Won't help my place, though."

"No, but you replace your old stove with mine. And if those double ovens are big enough maybe you don't need to bake in your house at all. You just come over here whenever you want. It's easier, with more counter space than at your place."

"We should talk to Stu about it."

"Of course. And I just had another thought, too. About the store building. We're already putting in washrooms so hoity-toity customers that don't like to use the outhouse won't have to run off as soon as they have to pee. Why don't we put in a kitchen while we're at it?"

"Wouldn't that add an awful lot to the cost?"

"It would. But thinking ahead... The pies are so popular, maybe Mom's right and we should up the production. Maybe we should see if one of our friends, Marcy maybe, would come and help out now, and at some point maybe we hire more people to do the baking, you just oversee it. With your recipes, of course."

"I dunno. I wouldn't mind gittin' some help. That's a good idea. But we don't have enough in the budget to add a kitchen, do we?" She chews at her bottom lip.

"Yeah, we'd have to increase the budget. And of course we'd need a bigger loan."

"Are they even gonna give us the loan we asked for?"

"I, um, hmmm. I don't know. I sure wish they'd get back to us. Problem is, we missed that big payment. They know we had a good reason and I thought they'd take it into consideration. I hate that they're leaving us in limbo like this. Anyway, if they won't give us enough, we should at least add a room even if we leave it unfinished so we can do it sometime in the future."

"I'll leave it up to you, Lindy." She's still frowning but at least she's quit chewing her lip. She gets down off her stool to get another cup of coffee, and checks the pies in the oven while she's up. "Another fifteen minutes or so. I'll go check on mine."

"You just poured a fresh coffee. You sit and drink it," I tell her. "I'll zip over and do that. They were in the oven after these so I'm sure they're fine."

"They need to be switched around, though. You know my oven has that hot area on the right."

"I know. I'll switch 'em." I slip into my boots. "I'll be right back. I need another coffee, too."

"And take that plant to my place before you kill it," Red says.

That's Red, for you. She solves the aspidistras problem. Now I just have to tell her about Jake.

TURNS OUT RED IS PLEASED I'm going out with Jake. I don't know why I'm surprised. She's always been one for giving people another chance.

True to his word, Jake arrives ten minutes early to pick me up. Conversation on the ride into town is a bit tentative but we manage to chat amiably about the new visitor's center the province is putting in up on the Trans Canada Highway and the expansion of the feed store to include a big hay barn that means they'll be buying more hay from Jake. I ask how things have been between him and Leo, and he tells me Leo moved out and is living with friends in Swift Current. He says it's good having him out of the house since they were fighting so much. I'm reluctant to pitch in my two cents worth after his reaction last time, but I bravely tell him I don't think Leo is too young to fly the nest, and—surprise!—he agrees.

Now we're at a small table in the corner of the dining room at The Jasper, tucked in next to a weeping fig that's not much bigger than the one in my living room that I've been trying to keep alive but with about five times as many leaves. I'm surprised and impressed that he made reservations. Good thing he did or we would have had to wait for a table, judging by how busy the place is.

After a couple of beers, Jake begins to look less like he's being tortured and more like he's glad to be here. Or maybe it's just my perception now that I'm on my second glass of what I call treat wine, actual Riesling and not rhubarb or saskatoon. Whatever. He's comfortable enough to tell a joke.

"Did you hear the one about the rancher who got audited by the govermint?"

"No."

"Well, the govermint guy phones up 'n' says the rancher's been reported for, um, unfair labour practices 'n' he's gunna need to talk to some of the hands. He asks fer a list of all the hands 'n' how much they git paid. So the rancher says, 'well, there's the guys who look after the cattle 'n' the guys who look after the horses. Them guys work ten or twelve hours a day. I pay 'em eight bucks a day. There's the cook. He works from six in the mornin' to eight at night 'n' I pay him ten bucks a day. They all git free room 'n' board 'n' Sundays off. Then there's the half-wit that works about eighteen hours a day, no days off. He gits nuthin' but room 'n' board 'n' a bottle of rye every Saturday night.' 'That's the guy I wanna speak to,' the govermint guy says. 'Yer talkin' to him,' the rancher says."

I know, it's predictable and not a knee-slapper, but I laugh anyway.

"I know it ain't that funny but it's the only one I got that's fit fer polite company," he says.

"It's funny," I assure him. "It would be a lot funnier if it wasn't so close to the truth, though."

"That's fer sure."

"Did you hear about the rancher that won a million bucks in the Irish Sweepstakes?" I ask.

"No."

"Yeah. They interviewed him on TV. They asked him what he was going to do with all that money. He said he's just going to keep on ranching until it's all gone."

"Also too close to the truth," Jake chuckles.

I notice the pleasant crinkling at the corners of his eyes. Nick would've looked like that if he'd lived to be Jake's age, because he already had the beginnings of crow's feet at twenty-seven. A twinge of sadness passes over me before I can push that memory away.

"How's the pie makin' goin'?" he asks. "You mentioned the little fire this morning. Git everything done you wanted to?"

"Pretty much. I'd like to've had time to go for a ride, but that didn't happen. Maybe Chica is just laid off, at least until I'm finished this Calgary stint. As it is, Mom wants more pies..."

"Your mom wants pies?"

"She has a store, in Calgary. Marie's Bulk Buy in Southridge Mall. If you know Calgary, it's just south of Chinook Centre on Macleod Trail. She sells Red's pies."

"Oh. What's a bulk buy?"

"Well, it's kind of like stores used to be, with everything in bins instead of in packages. So you buy just as much as you need. Everything from soup to nuts as the saying goes. Maybe an odd place to sell pies, but they sell so well she wants more. Also, we've been talking about expanding the new farm store to include a commercial kitchen. Trouble is, we need a bump in our loan to do it."

"Speakin' of keepin' on ranchin' until the million bucks is all gone," he says.

"Yeah, and it's not money we won. We have to pay it back. If we even get a loan for it."

"You know what they say, you gotta spend money to make money." He spears his last bite of prime rib, adds a dollop of horseradish, and pops it in his mouth. After he swallows, he says, "About the loan. If the bank won't give it to you, I have some contacts. Higher interest, sure, but not a lot, 'n' they're better at lookin' at the big picture."

"Oh, yeah?"

"Yeah. Let me know if you want me to put you together with them."

"Is it a finance company?"

"Not a company, really, just a group of high rollers who got together, pooled their money into a fund they loan out. I'd put in a good word fer you."

"Oh. But how can we, I mean, someone, be... If they aren't bound by banking rules..."

"They're honest people, Lindy. I wouldn't suggest it if there was any risk." He reaches across the table and takes my hand, fixing me with an intense gaze. "I've had enough trouble of my own, I would never suggest it if I didn't know it was all above board. You can trust me. You know that, right?"

He looks sincere. How devious could someone wanting to loan us money be? "Of course."

"Okay. Good." He gives a sharp nod, releases my hand and picks up the dessert card. The server comes around with a pot of coffee and we accept top ups while we decide if we should have dessert at all, and if so, what.

"I dunno," Jake says. He hands me the dessert card and asks, "Ever heard of Death By Chocolate?"

I read the description and say, "Hmmm, chocolate cake with chocolate butter cream. Probably pretty sweet. Put some whippy on that and I bet it's worth dying for. I'm pretty full though. Would you share one?"

"Um, sure, but you go ahead. I'm really more of an apple pie 'n' ice cream guy. Think that's what I'll go for."

"Hey, Jake," I say, "I don't have apple pie but I've got pie. Rhubarb or saskatoon, your choice. How about dessert at my place?"

He nearly jumps to his feet and says, "That's the best offer I've had this year. Maybe this decade."

I stand, pull my jacket off the back of my chair and start to put it on. Jake takes it by the collar to help. I pick up my purse, walk beside him to the hostess desk and hover in the background while he pays. As we walk out to his truck he takes my hand. I feel calluses on his palm and fingers; his hand feels strong and warm, and I like it.

When we get to my place, I make a pot of coffee and slice the saskatoon pie (the rhubarb is in the freezer) while he watches from his perch on a stool at the island. I dig out two pieces and set the plates on the island. "Would you like whippy or ice cream?" I ask as I slide his plate in front of him.

He takes my hand and pulls me to him. "I've been wanting to kiss you all night," he murmurs. "If you'd let me, that would be sweeter than any pie, even sweeter than Death by Chocolate."

His eyes are dark and intense. I realize I want him to kiss me, pretty badly in fact.

"Okay?" he coaxes.

I answer with a quick kiss. He slides his hand up my arm to my shoulder, strokes my jaw and tucks a stray lock of hair behind my ear before putting his hands behind my neck and kissing me with the intensity his eyes promised. He slides off the stool and pulls my body up tight against his, backing me against the counter and slipping his knees between mine. I tilt my head up and close my eyes as we kiss.

Pie and ice cream will have to wait.

Thirteen

MY LIBIDO MAY rule me at times, but I'm not so gullible as to take everyone at their word, not even a gorgeous, sweet-talking guy. When my stint at Regional Office is behind me and I'm back at my desk, the first time I have a few minutes to myself I pull Jake's account cards.

He has a two chequing accounts, one personal and one business, as well as a pretty impressive savings account. There have been substantial deposits from time to time, the most recent just a few weeks before our latest date. I imagine these deposits coincide with hay or farm equipment sales; I'm surprised at how large they are but aside from that, it all seems pretty routine. From what he's told me, his hay customers are feed stores or large ranching operations that buy semi-loads at a time. Ergo, big sales, big payments, big deposits. I put the apprehension I had about him out of my mind and leave for the day feeling optimistic about Jake.

THE WORK WEEK FINISHES with Jake picking me up (right on time) and taking me for burgers at Billie's, then a nightcap (and romp in bed) at my place. He says he could stay over if I invited him. I tell him it's too soon.

"Not too soon for me to fall in love with you, though," he murmurs.

What? We barely know each other! I like him and the sex is great, but I'm certainly not in love with him. I don't know what to say so I tease, "Yeah, it is!" I give his shoulder a little punch. "You haven't seen me at my worst yet! And anyway, Red and I are leaving bright and early to go to Swift Current to do some shopping. So get your pants on and get out of here."

He grumbles but gets dressed and leaves, with a promise to call me later in the week.

CHRISTMAS IS COMING. Red and I on our way to Walker's Tack and Feed. I thought I'd get Jake a new belt, but Red thinks it's too much to spend at this point in our relationship. She suggests something less personal, maybe Old Spice Soap on a Rope. I say a belt isn't all that personal, not being underwear after all, and it'll still be a reasonable price since I won't buy a buckle.

"He won a bunch of silver buckles back in his rodeo days but doesn't have belts for all of them. This way, he can wear one of his other buckles without switching belts," I tell Red.

"I still say it's too much to spend, bein' as you've only been on a few dates," Red declares. She's adamant. Soap on a rope it is.

"Wisht I could figger out what to git fer Stu that easy," she says.

"Maybe he could use a new belt? Maybe a couple inches longer?"

"Yeah, I've noticed he's puttin' on a beer belly, too. Maybe that's a good idea. He might not take it well if he thinks it's an insult to his manly physique though."

"Just say tell him his expanding waistline means there's more of him to love."

"Pffft! You know his nickname is Porky. He was pretty stout back in the day, got ribbed a lot 'specially by yer dad, so he's touchy about it. I don't care, 'cept him puttin' on weight makes me worry he'll come down with the diabetes."

"Yeah, it's a concern. What can you do?"

"Quit feedin' him's about all."

"And you're not going to do that. So, what about the boys? Got any idea what I should get for them?"

"I got no idea. But they're growin' like bad weeds. Both of them're gonna need new clothes. Boots too. I'd get 'em clothes anyway though. Sort of mean to make it their Christmas gift, don't you think?"

"I guess so," I agree.

We arrive at the store and I turn into the parking lot. Judging by the lack of empty stalls business is booming, but then the pile of snow from lot clearing is nearly as tall as the building and takes up a lot of space. There's a green pickup with the Walker's Tack logo on it parked right at the entrance.

"You'd think they'd park somewhere else and leave the parking lot for customers," I grumble. I have to turn around, not an easy task with a crew cab long box in a parking lot that's small at the best of times. I find a spot on the street and we hoof it through foot-deep snow to the cleared sidewalk leading to the store entrance.

We're greeted by the pleasant smell of new leather and a blast of Christmas songs issuing from speakers above the cashier desk. Tinsel adorns all the shelves and someone made a garland halter on the plastic horse head that usually displays show halters. Every aisle is crowded with shoppers.

We make our way to the belt rack. Red finds a nice one at a decent price. Then we move on to the kid's section and are sorting through the mark-down rack discussing the pros and cons of the boys having matching shirts, when I hear someone call out, "Martine?"

Hearing that unusual name, I look up and see it's the clerk at the cashier's desk that called. She's turned away from the customer that's at the counter and is facing a doorway that opens into a back room. A woman appears and rather more loudly than necessary since they're less than a dozen feet apart, demands, "what?"

I draw a quick breath and nudge Red with my elbow. "It's her!" I hiss.

"Who?" she asks, and pulls out a black shirt with a stylized thunderbird printed on the back, holding it up for my approval. "What d'ya think?"

"Look," I whisper. "It's the woman that was at Billie's the night of that awful first date I had with Jake."

Red turns her head to look as the Martine person speaks with the cashier, who has moved close. Their voices are hushed now but from the expression on Martine's face, it's a heated conversation. Martine waves her hand in a gesture of dismissal, turns on her heel and disappears back through the doorway. The cashier watches her retreating back for a moment as if collecting herself before returning to the waiting customer. She says, "I checked with the owner," and then her voice drops and we can't hear the rest.

"She's pretty," Red remarks. "Jake ever tell you why he called it quits with her?"

"No. I never thought to ask."

"Well it ain't 'cause she's ugly," Red concludes, "at least not to look at. I wouldn't want to be on the receiving end of that sharp tongue though." She turns back to the shirt and says, "I kinda like these dark ones. Won't show the stains so bad. Whaddaya think, a black one fer Charlie 'n' navy for Johnny?"

I'm still startled at seeing Martine here. It takes an effort for me to refocus my attention on the shirts. "I, um, sure, Red," I agree. "I've seen Felix in a shirt like that. The boys idolize their big cousin so they'll love these shirts and they're even on sale. Even though it's clothes, it's a good present from someone not their mother I think. I'll get them. You find something else."

"That's a cop out, Lindy, lettin' me pick 'em out fer you. But all right. Maybe we should go somewheres else, like Toys R Us, 'n' git 'em somethin' they can play with. They're still kids, after all. New cars for that track of theirs fer their stockin's. Or maybe a couple new games fer their Nintendo."

"Done," I agree. "You want to go upstairs?"

"It's just ladies stuff up there, ain't it?"

"Yeah. Ladies shirts and jeans."

"Could use a new pair of jeans. Might as well take a look since we're here."

We trot up the stairs and take a quick tour through. "Don't see nuthin' I need up here but you look all you want," Red says. "I'm goin' back downstairs. Gonna see what they got fer saddle pads."

I admire jeans that have a row of small brass beads down the side but they're too nice for around-the-ranch jeans and I can't wear jeans to the bank no matter how cute they are. I gasp at the price tag. I sure don't want to spend that much, not this close to Christmas, anyway. When I think I've seen everything, I go back to the cashier's desk downstairs, where Red is waiting with her purchases already in a bag.

"Didn't find nuthin else?" she asks as I hand the boys' shirts to the cashier.

"Nope." I pay and turn to Red to whisper, "Let's get outta here before Martine comes back out of her lair, just in case she recognizes me."

Fourteen

ARNIE'S GIRLFRIEND'S NAME is Anita. In a five-minute phone conversation with Arnie before he passed the phone to her, he must've said it a dozen times, so I'm not likely to forget it. Turns out her brother Jerry lives just an hour or so from Wacasko-Wâti and we're congregating at his place the Saturday before Christmas. Saturday being too busy at the store for them to get away, Mom and Wiggles have to pass. Arnie promised to take Anita to the store to introduce her to them.

Naturally Red is bringing pies and as requested I'm bringing sweet potatoes with marshmallow topping. I hate the stuff but Anita, who must be a whole lot more organized than I've ever been, offered me a choice of two items to contribute to the dinner and that was the one I had a hope of not screwing up. All it involves is boiling and mashing the potatoes, topping them with marshmallows in a Corning Ware dish, and sticking them under the broiler just before dinner's ready. As long as someone's watching the broiler, I'm confident it'll be fine.

My other choice was brussels sprouts in cheese sauce, with the added stipulation the sprouts should be caramelized and there should be bacon in the sauce. Anita would be happy to give me detailed instructions right then, over the phone, if I didn't have my own recipe. She obviously hasn't heard the jokes about my cheese glue. In her defence, it's early in her relationship with Melon so she hasn't been to my place for a meal. Still, it's kind of surprising he didn't warn her. I can only conclude she didn't run the list by him.

It's early in my relationship with Jake, too. In fact, maybe it's too soon to introduce him to Melon. I wouldn't have invited him except as he was getting dressed to leave last night, he asked what I was doing today. So far we've only seen each other once a week so I didn't expect it, but of course I told him and then had no choice but to ask if he wanted to come along. He surprised me by saying he would. I realize I'm happy about it. I'm starting to like him. Quite a lot, actually. Maybe if he says he loves me again, I'll say I love him too. It's still early but by then it might be true.

Red and family left Wacasko-Wâti a few minutes before we did. When we get to the full size statue of a Hereford bull we were told marked the driveway, we turn in and see them on the porch going in the door of the large, modern-looking two storey house.

"Jeez, the ranching business must be better here than around Maple Creek," I comment. "Look at the size of the house! And the barn!" I point to an equally imposing gambrel-roof barn surrounded by corrals teeming with cattle a few hundred meters off.

"Maybe they're just better at it," Jake says, and parks the truck at the low hedge.

I'm puzzled by that remark but he doesn't look at me. I follow him up onto the porch, where we put his six pack of Labatt's and one of my two bottles of wine (one for me and one for sharing) on the floor next to the others to keep cold. I ring the doorbell.

Almost instantly the door is opened by a petite brunette. An expression of surprise flickers across her face. Should I have called to let them know I was bringing someone?

She recovers quickly and says, "Hello! Come in! Come in! You must be Lindy!" she gushes. "And...?"

"Jake," he says.

"I'm Hazel. Welcome."

She's wearing what look to be go-to-church clothes and has done an impressive job on her hair and make-up. I'm reminded of the wife of the Amway recruiter who wanted to get me into their pyramid scheme a few years ago and I suddenly feel under-made-up, under-coiffed and under-dressed even though I brushed my hair before I put it into a scrunchie and I'm in my best jeans and best, never-barn-worn pullover.

In the kitchen there's another brunette woman, equally well made-up and pretty despite being quite a few pounds overweight, busy slicing some kind of sausage.

"This is Anita," Hazel says. "Anita, this is Lindy and Jake."

"Oh, hi," Anita says, giving me the once-over. "You know how you picture someone when you're talking to them on the phone? You don't look anything like I pictured you, Linda." Before I can correct her on my name, she continues, "Are you ever tall! I thought you'd be small and dark-haired. How tall are you, anyway?"

"Um, five eight and a half."

"Wow! Good thing your husband is tall."

"Well, um, he's not my husband..."

"Boyfriend, then. Good thing you found a tall boyfriend. You must come from big people."

"He found me, actually. And I'm a lot taller than my mother. My dad was tall. Norwegian, you know." So now I feel big as well as unkempt. I halfway expect her to ask "how's the weather up there?" This on top of the brussels sprouts recipe thing and I'm starting to think I'm not going to like Arnie's girlfriend.

Thankfully, Hazel steps in. "Let's get you drinks and we'll join the others."

"Nice place," I mumble, and hand her the shopping bag containing the casserole.

"Thank you. We like it," she says. She sets the bag on the island and points to the bottle of wine I'm holding awkwardly. "Shall I open that or would you like a highball instead?"

"Thanks, I'll open it, but I forgot to bring a corkscrew. Hope you have one."

"For sure!" She opens a drawer and roots through it, coming up with the utensil in question. As she hands it to me she says, "I'll get you a glass. What about you, Jake?"

Jake, who has just been standing there mute, lifts the bottle in his hand and responds, "I got a beer, thanks."

Given how this party started off I'm tempted to drink out of the damn bottle, but after determining Hazel isn't a wine drinker and Anita doesn't want to try Wacasko-Wâti Saskatoon Berry Dry (eww! Wacasko-Wâti means Rat Hole? No thanks! Giggle) good sense prevails. I fill a glass and put the bottle in an out-of-the-way spot on the counter.

We leave Anita preparing the trays of meat, cheese and crackers and join the others in the spacious living room. The room has wall-to-wall, ceiling-to-floor windows on three sides looking out onto the verandah, and a massive stone fireplace on the fourth wall, so the three couches and twice that number of armchairs stand around a large, low table in the middle of the room. It appears Jerry and Hazel are well-fixed financially and are no strangers to big gatherings. Jake and I head for the empty couch. After a few minutes of polite conversation, I realize the boys are nowhere to be seen. "Where are the kids?" I ask.

Hazel replies, "They wasted no time getting downstairs to play video games with my kids. So they're out of our hair for a while."

Anita comes into the room with a platter of snacks and a handful of cocktail napkins just as Hazel says this. "I took a tray down to them. These are for us. Help yourselves, everyone! It'll be a while before we eat." She graciously passes the plate around before putting it on the table, then instead of taking one of the vacant chairs, goes to sit on the arm of Arnie's. His arm goes around her and he pulls her down into his lap. She giggles adorably and he doesn't grimace so probably his legs aren't broken. Still, I doubt that's going to be comfortable for long.

"What time will that turkey be ready, Hazel?" Jerry asks.

"Not for hours yet. We'll eat around six."

"Oh," Red says, "I hate to say it, but we might have to leave right after, then. We got chores."

"Hazel, I told you that might be too late for dinner if folks have chores to do," Jerry says. "Can't you hurry things up?"

"You know that's a big bird and it can't be hurried up," Hazel tells her husband. Then she says, "Red, I'm sorry, but I didn't get it in the oven until we got home. I should've stayed home and got it going sooner but we had an important meeting this morning. About church."

"Can't be helped," Red says. "We might sneak out right after we eat, is all."

Hazel continues, "Too bad our church is so far away. Over two hours each way, and that's in good road conditions."

"Good grief! Where's your church?" I ask.

"In Pillerton," Hazel replies.

"Pillerton? Where's that?"

"A little south of Regina," Jerry says. "I'd call it a whistle stop but for quite a while now the train doesn't stop, it just whistles. Since they moved the highway even the Greyhound doesn't stop there. If you want to get on, you have to go out to the highway and flag it down."

"There must be a church closer."

"There's just one true religion, and one church, so we got no choice. Wouldn't be so bad if the goddamn P.C.s would get their act together and get a decent road maintenance program. You must of noticed even the main roads ain't been plowed. The road to the Reserve, that's plowed, though. Goddamn natives get their road plowed while the good people who pay taxes have to wait."

I draw a quick breath and look at Red. A look of surprise, then anger, flickers across her face and is gone. Stu picks up her hand and gives it a squeeze. I'm not worried about her saying something rude because she never would, but she stiffens visibly.

I ask, "Isn't it up to the municipality?"

"Conservatives won't spend a nickel unless it goes to one of their cronies," Jerry replies, dismissing me with a wave of his hand. "Anyhow, our church is a religion on its own, called the Children of Noah. We're going to start having services here soon as we get enough people interested in joining, and of course we'll need another Elder. I'll be one, and one of the Pillerton Elders lives closer to us here than to Pillerton so he's happy to switch and come here instead."

"I still wish we could have the other one," Hazel says.

"Give it up, Hazel, it's a done deal," Jerry says, and for the enlightenment of the ignoramuses in the room, explains, "She wants the young, good-lookin' one. We're lucky to have the one we got. And we got another one interested, just have to get him Purified, which is happening soon. Then we'll have three 'n' we'll start services here. We still need a bigger congregation than what we got, of course."

"Wouldn't be a problem if they gave us the young one. He's smart, and has a real nice voice. I love his sermons! If we had him, I bet we'd have a bigger congregation, too."

"I said, give it up," he snaps. Hazel presses her lips together, drops her chin and studies her folded hands. In a moment, Jerry addresses all of us in a softer tone: "I doubt she ever hears a word he's sayin', she's so busy eyeballing him. But it's Catch 22. You heard of that book? Know what that is? If we could offer a bigger congregation, he might come, but we need him to get a bigger congregation." Jerry looks around, his eyes settling on me, and asks, "What about you, Lindy? Maybe you'd be interested in joining our congregation?"

What? Why me? I stutter then say, "Thanks, but, um—"

"Children of Noah isn't like other religions," he continues before I have to come up with an excuse. "We don't believe in false idols, which is why we don't have a Christmas tree or lights all over the place. No church service, just meetings. We're like the Jehovah's Witnesses that way. And we're like Jews in a way too. we don't believe Jesus is the Messiah or anything else in the New Testament, because it's all false. All made up by King James. He had—"

"Politics and religion!" Anita interrupts. "Two things that shouldn't be discussed with people we've just met!"

I'm not sure about the others but I'm grateful she put a stop to that! And I see Red still frowning in a most un-Red way. I glance at Jake. He makes eye contact with me, but just briefly.

"You guys got quite a bunch of cattle in yer corrals, there," Stu says, breaking the awkward lull in the conversation. "You had any problems with rustlers?"

"Rustlers? No, but there's been some of it down around Pangman and Ogema, I heard. And up at Watrous."

"That right, eh?" Stu says. "Sounds like it's a lot more widespread than I thought."

After another uncomfortable silence Melon says, "Well, Anita has news." He prods her off his lap and back onto the arm of the chair.

"Yeah." She looks around the group and says, "My daughter Ellie will be going to Olds College in September."

"So she's decided?" Hazel asks.

"Goddamn waste of time 'n' money," Jerry opines. "What kind of a job can she get when she's done at that horse school? Nothing but shovelling shit, at Spruce Meadows if she's lucky."

"It's what she wants, Jerry," Anita says. "You know she's always loved horses."

"She should follow her dreams," I say. Maybe I'm remembering myself at that age, unable to break out of a path chosen for me by others. Jerry gives me such a sharp look I draw a quick breath.

"If she gets a useful education and a good job, she can follow her dreams like you say, Lindy, without being a barn slave. By having all the horses she wants. I bet her dad would agree," Jerry declares. "He's got them all week, right Anita? Maybe he can talk sense into her."

"I support her decision. If she doesn't want it bad enough that her dad can change her mind, I'll support that."

"You're way too soft on those girls," Jerry declares with a snort. "I need another beer." He starts to get up but Hazel jumps to her feet and says, "I'll get it."

"You going to take a piss for me too?"

She shakes her head and looks down at her feet as she stands aside to let Jerry pass through the doorway ahead of her.

We watch them leave the room. After a moment, Melon turns to us and says, "Anyway, Anita's thinkin' she'll leave Kamloops. Come to Calgary so she'll be closer to Ellie. I've asked her to move in with me."

"Oh!" I gasp. This is sudden and unexpected. Dating two months and they're making a big decision like that? I know I should congratulate them or whatever is expected in the circumstances, but I'm speechless.

Red says, "Well, ain't that somethin'!"

"I hope you know what yer takin' on, 'Nita," Stu says.

"Stu!" Red scolds.

"Well, she better have her eyes open," Stu says. "Ol' hoss like him, set in his ways."

"Hoss?" Melon says. "You mean stud."

"See what I mean?" Stu says. "He thinks he's a stud when he couldn't git up outta that chair without his knees creakin'."

"Okay, I'm a old stud, then. Don't matter if my knees creak when I can git the filly to do the work."

"Well, if you think this filly will do the work, you got another thing coming," Anita says.

"See? She's spunky, just how I like 'em," Melon says, looking at the four of us. "She's the gal fer me. I might even git married again. I been happy long enough."

"Arnie!" I exclaim.

"It's all right, Linda," Anita says, "he tells everyone that. I always ask who he's dating. He can't mean me because I plan on staying happy. And besides, I haven't decided to leave Kamloops. Kaylie, my younger daughter, is still in school and I don't think she should have to change schools now just because her sister is going off to college."

"Makes sense," I agree.

Jerry, fresh beer in hand, appears in the doorway and says, "Okay, then, who's up fer a game of Asshole while we're waiting for that turkey to cook?"

"What's Asshole?" Anita asks.

"You probably know it as Gopher," I tell her, and declare to the room at large, "I'm in if Annette is." Although I don't like the game because I always end up being either the Asshole or the Beer Bitch, I ignore the glare Arnie gives me for purposely screwing with his new lover's name and enthusiastically join the group heading for the big table in the dining room. Anything to lighten the mood.

THANKFULLY, THE REST of the visit is pleasant enough. Other than a lengthy grace delivered by Jerry thanking the lord for not only the food but for anything else he could think of and bestowing multiple blessings upon us, there is no more proselytizing. We also steer away from politics and no one comes up with another racist comment. Still, I breathe a sigh of relief when we say our goodbyes and the farmhouse/mansion is in the rear view.

"That was really—well, let's just say I don't need to see any more of Jerry and Hazel," I say, and lay my hand on Jake's thigh.

He pats it, but returns both hands to the wheel to negotiate the ruts in the snow. "Or Annette," he says. "You called her that on purpose."

"We didn't really hit it off."

"No shit."

"I think they had an agenda when they agreed to put on this dinner. Like it was a set up to get converts to their new church."

"Hmmf," Jake says. "Sounds like it might be all right, I thought. You interested?"

"Gawd no! You mean you are?"

"Well, I ain't drivin' to here to go to church when there's dozens closer, that's fer sure." He shrugs. "What about Red 'n' Stu?"

"Red is spiritual. She believes in the Creator and vision quests and smudging and spirit animals, stuff like that. But Stu? You have obviously never heard him talk about religion."

We're at the end of the driveway now, and Jake waits for traffic to clear before pulling out. The highway has been plowed and sanded since we came in so the going is much easier. He remarks, "We should be home before nine. At yer place, anyway."

"Jake, when you met Red, did you realize she's Indian?"

"No. I guess I wondered, though. Thought maybe part Chinese or somethin'. I always wondered why her name is Red. Expected someone with red hair 'n' freckles, which sure ain't her."

"I think her mother was Swedish. And Red's a nickname she got when she was a cook on a fishboat. Something about Red Snapper fish. But why would Jerry make a comment about Indians, though? Not knowing us from Adam? And didn't he see the boys? You'd never mistake them for anything else. And the way he treats his wife, like she's a child. And she just takes it." When Jake says nothing, I prod: "You didn't like them either, did you? I noticed you were pretty quiet."

"I just thought to stay right outta it."

He glances my way but quickly returns his attention to the road. It's starting to snow again, big flakes, no doubt just floating down but seeming to be blowing toward our headlights. Of course visibility is decreased considerably, making driving a full-time occupation.

"Wonder how Jerry lost his finger."

"Never know. Pretty common fer farmers to be missing fingers."

"Yeah." I study Jake's profile, feel the muscles of his thigh tense under my hand as he brakes for a second to slow in consideration of the increasingly bad driving conditions. We ride along in silence for minutes. Finally, I say, "Anita's pretty, though."

"Not as pretty as you, baby."

"Thank you, sweetie." The warm glow I'm experiencing makes me think maybe I do love him. I give his thigh a pat. "I hope she's not involved in that crazy church, though."

"She didn't say nuthin' about it."

"True. She just shut the conversation down. Thankfully. But maybe she's better at reading people, although I doubt that given her comments about my size."

"Askin' how tall you are ain't a comment about yer size, Lindy."

"What would you call it?"

"Er, maybe it's a compliment. She prob'ly wishes she wasn't so short."

"Hmm." After a moment, I ask, "Could she still be one of the, what did he call it? Noah's children?"

"Children of Noah," Jake answers.

"Children of Noah. Maybe she's in that, er, church and I won't have to try and like her."

"Why not?"

"Well, if she's one of them, it's not going to last with Arnie. I hope he doesn't get his heart broken again."

"He's a big boy."

"So, big boys are too tough to get their hearts broken? Don't you listen to country songs?"

"I'm just sayin'. He knows what he's gittin' into or he'll find out soon enough 'n' whatever happens he'll survive." He clicks his tongue and staring straight ahead as the wipers slap back and forth across the windshield, adds, "Just like the rest of us."

Fifteen

S TU IS IN MY kitchen taking down cabinets, preparing for his electrician friend Pete to come and wire in the new double wall oven. I'm sweeping to keep ahead of the sawdust. The new propane cooktop is already in place and Stu is working on switching the upper cabinets around so the shorter one with the range hood will be above the cooktop.

My old stove is on the porch, waiting to be moved over to Red's. It was new when my house was built a couple of years ago so it's decades newer than Red's, which came with the trailer when my father won it in a poker game.

The new oven is also on my porch. If Red is happy about getting a nearly-new stove, I'm ecstatic about my kitchen renovation because besides being such a boon to pie production, the new oven is really sleek and modern-looking, all stainless steel and black glass. I'm happy about the new propane cooktop, too, even though I had to give up two shallow drawers for it. I lose counterspace because of the cooktop being separate from the oven but the island has more than enough work space, especially since I got rid of the aspidistras.

The problem is that Pete can't come until after Christmas, although Stu is still working on him and can be persuasive. If Pete can't be convinced, pie production isn't worth talking about with only one oven, a poor one at that, so we've decided to shut it down until after the New Year.

Since we already had turkey at Jerry and Hazel's, Red is planning on ham for Christmas dinner and will make that and scalloped potatoes at her house. There's more room both in the kitchen and around the table at my house, but rather than hauling everything from there to here, we've agreed we don't mind cozying up to eat at her place. With Mom and Wiggles and possibly Leo, there will be a lot of people to cram into the dinette of a twelve-foot wide mobile.

Jake seems reluctant to include Leo. I remind him he's about the same age as Red's cousin Felix and they know each other from school, so it's not like he'd be thrust into the midst of a bunch of complete strangers. But Jake says he's got an invite to a friend's place and will likely go there. It's a shame, as it would be a chance for us to get to know each other.

As sweet as he's been and as well as things seem to be going between us, I have niggling concerns because of Jake's many absences. I don't want to see him every day, it's just that he never talks about his life away from me, even when I ask. I feel like I'm shut out, like we're not connected, and wonder why he's so secretive. Red tells me not being talkative doesn't mean secretive and says I should lighten up and be glad he's not yappy like Stu, who never gives her a moment's quiet. She doesn't mean it, of course. Not really.

Now there's the usual mumbling and grumbling from Stu, just the background noise I've gotten used to when he's around, until a spate of swearing brings my attention back to him.

"What's wrong?"

"Goddamn Phillips screws! They used Robertsons to put this up but were they happy with one kind of screw? No. They hadda use Phillips to put it together. Who uses these goddamn Yankee things? Now I gotta make another trip down to the shop fer a Phillips screwdriver."

"For one, I'll go. And for two, I'm surprised you don't have one in your toolbox. And for three, that's a lot of swearing for such a minor problem, Stu."

"Sorry, Princess."

"It's not like I haven't heard those words before," I assure him. I lean the broom up against the fridge and as I'm passing Stu on the way to the door, give his shoulder a rub. "Stand down. Have a coffee and a cookie while I run down to the shop."

The way he tosses his screwdriver into his tool box tells me he's still irritated, but at least he heads for the coffee maker and the cookie jar. Apparently I'm not the only one who gets grouchy when their blood sugar is low.

I pull on my snow boots and ski jacket and head out, hurrying along the path worn through the snow to the barn, and past it, to the shop. I find the screwdrivers and decide to bring three of the Phillips type to be sure I have the right size. I'm just coming back out and closing the door when Jake drives into the yard. This is unexpected. I wasn't planning on seeing him until Christmas Eve.

"Hey!" I reply. I catch up with him as he's climbing up to my porch. "This is a nice surprise," I tell him, and we go into my house together. Stu and Jake exchange hellos as I put the screwdrivers on the island, then remove my boots and jacket. I motion to the stool next to Stu and say, "Take a seat, Jake. I'll get you a coffee."

"No thanks, I can't stay. I just came to drop this off." He pulls a small gift from his pocket and lays it carefully on the island.

"Oh, thanks," I say. "You didn't have to bring it today, though."

"I, uhh, yeah, I did." He hasn't moved off the door mat but shifts his weight from one foot to the other. "Lindy, I'm sorry but I ain't gonna make it fer Christmas after all."

"Oh no! Why not?"

"Turns out I got an emergency hay order I gotta deliver."

"Won't you'll be back in time for Christmas?"

"No. Damned nuisance. But this order, it's a good one. Can't turn it down."

"Well, I git it," Stu says between bites of cookie. "Not great bein' away from home over Christmas, though. Whole trailer load?"

"Whole B-train load."

"Where are you taking it to, that you'll be away so long?" I ask.

"Vancouver Island."

This is stunning. All I can think of is that it's a bad time, weather-wise, to be travelling through the mountains, especially driving a B-train. I've only been to Vancouver Island once and remember it being a long trip made extra difficult because of having to tee up with the ferry schedule.

"Folks gotta have feed fer their animals," Stu says, and digs another cookie out of the jar.

That's Stu for you, never passes up a chance to state the obvious. I give him a *'really?'* look, then say to Jake, "You'd think they could've let you know a little sooner, though. It's not like they went out to their hay barn one day and were surprised to find it empty."

"I think they were dickin' around tryin' to git it cheaper before they called me."

"So they expect you to be away from home over Christmas because of their, er, I dunno... Lack of planning? Because they're cheap?"

"Can't blame 'em," Stu opines. "They gotta pass their added costs on to their customers so they owe it to them to git the best price they can."

"It sucks," Jake says. "I'm disappointed, too."

"Can't be helped, I guess." I push away from the counter and go into the living room to get Jake's gift from under the tree. I come back and hold it out to him, but he doesn't take it.

"No, Lindy, I won't take that now." He pulls me into a hug and promises, "We'll do our Christmas together when I'm back, okay?"

"Okay," I agree.

"Okay. Now, sorry to rush off, but I got things to do before I leave."

I give him a quick goodbye kiss but he tugs me out onto the porch with him. When the door closes behind us, he puts his arms around me and kisses my forehead and nose before finally settling on my mouth to kiss me properly.

"That's better," he says. "See you Wednesday."

I stand on the porch watching his tail lights disappear over the rise.

When I'm back inside Stu says, "Them folks on Vancouver Island must pay a pretty penny fer their hay."

"At least it won't be crowded around the table," is all I can come up with.

Sixteen

"**I** DON'T BELIEVE it! Brand new and it already needs a part? We have to go all the way to Regina to pick up a part for the damn thing, on Christmas Eve yet?" I blow a loud breath in frustration and pace around the island.

"Well, *you're* peeved," Pete says. "I wouldn't of had to come today after all. I planned to go shoppin' for my wife's present but Stu said you really needed this done before Christmas. Instead of gittin' the job done I spend an hour figuring out what's wrong. Which ain't easy 'cause I ain't an appliance repairman."

I sigh and say, "I'm sorry. You better go now, before the stores close. We're grateful you came and at least you got Red's stove and my range hood wired in. It sucks, all the way around. Why are there always problems? It's not like this thing was cheap." I'm tempted to give the pretty oven a good swift kick. It's just sitting there looking innocent next to the hole in the cabinets where it was before it had to be pulled out again to see why it wouldn't heat up.

Pete closes his tool box and pulls his jacket off the back of a stool. "Don't want to mess with tryin' to fix it when I'm sure I can't anyhow. Good thing we tested it before you had it full of pies."

"When I called the dealer, they couldn't of been sorrier," Stu says. "But they also said it's not their fault because they don't unpack 'em 'n' test 'em 'n' so on. At least they have the part in stock so they don't have to order it. They're gonna replace it at no cost to us."

"Except they're not sending someone to fix it, they're just giving us the damn part and we not only have to go get it but have to hire someone to come and put it in," I point out.

"I think I can do it," Stu says. "Sounds like it's a component you just switch out."

"That's what it looks like," Pete agrees.

"Whatever, we gotta go git it. But they're closin' at three today."

"So it's too late for today," I conclude.

The door opens and Red comes in with a swoosh of cold air and a pie. "Merry Christmas, Pete," she says, and hands it to him. "Just a little thank you fer comin' today. It's froze, but just stick it in the oven for a half hour or so."

"Aww, thanks, Red. Sorry I can't be of more help."

"What's that? Yer leavin' already?"

Pete explains the problem and ends with, "But I'll keep the pie, with thanks, anyhow."

"For sure," Red says.

"Well, there's nothing to be done about it," I say. "We need it ready to go PDQ, though. That dealer say if they'll be open Boxing Day, Stu?"

"Ay-yuh, they said they would be, if we could wait until then."

"We've got no choice but to wait till then," I point out.

"We could make a day of it," Red says. "We'll all go. The boys will have Christmas money to spend. They'd love an hour or so at Cow Town. I wouldn't mind seein' the Boxing Day sales. Maybe git a new shirt myself."

MOM AND WIGGLES SHOW up soon after Pete leaves on Christmas Eve, planning to stay a couple of nights. As is usual in our family, we do Christmas dinner and the gift opening on Christmas Eve. It's a Norwegian thing. Another Norwegian thing: lefse. Red started making it for my dad and Stu years ago and everyone loves it, so she's continued. Mmmm! Even thinking about those tasty potato flatbreads is enough to make my mouth water and imagining one with turkey or ham rolled up in it or even just buttered and salted is practically orgasmic. I draw the line at lutefisk, though.

I decide against opening Jake's gift until he's back and we can open our gifts together. I have enough gifts anyway. I get a nice silk blouse, some very nice dress pants and a Kodak Ektralite camera from Mom and Reggie, and a bracelet I remember admiring when we were at Walker's from Red and Stu. So that's why she went downstairs before me!

Charlie and Johnny each give me school projects. A clay ashtray with a horse head painted on it is from Charlie (I correctly guess it's Chica), and Johnny gives me a popsicle stick basket.

"You're supposed to put a plant in a little pot in it," he explains, his expression is so serious I bite my lip to keep from laughing, tousle his hair and pull him close. I don't remind him of my miserable history with plants. Maybe I'll try one of those air plants. I think they're dead to start with.

"It's really nice! You did such a good job. Thank you, sweetie," I say, and kiss the top of his head. I reach for Charlie and give him a kiss and a thank you too.

The boys are mildly pleased with the shirts but really excited about the new Nintendo games. I wish I had let Red give them the shirts so I could be the cool auntie who gave them cool video games. I'll keep that in mind for next year. To assuage my guilt at buying their shirts off the markdown rack, I had tucked a ten dollar bill inside a Christmas card for each of them. They're ecstatic about that.

Christmas day the boys have their stockings and we eat leftovers, including lefse with ham rolled up in it. Time passes very pleasantly. Adults drink plenty of wine and more than a few rum and Cokes. Wiggles pours multiple tequila shooters. The kids are allowed all the potato chips, home-made root beer and cookies they can stand, and we all play Uno and Crokinole.

The boys are thrilled to have Felix visiting. Despite the cold they saddle their project horses, put Felix up on another rescue horse and go out into the pasture to chase cows. With the kids otherwise occupied, Stu gets up a game of stook and I manage to lose all the loose change I've been collecting in a jar on my dresser, which amounts to at least ten bucks. Wiggles is the big winner. He always wants to stook the pot, something I never have the nerve to do, and he usually wins. When I was the dealer and it was my turn to play him, of course he stooked the pot. I was feeling pretty smug, holding an ace, thinking I'd beat him for once. He drew 18 in 3 cards. Everyone knows you don't hit eighteen. Astonishingly, he hits it and draws an ace. So now I have to draw a 10, a face or another ace. I draw an 8. I don't give up. I call it 9 and draw another card. A 7. So, 16 in 3 cards. My next card is the Jack of Clubs, the card I needed when I drew the 8, and I'm bust. There goes my pot. You'd think I'd know better by now.

"You know what they say, Princess," Wiggles says with a chuckle as he mounds up my pot and pulls it to his side, "unlucky in cards, lucky in love. If you wanna keep playin', I'll loan you some change."

"Don't gloat, Reggie," Mom says.

"Thanks, but no thanks," I tell him. I'm unlucky in cards, that's for sure, but lucky in love? I'm about the farthest thing from it. Not even a phone call from Jake.

IT'S EARLY BOXING DAY. Mom and Reggie leave for home at the same time as we head out to Regina. Stu isn't a shopper so he was happy to stay home, and I'm at the wheel. Red and I made a deal that I would drive on the way there and she'll drive home.

The weather is sunny and cold, and the road is clear, so we make the trip in the usual two and a half hours, arriving in Regina just after ten. You'd think most people would still be at home, but with throngs of people out to take advantage of the big sales, there's traffic. Lots of pedestrians, too. We plan to go to a couple of stores downtown before heading to Eaton's, which is on the way to Cow Town. Those stores both have lots of parking, but downtown is another story. I find a parking spot a few blocks away from the main drag and we walk from there.

The boys like Kresge's. As if there weren't enough sweets over the past few days, Johnny spends a good whack of his Christmas money at the bulk candy counter and happily shares it with everyone. Charlie buys no candy but happily helps Johnny eat his. Both boys are good about Red and me having a look through Simpson's and what trip to Regina would be complete without stopping at Army & Navy? At least that store has more to interest the kids. Charlie finds a "rad", "cool" and "awesome" pocket knife but since he spent too much on candy, Johnny doesn't have enough money left to get one for himself. I'm tempted to chip in on it but Red won't let me, saying it's a lesson he needs to learn. Red buys the boys each a couple pairs of jeans. They find boots they like, but Red insists they wait until they see what Cowtown has, with a promise we'll go back to Army & Navy if they don't find something there.

At Eaton's, I treat myself to a fuchsia bath mat and towels at half price, a nice update to my bathroom. At Cowtown, the boys both find gorgeous Tony Lama boots, marked down, and elect to wear them right away. Red gets her new shirt and I get a pair of the same jeans I admired at Walker's Tack before Christmas, but now 50% off.

We've all had enough shopping, pack our purchases in the truck, and head out. We brought ham sandwiches with us but the walking stomachs in the back seat polished those off between Eaton's and Cowtown and are hungry again. We head for the appliance store to get that part for the oven with a promise to get a meal right after.

The appliance dealer is in an industrial area so far south of the last signs of civilization it doesn't even seem part of town despite having a Regina address. This is unexpected and by now I'm getting hungry, too. I thought we'd see a diner or something on our way here, but since we left the last residential area all we've seen is a gas station with a faded sign offering coffee and snacks.

We find the Prairie Appliances warehouse and don't have to wait long for the staffer to locate our part. "Is there anywhere to have lunch around here?" I ask as he hands it to me.

"Naw, not around here," he says. "There's Big Al's or Rosie's Diner over in Pillerton. That's where I'd go."

Pillerton? In my whole life I'd never heard of the place and now twice in little more than a week. "How far is it?" I ask.

"About ten minutes. Not far off the highway. You say you're from Maple Creek? That's over by Swift Current, right?"

"Uhh, well, sort of."

"So, if you're heading home from here, you can take Number 39 West and get back to the Trans Canada before Moose Jaw so you don't have to back track through Regina. It's a decent road. And it's about the same distance from here as if you went back and got on the Trans Canada in Regina."

I look at Red and shrug. "Sounds great. Thank you."

We go back out to the truck and I get behind the wheel again. "So," I say, "are you okay with us going to Pillerton, Red?"

"Might as well," she says. "Maybe we have a look at that church Hazel and Jerry talked about."

"Exactly what I was thinking. Although I guess it doesn't really matter since I'm not going to join. Surely not you...?"

"God, no! But if Arnie ends up livin' with that gal, I'd like to know more about it. Just in case."

"In case...?"

"In case it's some crazy cult. Think about it. The one true religion? Only one place to git it? Needs elders? Sounds like a cult to me 'n' if he gits roped into it we might hafta haul him out."

"I doubt Melon would get sucked into something like that."

"Depends on which head he's thinkin' with, right? 'N' we're almost there anyhow."

"Okay." I put the truck in gear and we leave the industrial park, turning left onto Number 6 heading for Pillerton. Ten minutes farther on we come to the turnoff. I make the turn and once we're over the train tracks, Pillerton is before us. I'm surprised to see a wide boulevard in such a small town. It seems excessive given the lack of traffic. There's angle parking on both sides and the travel portion of the road is divided by a ridge of snow. It's probably a grassy median in summer but now all that's visible is a row of leafless trees half buried in snow.

The first building we come to is an old three-story sandstone. The upper windows are dark and look deserted but there's a neon sign above the ground floor windows reading "Big Al's", which looks to be a pub. There are enough trucks parked in front to indicate it's a popular place. I love pub grub but the boys wouldn't be allowed in, so I keep driving.

We get to the end of the street without coming upon either a church, Rosie's Diner or a break in the snow pile in the middle of the street so I can turn back. Fortunately just a couple blocks on there's a cenotaph in the middle of a round-about, so I negotiate the truck around that and head back in the opposite direction. I'm considering stopping to ask for directions to Rosie's when I see a familiar truck parked at the curb. I'm so surprised I hit the brakes and the truck slides to a halt.

Red exclaims, "Well, I'll be go to hell! What's Walker's Feed doin' here?"

Apparently she noticed the dark green truck with Walker's Feed logo on the door about the same time I did. And worse, Jake's truck is parked next to it. I gasp. It can't be his truck. It just can't be! I tell myself there are lots of pick-ups that look the same.

"Hey," Charlie pipes up from the back seat, "there's Jake's truck!"

"Are you sure?"

"Yeah. CPRA sticker in the window," he points out.

"I, er, probably lots of trucks with Canadian Professional Rodeo Association—"

"Pull over," Red orders.

I do as she says, pointing the nose of the truck to the sidewalk. When the tires bump up against the curb, I put it in park and sit in stunned silence.

"You think him 'n' that Martini woman're both in there?" Red asks, indicating with a lift of her chin the very dated-looking storefront.

"Probably. No other reason to park there, not with all these other empty parking stalls and everything else shut."

"You wanna go in there 'n' confront him?"

I shake my head. "No. I don't know. I don't think so. There must be an explanation for this."

"Yeah, like he's a liar," she hisses under her breath. "Git out," she commands, and slides across the seat toward me. "I'll take it from here."

I go around the front of the truck to the passenger side and have just barely shut the door behind me when Red reverses the truck out into the street and heads back the way we came.

There's an older man just getting out of his car in front of the Co-op Store. Red stops the truck and tells me to roll down my window. "Ask him how to git to Rosie's."

"Excuse me," I call out. When the man looks up, I ask, "Can you tell me how to get to Rosie's Diner?"

"Sure, honey. Just make a left at Big Al's there, and follow Front Street until you get to the sign that points you to Highway 39. Turn right, and you'll see Rosie's, right beside the Gas 'N' Go."

"Thank you," I say, and roll up my window. Red hits the accelerator and the big V-8 hums away down the street.

We no longer care about the church.

I sure hope Rosie's Diner is licenced.

Seventeen

SINCE PILLERTON, MY moods have been all over the place. What could Jake possibly be doing there? Was he with Martine? I don't care. He must have been. I do care.

What should I say when Jake calls? I don't want to see him, so our confrontation will have to be over the phone. It always happens that I only think of what I should have said after the fact, so this time I'll be prepared.

I even thought to call him instead of waiting for him to call me. I dialed his number but hung up after five rings, relieved both that he wasn't home when he wasn't supposed to be and that I could postpone the inevitable. What's that saying? I'm a procrastinator of no mean magnitude? Never do today what you can put off until tomorrow? I've rehearsed what I'm going to say dozens or hundreds of times so when tomorrow comes, I'll be ready.

At work, a surge of adrenalin courses through me every time my phone rings. When it's four p.m. and he hasn't called, I conclude he must be dumping me for Martine. Then I tell myself that's ridiculous. They never really were a couple, just dated a couple of times and he broke up with her months ago. Then I think maybe they have reconciled. Or maybe they've been together all this time and she is the real reason for all his absences. Why else would both trucks be at the same place at the same time?

At home, I hover around the phone all evening but still no call. It's nine-thirty and I'm getting out of the shower when the doorbell rings. It's late for the Pedersens and it can't be one of them anyway because they never bother to ring the bell, they just come right in. This is such an unusual event the first thing that comes to mind is that it's the cops, come to tell me someone has been killed in an accident. Mom? I whip on my robe, snugging the belt, tying it as I hurry to the door and open it. And there stands Jake, hat in hand.

"Jake!" I'm relieved it's not cops, but I was prepared for a phone conversation, not him just showing up. Before I can think about all the things I planned to say or even react, he steps inside and bumps the door shut behind him as he pulls me into an embrace.

"Merry Christmas, baby," he says. "Man, did I miss you!" He kisses me, but by now I've gathered my wits and squirm away.

"Lindy? Somethin' wrong, baby?"

"So, you've never been to Pillerton?"

"What? Pillerton? What do you mean...?"

"I saw—*we* saw—your truck in Pillerton."

"You were in Pillerton?"

"Yeah, we were in Pillerton! And don't you *goddamn dare* tell me you've never been there!"

"I um, yeah, honestly, I really have never been there. What's goin' on?"

"Don't lie, for chrissakes, Jake! We saw your truck! Right next to your so-called ex-girlfriend Martine's. I suppose that wasn't your truck?"

"I um..."

"Go away, Jake! And don't come back! I don't need a lying, cheating asshole in my life! I don't need *you* in my life."

"Lindy, please!" He takes a step toward me and cups my shoulders. "Lindy, that wasn't my truck! It couldn't of been my truck."

"We all saw it, Jake! We're not stupid!"

"Okay, well, maybe it was my truck, then. My *old* truck. The one I traded in." He takes my arm and pulls me out onto the porch.

Parked by my sidewalk is a black step-side Chevy with clearance lights across the roof. "There's my new truck."

Still a Chevy, but different model and colour.

"Your new truck?"

"Well, it ain't brand new. Newer than my old one, though. Someone traded it in. Only has five thousand klicks on it. That's one of the things I had to do the afternoon I came here to drop off your present. I had a deal cookin' with the dealer."

I feel resistance leaving my body as he continues, "I wasn't sure he'd accept my offer or I would of said something when I was here. I might of anyway 'cept I really didn't have time to start talkin' trucks with Stu. And you seen it in Pillerton? Goddammit, if I'd knew they could sell it so quick, I would of held out fer a better trade in."

A shiver courses through me, as much from embarrassment at being so wrong as from the cold. I turn and go back inside. Jake is right behind me and pushes the door shut.

"Okay?" he asks.

I turn to face him and nod. "Sorry."

"Not your fault. I'm sorry if it made you, er, unhappy." He kisses me, long and sweet, then asks, "You were in Pillerton? What on earth for?"

"Because of that thing." I point to the newly-installed double wall oven and I say, "Long story. Maybe we can do our Christmas Eve tonight. Do you want something? A beer, maybe?"

"Baby, I'm lookin' at what I want," he murmurs, and kisses me again. Unwilling to let go of each other and already working on undressing, we make our way down the hall to my bedroom.

When I'm helping him shed his shirt I notice his hand is bandaged. No Band-Aid this—it's the type they put on you at the hospital. "Oh, my god, Jake!" I gasp, and carefully take his hand to examine the dressing. It has a metal hoop over the end of a shorter-than-it-should-be index finger; it and his middle finger are bound together. "What happened?"

He pulls his shirt off, using his good hand to carefully work the sleeve over his bandaged one, and doesn't answer my question for a moment.

"Jake!"

"I, er. Well, remember when we talked about how it's not unusual for farmers and cowboys to be missing fingers?"

"You lost a finger?"

"Only to the first knuckle."

"Oh my god! How?"

"Doin' somethin' stupid, like most accidents." He pulls on my belt to loosen it and slides his hands over my shoulders to push my robe off. It falls to the floor in a puddle around my feet. "Can we talk about it later, beautiful?" he murmurs.

"No we can't talk about it later! You lost your finger, and on your right hand, too."

"Like I said, just to the first knuckle. Won't hardly bother me ay-tall." He chuckles, but it sounds forced. I sit on the bed and fold my arms over my breasts.

"Okay, if you have to know. It's embarrassing, really." He sits beside me on the bed and focuses his attention on the carpet. "I was at the feed store watchin' their crew unload my rig without my help, which is unusual in itself 'n' I admit I was enjoyin' it. Out in the parkin' lot a gal was tryin' to hitch her truck to her trailer. Don't ask me why it was there 'n' not hitched to her truck in the first place. I went out to give her a hand, guidin' her, you know? I thought the hitch was right over the ball 'n' it nearly was, but it was bindin' on it 'n' wouldn't just quite slide down over it like it should of. Instead of having her go forward 'n' try again since it was so close, I give 'er a tug. I shouldn't of grabbed it there or at least I should of gone to the other side and gave it a push with my foot but not thinkin' 'n' it slid down and smashed my finger. 'Course then she had to come 'n' jack the trailer off it before I was freed. I might of been squealin' like a stuck pig. Talk about embarassin'! 'N' my finger flattened so bad it didn't look like a finger so much as hamburger meat so they just lopped it off." He sighs. "I would of been home yesterday, a day early 'n' I thought to surprise you but it set me back a day. 'N' I sure don't like admittin' I was that goddamn stupid."

I'm confused at how what he described could happen. I'll get him to explain it again another time. For now I just rub his arm and say, "It must really hurt!"

He turns to face me and says, "It did at first but it ain't too bad now. And I got a beautiful naked young gal sittin' right beside me 'n' I missed her so bad I couldn't think of nuthin' else 'n' I know somethin' that would take my mind off it."

He gets to his feet and steps up so he's right in front of me, his crotch just inches from my face, and begins fussing with his belt buckle. I help him with that. What could else can I do? He is having such a hard time of it, what with one hand mostly out of commission.

Eighteen

I F WE THOUGHT the problem with rustlers was over, or at least that they wouldn't be active in the winter, we were mistaken. On a freezing cold Saturday, Stu comes home from the Weyburn auction with a trailer full of horses, a spotted mule, and bad news.

Red, the boys and I watch from a perch on the fence as Stu backs the trailer into the corral. As soon as the vehicle stops, the boys jump down off the fence and run to the trailer to open the door. One by one, the new arrivals come out and cautiously check their new surroundings. When they're all out and truck and trailer are out of the corral, Stu gives Charlie and Johnny the task of putting out hay for the newcomers while we go to my house for a glass of wine before supper and to check on the pies.

Earlier, Red brought a roast and rearranged the pies to fit the roaster into the larger of the two ovens, so along with the rush of warm air, we're greeted with aromas of rhubarb pie and roast beef. While I make coffee, Stu takes a stool at the counter and Red checks the pies.

Stu says, "Yeah, like I said, there's new talk 'bout rustlers. Some fellas were at the auction to see if any of their stock was goin' through. Wasn't none, of course. But the news is, remember that fella from over around Indian Head that went missin' along with his cattle a few months back?"

"Of course," I reply.

"Well, some photography club was on some kinda pitcher-takin' hike out in the Badlands 'n' found his truck at the bottom of a cliff, torched. And him in it."

"Oh my god!" I gasp. "He was murdered?"

"Yup. Bullet to his head. Guess they thought burnin' his truck would hide it. Prob'ly thought the truck would never be found, neither. I seem to remember some talk about him shippin' his cattle 'n' runnin' off with a bag fulla money, like the guy who goes out to buy cigarettes 'n' never comes home. 'Course no one thought about rustlers back then. Now they're thinkin' he caught 'em in the act." Stu clicks his tongue and sucks in a breath.

Red and I stand motionless, stunned. I feel like I've been punched in the stomach. "It could've been one of us! We're all vulnerable."

"I'm gonna talk with Bud 'n' Larry 'n' see what they think. But after this, when we start up patrols agin, I think it ought to be in pairs and maybe take a rifle along."

"A rifle? Goddamn! I hate to think of that," Red says.

"I know. Better to let 'em have the cows," Stu says. "But it's tens of thousands of dollars we're talkin' 'bout 'n' enough to put a lot of smaller outfits under. Lookit what a punch to the gut it was fer us to lose what we did last fall. Nearly cost us our financin.'"

We sit quietly, sipping coffee, each lost in thought. Then Red says, "Well, from now on the boys don't ride out on the community pasture no more 'n' neither do you two."

"I wonder if we're even safe in our home pastures," I muse. "The guy that was murdered was on his own land, right? Taken from his own land?"

"That's what I heard," Stu says. "Jake gits around all over the place. He ain't said nuthin'?"

"He's around home more since he's got no hay to sell until the new crop comes off so he hasn't been on the road much. He's coming for supper tonight. You can ask him if he's heard anything then."

"Wisht our construction project was goin' forward like Jake's hay barn," Red says.

"It will, just as soon as they increase our line of credit."

"You mean *if* they do. Why're they draggin' their feet?"

"I don't know, Red. Everett says he thinks since we missed that payment, they're nervous. He doesn't think we have enough collateral. I don't know what else we could give them. But I'll go over the income projections for the store again. I know from talking to people at Regional Office that the bank will open a new branch if they can predict a break-even point in five years. I have no data to make a prediction. Doubt if we'll get any walk-in traffic. We have to become a destination, and who knows if we can make that happen? We're willing to take a chance, but the bank isn't."

"I know yer loyal to yer bank, Lindy," Red says, "but maybe we should shop it around? FCC, maybe?"

"Farm Credit won't look at it because it's retail. They'd like to help but until the government changes the rules, their hands are tied."

"Oh well. We'll just have to wait 'n' see. Maybe give them pals of yers at Regional Office a little nudge, though?" Stu suggests.

"Will do, for sure," I agree. "I'll be there for the next two weeks. That should give me lots of time to plead our case."

"If that don't work, try a kick in the ass," Red says. Then she grins.

I smile back, even though it's not funny. Too much depends on it.

Nineteen

IT'S THE LAST day of my last training session at Regional Office. I breathe a sigh of relief when the TRW Information Services report on Jacob Jordan arrives on my desk. I was on pins and needles waiting for it, worried it might not come before I left and I wouldn't be there to intercept it to make like it was for one of the files I was working on. Being a spy is nerve-wracking.

It looks like Jake got into trouble with too much debt a few years ago. There was a large farm loan I assume was when his wife was a joint borrower. Then their credit card debt started to climb, there was a debt consolidation loan with a finance company at a higher interest rate but it soon went into arrears. His credit score tanked. Then just last fall, a company by the name of Prairie Equity and Wealth Management bought all his notes. Smooth sailing since then, apparently; they're not documenting missed or late payments, and that was enough for GMAC to give him a loan for his new truck.

The date on the GMAC loan seems odd, though: December 27. That's after Boxing Day, and Jake said he bought the truck before Christmas. I can only assume there was a delay in either the dealer or General Motors Acceptance Corporation filing their paperwork because of Christmas.

But, Prairie Equity and Wealth Management? If they loaned all that money to Jake, maybe they'd give Wacasko-Wâti a loan, too. I've never heard of them before, so I ask the supervisor I'm shadowing, Mr. Jensen, what he knows about them.

"Where'd you hear that name, Lindy?" he asks. He pulls a cigarette out of the pack on his desk, puts it between his lips and lights it, exhaling a cloud of smoke.

"It's on this TRW."

"Take a seat and let's have a look." He reaches across the desk and I hand it to him, then perch on the edge of a chair. After studying the documents for a minute or two, he looks up and says, "he got in trouble a while back and Prairie Equity bailed him out, eh?"

"Looks that way. A lot of credit card debt on top of operating loans."

"But it was manageable until the interest on the farm loan went crazy. Suddenly prime plus one isn't nine percent, it's twenty percent. Interest on that farm loan nearly killed him, looks like."

"So why would Prairie Equity bail him out?"

He takes another drag on his cigarette then holds it in his lips as he flips the pages of the credit report. At last he removes the cigarette from his mouth so he can stop squinting from the smoke curling up into his eye. "That's what they do. Look at that interest rate, worse than any finance company. And they probably have it set up so if he defaults, they get everything, for far less than what they've loaned him. Not a bank, so they aren't covered by The Bank Act. No paying him the difference between what they sell it for and what he owed. And they never call a loan until it's nearly paid off."

"That's criminal!"

"Yup. They've been investigated a few times and if memory serves they even got charged, but nothing came of it. They're Teflon." He hands the report back to me. "Some pretty shady characters. Too bad he got hooked up with them."

I study the document for a moment, and note the address of the lender. Pillerton? That town again? Why would their office be there instead of in Regina?

Mr. Jensen continues, breaking into my thoughts: "A few borrowers end up doing well enough to qualify for conventional financing and retire their Prairie Equity loans before they lose their farm, so they actually help some folks I guess." He takes another drag then butts his cigarette in the overflowing ashtray. "Your customer—what's he applying for?"

The moment of truth. I can't admit Jake isn't a customer, at least not for a loan, and I ordered this credit report because I'm snooping on him.

"I, umm, he hasn't actually applied yet, just mentioned he was going to."

"He talked to Everett about this?"

"No, um...It's a small town. Everyone knows everyone." I focus my attention on the nickel-sized patch of white whiskers on his jaw that he missed when he shaved this morning and hope he doesn't realize I'm avoiding eye contact. "He was in the line-up waiting for a teller when I walked by and I guess he thought I was Everett's secretary because he asked how long he'd have to wait to see him because he wanted to talk about a loan because he was thinking about expanding his hay business and would need more financing for some equipment and a bigger hay barn but he didn't have enough time to wait that day." I pause to take a breath and tell myself to slow down and quit babbling. "So I thought while I was here, I might as well check his credit to see if he should be encouraged."

"Hmm. I see. You're being pro-active. Maybe next time don't spend the money on a credit report until there's an actual application, though."

I nod and say, "I will." I had no idea I could lie like that. I probably shouldn't be as proud of it as I am.

"Well, unless his cash flow projections are really strong, I couldn't approve it. He'd be best off going to FCC because—"

"Because Farm Credit loans have the government guarantee so they can take riskier accounts, right?"

"Right."

"Okay! Thanks, Mr. Jensen!"

"You're going to have a lot of dealings with me now that you're a lending officer. You better start calling me Glen."

"Thanks, *Glen*!" I tuck the credit report into the folder, stand up and start to leave his office.

"Lindy," he calls out. I stop in the doorway and turn back.

He says, "this is your last day here, right?"

"That's right."

"Let me say again how sorry I am we can't loan Wacasko-Wâti as much as you wanted. Next fall after you sell some cattle and pay down that line of credit, I'll look at it again."

"Thank you."

"You're welcome. You can leave now, Lindy. Get out of town ahead of rush hour."

"Great! Thanks again." I give him a smile and escape. I pack up the desk I used for the past two weeks, get my boots and coat on, and breeze out of the office calling out good-byes to the girls in the steno pool as go.

As happy as I am and as fortunate as I feel to be propelled into what has traditionally been a man's job, I'm glad to get this Regional Office gig behind me, get home to stay, and see Jake. I said good-bye to Mom and Reggie and put my suitcase in my truck this morning, so now I head straight out of town.

As I drive up Edmonton Trail to connect with 16th Ave and the Trans Canada Highway, I mull over Jake's finances. The bailout from Prairie Equity and Wealth Management is troubling. Is he going to be able to keep up the payments? He's got what looks like enough cash now but at this time of year, he should have. He has little in the way of operating expenses and has sold most of his hay. But what happens in spring when there are expenses for fertilizer, diesel for tractors, repairs and so on?

What about Prairie Equity and Wealth Management? If he's got an in with those other guys, the high rollers he talked about, why wouldn't he go to them instead? I can't ask him because it's something I shouldn't know about.

And that lie I fabricated when Glen asked me why I ordered the credit report—more accurately the pride I felt at coming up with it on short notice and being able to tell it—what have I become?

Twenty

"**S**O THEY TURNED us down," Stu says. He roots in his ear with his little finger, then sighs and takes another sip of coffee. "Wisht the hell they'd of said somethin' sooner."

Red brings the carafe from the coffee maker and tops up our mugs. She returns the carafe to the warmer and resumes her seat at the table. "Are we gonna apply somewhere else, Lindy?"

"Yes. I'll do some more work on the books. Maybe I can boost the value of our assets."

"Maybe we should git an appraisal," Stu suggests.

"Maybe. But that costs money. I've been using the land value from the provincial property tax assessment, which you know is lower than actual value. So it's reasonable to bump up the valuation by ten per cent maybe. That goddamn new oven!" I exclaim. "Poor time to be laying out that kind of money on it instead of paying down the loan. I'm sorry, guys. I really thought we had a shot at getting the financing."

"It's okay, Princess," Stu says. "What was the total cost includin' the cooktop 'n' the gasfitter? A thousand bucks. Wouldn't make that much difference 'n' it's a expense that'll pay fer itself now that we got the pie production spinnin' along."

"Sure, but we've also got added expenses now, for Marcy's paycheque and for Loomis delivering the pies." I shrug and sip my coffee. "I really want to get the store going, though. I don't want to put it off another year. We didn't spend to get that basement poured and ready for the rest of the build to have it sitting there another year."

"Need it to store the wine, anyhow. Worse comes to worse, it's never nuthin' but a wine cellar," Stu says as adds more sugar to his coffee, earning him a disapproving frown from Red. He shrugs and gives me a wink.

"I appreciate you trying to make me feel less like an idiot for insisting we put in that basement, Stu. I know we needed it for the wine, but it really was putting the cart before the horse and taking more dollars out of the line of credit to pay for it is going against us now. And now we got these damn rustlers to worry about on top of it."

"Dunno why the cops can't git a handle on that," Red says. "How do they git away with it, that big rig they got 'n' loadin' up whole herds?"

"They must be connected somehow," I suggest. "You know what I mean, they have connections, someone that'll let them keep the cattle on their property until they're ready to ship. I think they've refined their modus operendi, not taking the time to overbrand them where they steal them. They could be offloading them, branding them, and shipping them from any of the ranches around here, especially the ones more toward the Badlands. They could be in a corral a hundred meters from the road down a ravine and you'd never know it driving by."

"Well, maybe we change our operendi 'n' don't put no more of ours out on the community pasture," Stu declares, and takes a noisy slurp of coffee. "Way too much territory to cover to keep an eye on 'em. Bad enough with our own."

"But if we don't, we'll run outta pasture by August," Red points out.

"Yeah. We'll have to cull," Stu agrees.

"We'd have to cull a helluva a lot. If we do that, make our herd that much smaller, what'll we live on?"

"We're sellin' a fair amount of wine. 'N' I can pick up some work here 'n' there haulin' livestock fer other folks, maybe."

"You know, worst case scenario, we can be self-sufficient," I say. "All we need is enough cash flow to pay utilities, really. We have the big garden, as much beef as we want, and we even have our own eggs now. Maybe we get a milk cow. The only problem is the loan. If the store goes as well as I think it will, we'll get that paid down in under five years."

We hear a vehicle on the road and look out to see Jake's truck turn in.

"Jake's here," Stu says. "You expectin' him?"

"Not this early," I reply. I get up and go out onto the porch in time to see him park the truck by my sidewalk. When he gets out of the cab, I call out, "Over here, Jake!"

He looks up and with a short wave, trots along the path through the snow to where I'm waiting. I start to go back inside but he pulls me into a hug and backs me up against the door. "Hi, beautiful," he murmurs, then we share a lengthy, gentle kiss. "Did I ever tell you how much I miss you when I don't see you fer even a few days? One day, even?" His eyes are intense. "I mean it. Say you miss me, too."

"I miss you, too," I concede with a short nod.

"I love you, baby. Say you love me, too."

"I love you too," I say. It's the first time I've said it and it feels like it's true. Now our kisses are intense. Finally I pull away and say, "We better go in. They'll be wondering what we're doing."

"I think they can figger it out." He chuckles, releases me and follows me inside. Greetings are exchanged as Jake takes off his jacket.

"Sit," Red orders. She fills a mug with coffee and sets it in front of the chair next to Stu.

"Great, thanks," Jake says as he slides onto the seat.

"What's up?" I ask him as I go back to my coffee. "I wasn't expecting you this early."

"Nuthin' much. Just slow around home, thought I'd pick up some beer 'n' when I was out, decided to swing by here to see you even though it's a little early," he replies. "Thought we could take a run down to Billie's for an early supper, then go up to the Starlight 'n' see what's playin' tonight."

"The drive-in? Is it even open?"

"Well, if it ain't, we won't be distracted by a movie, then," he says, and winks.

His grin is infectious and I feel that familiar stirring inside. I don't know that we'll make it out of my house, but, "Billie's it is," I say.

"So if yer summer of love is over, can we talk about real problems?" Stu asks.

"Problems?" Jake asks. "What problems? I got no problems. I got a heater in my truck, a cold six pack and a hot girl."

"Well, *we* still got problems."

"Oh?" Jake says.

"Goddamn rustlers. Dunno if it'll be safe to run cattle out on the community pasture this summer 'n' if it ain't, 'n' we end up keepin' our cows home, we're gonna run outta pasture mid-summer. And can't afford to buy the extra feed we'd hafta have."

"Ain't you got patrols organized?"

"Sure, but we can't have guys goin' out alone 'n' unarmed no more. That means we need twice as many riders 'n' we ain't got enough guys who can commit to patrollin' that much. A few dropped out when we heard the news 'bout that fella's body bein' found, not anxious to sign up fer somethin' that might git 'em killed. Can't blame nobody fer that. So we were just talkin' 'bout cullin' our herd down to a size we can keep on our home pasture."

"Least here we can keep an eye on it ourselves. Although with Lindy away workin' all week now..." Red clicks her tongue.

"And the bank turned us down," I add. Stu gives me a sharp look. I realize he's sensitive about outsiders being privy to our finances, but he did mention we couldn't afford to buy hay, so he opened the door. I give him a smile and make a mental note to tell him how close Jake and I have become, so it's not like he's really an outsider.

"Well, you know," Jake begins as Red refills his mug, "thanks, Red. You know, I only got a few cows now. Most all I do is raise hay, which is busy for a few weeks here 'n' there. I'd be glad to help with patrols."

"Well, that'd be a big help, Jake," Stu says. "You wanna bring yer horse 'n' keep him here while patrollin' or ride one of our rescues?"

"I dunno. How crazy are they?"

"They ain't crazy," Red tells him. "Ain't you a bronc rider? Why d'you care if there's still a buck in 'em?"

"Ex-bronc rider. 'N' I don't bounce so good no more, Red," he says. "Can't do my job with a busted leg."

"My kids ride 'em. You'd be fine."

"We can work out the details when the patrols start," I suggest. "For now, finish your coffee and we'll go look at the rescue horses. See if there's one you like."

"Take the boys with you," Red says. "They been playin' that video game long enough."

"It's a good idea to take them with us anyway," I agree. "They know everything about every horse in the herd."

LATER, AFTER A NICE meal at Billie's, we're snuggling in my bed after an even nicer lovemaking session with more love declarations, and Jake says, "You know, Lindy, about yer bank turnin' you down. 'Member I told you about them guys who are lookin' to make loans? Yers is just the sort of operation I think they'd be interested in."

"There's still a couple of other banks I want to approach first. I went over our income projections again, and the valuation of our property. You know I was using the provincial property tax valuation? I think it's too low. I increased the value based on inflation and recent sales of similar properties. The Remax Realty lady helped me with that. Then I bumped it up a few percentage points because, you know, land values keep going up so it'll soon be accurate."

"Smart," he approves. "Well, it don't cost nuthin to talk to them. Just think about it."

"Okay."

"And also baby, it shore would be sweet if you didn't chase me home tonight. Just this once? Ain't it silly? If it's to keep them boys from catchin' on, they ain't that stupid."

"I guess that's right."

"Think about that, too, please?"

"Okay. I will."

He pulls me closer, fondling my breasts as he cuddles up against my back. I feel something pushing against my buttocks.

"See what you do to me?" he murmurs.

"Again?" I whisper. "At your age?"

"I'm crazy fer you, Lindy."

"Okay, I've thought about it. You don't have to go."

Twenty-One

ONE MONTH INTO my new job I still feel like a fraud. I don't know nearly enough. I've had several applications declined so either I don't understand the necessary qualifications or I'm not good enough at writing up what amounts to a sales pitch.

Everett says it's normal to have applications denied. We don't want to turn people down at branch level unless it's obvious they'd have trouble making payments if they got what they asked for, in which case we'd look like idiots presenting it to Regional Office. It's always better to let R.O. be the bad guys. Like buying a car and the salesman has to keep going back to talk to his manager instead of admitting he's the one trying to hose you.

Other than that, I mostly like the work. I mostly like dealing with people. I seriously enjoy the evil glares from Irene, but I wish she'd do more to train Maureen, the typist who took my old job, instead of ignoring her so she has to interrupt me with questions. I've already told Maureen about six times I can't help her get a new pen, though. She'll just have to prostrate herself at Irene's feet along with everyone else.

I'm at my desk reviewing the latest financial statements from Bar O R Ranch in hopes I can see a way to get them the requested bump in their line of credit. They need it to branch out from their cow-calf operation and start finishing the feeder calves themselves. I'm deep into calculating a restructuring that would make the application palatable to Glen Jensen (not an easy task since he always counsels borrowers to do the opposite) and naturally I have to run it by

Everett before I can get it sent off to Regional office. It's too late to-day and Everett left early for a doctor's appointment anyway, but I want to have it ready to show him first thing in the morning. I glance at my watch and see that it's already closing time. Of course this is when Josie comes to interrupt me.

"Hey, Lindy, would you have time to talk to Mr. Baxter? Remember him from that time—"

"I remember," I tell her, and look up and see him waiting on the other side of the counter, looking our way expectantly. I smile and wave him in.

"I'll get his file for you," Josie says, and heads for the file cabinets on the other side of Everett's office.

I may not have seen him since before Christmas but I certainly remember him. A big, handsome man is nothing if not memorable. I stand as he approaches; when we make eye contact and he reaches out to take my hand, I feel a warm glow. Apparently his over-abundant pheromones are pumping away big time and my receptors are wide open. It's suddenly very warm in here.

"Hey, Dan! Nice to see you. Have a seat."

"Hi, uh, Lindy," he says. "You, too. Thanks for seeing me. I know it's late and I should've made an appointment but I was in town..."

"No problem. You don't need an appointment," I tell him, and sit down. He takes the chair across from me. I ask, "What can I do for you today?"

"Well, I'm thinking of getting a new tractor. Not brand new, I mean. The New Holland dealer in Medicine Hat got a nice one in on trade."

"Is yours too old? It might be better to keep it, even if it needs work."

"Oh no, it's getting up there but it still runs good. I'm keeping it as a second tractor. It's just that it's not big enough for what I need. I'm going to expand my operation. Keep the calves longer so they don't go to a feedlot for finishing. Which means buying grain, building new corrals with feed troughs. A grain silo. You know."

Another rancher making room for more cattle? Another rancher wanting to cut out the feedlot and finish the feeders on site? This sounds like the file I was working on when he came in. Wacasko-Wâti must be the only ranch around that's culling instead of expanding cattle operations.

"Okay," I say slowly. "You know if you can get dealer financing or financing through FCC, you'd be better off because we probably can't match the rate."

"No, I know. I don't want the tractor loan from you guys," he explains. "There's room on my line of credit but I need that for the other stuff I can't get loans for, like the building materials."

"Does Sun Glo or wherever you plan on buying your building materials, do they offer credit terms?"

"I guess they do." He frowns for a second, shrugs, then says, "But I just want to know... Well, there's another review of my line of credit coming up and I was wondering if having another loan like that would tank my chances again, maybe you'd refuse to renew altogether, forget about the increase."

"Hmmm. I'll look at it, but you know it's above our branch lending limit so it has to go to Regional Office. How soon would you need an answer?"

"Well, pretty soon I guess. I wouldn't want that tractor to be sold to someone else while I'm waiting for them to make up their minds."

"How about I phone them? They're an hour behind us so there should still be a manager there. I think I could have an answer for you by tomorrow. Let me just take down some more information, enough to give us an idea of how likely they are to approve your LOC if there's another loan skewing your debt service ratio." I smile. He smiles back. I get a quivery feeling deep inside and I'm glad when Josie brings his file to give me something to focus on other than that dimple and the slightly out-of-alignment eye tooth that makes his smile so appealing. I rifle through a few pages, then ask, "How's business? You got calves on the ground yet?"

"Yeah, calves are coming thick and fast. With the decent weather we've had so far the calves are thriving. No problems in particular. My old man, he's living on the ranch now. He's a big help."

"That's great! For both of you." I nod and he smiles. Why is that so ridiculously sexy? I draw a breath and force my attention back on business. "Have you had any trouble with rustlers?"

"Well, no, I haven't but why does the bank care? I mean, I have no control over that."

"It's not for the bank, it's just that I'm curious. We had some stolen last fall. Some other ranches have been hit, too. We're wondering if we should put any of ours out on the community pasture this year."

"Oh yeah, I heard about that, took a bunch right off the community pasture. Some of those were yours?"

"Yeah."

"I also heard that guy that was supposed to have run off but it turned out he was murdered and his whole herd stolen."

"That wasn't around here, it was in the Qu'Appelle Valley," I say, "but likely the same outfit and too close for comfort. We're setting up patrols again."

"I was thinking of putting a bunch of my pairs out on the community pasture as soon as calving's over. If there's rustlers around and you're starting patrols, I'll sign up."

"Oh, you will? That's great."

"Um, I guess since you're working full time here now, you won't be on any of the patrols."

"I'll join some weekend patrols, though."

"Good," he says.

He sits watching me as if he's going to say something else. When he doesn't, I say, "Okay, let me get my thoughts organized so I can call Regional Office before they close. I'll call you tomorrow with their answer." I stand and he does likewise. I look toward the customer area and realize the branch closed while we were talking. "I see they've locked the door," I tell him. "I'll walk you out."

We walk to the door together. Standing beside him I realize he's nearly as tall as Jake. His breath smells of peppermints. I'm close enough to smell his breath? I think my face must be turning pink. I quickly unlock the door and he pushes it open, then backs away a couple of steps and says, "Thanks, Lindy. I'll hear from you soon, then?"

"For sure."

"Let me know when the patrols start and where they start from."

"Don't know when we're going to start or where all the groups form up, but we have a group that meets up at Wacasko-Wâti."

"Oh yeah? Well, great. I'll see you, then." He smiles and with a nod, turns and heads down the sidewalk. I stand holding the door open and watch him walk away, his stride purposeful and athletic as if he's comfortable with his body and in his own skin.

The first time I met Dan I thought he was married, but that didn't stop me from checking him out. My impression of him then was correct: he's smokin' hot. And it seems he might be interested in me. And now I'm with Jake.

I can't believe I'm thinking this, but goddamn! What lousy timing.

Twenty-Two

H AVING RUN OUT of conventional options, I tell Red and Stu what Jake said about getting financing for the farmgate store from those high rollers he knows. Stu seems interested but Red's frown tells me she's skeptical.

"Well, who the hell are they, if they got no company name?"

"I didn't say they don't have a name, Red, just that I don't know it," I reply. "I think Jake told me, but it's just a number and I don't remember it. He said they're a bunch of guys that have money to invest."

"So why don't they buy stocks or an apartment building or somethin', like normal people?"

"I don't know, Red!" I hear the tone of exasperation creeping into my voice, and take a breath. "Look. Why don't we at least meet with the guys and let them explain it."

"I dunno if I want 'em comin' around. Next thing you know, they show up here botherin' us, pesterin' us until we give in."

"Jeez, Red, it's not like you to be such a pessimist."

"I'm a pessimist? I guess I am, after bein' turned down by every bank there is."

"So that's a good reason to hear what they have to say," Stu says. "They wouldn't have to come here."

"And make us drive to Swift Current or wherever their damn office is?"

"Maybe we can meet them at the Husky over a coffee," I suggest.

Red frowns and takes a deep breath.

"Okay?" I prod.

"I guess," she agrees, then spins on her heel and heads in the direction of the hen house, egg collecting basket in hand.

I turn to Stu and remark, "There's something about this she doesn't like."

"There's plenty about it I don't like, but I still think it's worth hearin' them guys out."

"Okay, then, I'll let Jake know. The meeting will have to fit into my work schedule, though. I wonder if they work evenings or weekends. But I better get a move on. If I'm late, Irene will give me a demerit, and there goes any chance of getting a red pen." It's a joke, really, because I already bought my own red pen. Turns out I don't use it as much as I thought I would. But I exchange a chuckle with Stu and head for my truck.

THEY DO, INDEED, WORK weekends and evenings. Or at least one of them does. I'm surprised at his prompt response. On the phone, he introduces himself as Nick Reeves and agrees to meet with us in the coffee shop at the Husky at seven p.m. Felix stays for supper after his chores in the wine shed are done and will keep the boys company while we're gone.

Stu, Red and I are headed out now. At the first Husky entrance, Stu turns the truck in. As usual, the lot is filled with big rigs and pickups covered in mud. Stu finds a parking spot and we go inside.

There's no trouble identifying Mr. Reeves, who's wearing a tan sports coat, navy button-up shirt and tan and blue paisley tie. He might look less out of place among the truckers and ranchers and oil patch workers if he wore his hair in a Mohawk and had bangle earrings.

He stands as we approach and when introductions have been made, Red and Stu take the bench across from him and I slide in be-

side him. In retrospect, it might have been better to choose a location for this meeting that had tables rather than booths, but I don't
mind sharing the bench with him. He's younger than I expected and
he looks and smells good. Maybe his name being Nick predisposes
me to liking him. I sit close enough to follow along in the paperwork.
At least I tell myself that's the reason, and that it's important. Red
looks at me with a knowing expression. If she doesn't remark on me
sitting so close to him as soon as we're alone, I'll be surprised.

He hands us each a business card with his name in raised lettering, then picks up a pen and opens his portfolio to a lined pad. He
begins the conversation by asking, "So, how much financing are you
seeking and what do you want it for?"

WE SPEND OVER AN HOUR drinking coffee and discussing our
plans, explaining where our current financing falls short. Jake was
right, switching to Nick's group would mean a higher interest rate.
Instead of having his group assume our existing line of credit and just
bump it up, I ask for bridge financing for just enough to build the
store and get it up and running. I'd like a one year term with option
to renew. He says all he can offer is a six month term with an option for a further six months, and he wants a second mortgage on
the ranch. I'm not naïve enough to think we can get anything without collateral but a charge against the ranch for a comparatively small
loan is a deal breaker. He pushes his offer to assume our operating
credit so it would just be one big loan and just one mortgage. While
I like the idea, the interest rate on our line of credit is five points lower. He says he can shave the rate by one percent. We say that's not
enough so no thanks, we'd rather have the second, smaller loan. I offer the herd as collateral. He says he has to run it by his partners. I say
we need to think on it anyway.

We leave with no deal, and I don't think any of us is happy. Except maybe Red. For some reason, she hardly said a word throughout the meeting and when I glanced at her from time to time, I wondered if she had something really awful-tasting in her mouth.

To my surprise, when we're back in the truck heading home she says nothing about me crowding the movie-star handsome Mr. Reeves. I wonder if I could have sat even closer, but our thighs touched a few times so any closer and I'd have been in his lap. Not a good negotiating posture. I broach the subject by saying, "He sure is good looking. I guess jeans instead of dress pants is his idea of going casual."

"That money fer that git-up of his would buy my whole family's clothes. 'N' he's too good lookin'," Red says. "Smooth talker, too."

"I take it you don't trust him."

"Not as far as I could throw him."

"The thing is, though, Red, if we can agree to terms, we can have the money as soon as Friday. We could phone SunGlo tomorrow to have them get our lumber order ready for delivery, and get the guys that're going to help Stu set to come as soon as they can clear their schedules. We got to get going on the building if we're going to be up and running by the end of May."

"I know yer right, Lindy. I guess I'm just a real Nervous Nelly but when I was listenin' to that smooth as silk voice of his that's enough to set you to dreamin' 'n' while I'm some glad you drew the line at puttin' another mortgage or a bigger mortgage on the ranch I can't stop thinkin' 'bout all our cows bein' took and then how would we make our payment on the loan we already got? What if we couldn't make the payments and yer bank called the loan? We'd end up in real trouble."

I take a deep breath and blow it out slowly.

"I'm sorry, Lindy. I know how much you want this."

"Don't be sorry, Red. You're right, there is a big downside if everything goes sideways. But I've got a good job now and if worse comes to worse, I think I can manage the payments on the bridge loan. We'd only need to generate enough cash flow from the ranch to service the mortgage and line of credit we've got, and we've been doing that without a problem. We only ran into trouble because of the rustlers and we've pretty well recovered from that now."

"So what if they hit us again? The rustlers?"

"Come on, darlin'," Stu says, "it's not like you to be Miss Doom 'n' Gloom. We ain't gonna lose no more cattle to rustlers, not with the patrols 'n' keepin' our herd home."

"Yer fergettin' how much of our land we can't see from the house 'n' the patrols don't go out at night, do they!"

"You think the bastards're gonna find the cows, round 'em up 'n' load 'em into trucks in the dark?" Stu says. He glances at his wife, takes her hand and gives it a squeeze. "Yer worryin' too much."

"I think they could, if there was a full moon 'n' if they had big lights, like flood lights."

"Hmm." Stu says.

From the look on Stu's face he has more to say, none of it in support of Red's fears, but he doesn't want to argue. Or maybe he doesn't think it's so far-fetched. I don't mention it now but as Arnie pointed out, there are headlights on ATVs. To me it seems like a reach to think the rustlers drive around in that rough country in the dark, headlights or no headlights, or would go to the trouble of putting up flood lights to steal our cattle when there are ranches everywhere they can steal from during the day. It's on the tip of my tongue to tell her not to be stupid about it, not in those words of course, but it's like telling someone who got bucked off the horse and is afraid to get back on, to suck it up. They may get back on, but they're still afraid. I fume silently for a few minutes and just watch the fields with their ever-shrinking patches of dirty snow sliding by the truck window.

"Red," I say at last, "I don't want to do anything you're uncomfortable with. We'll talk some more about the pros and cons, sleep on it, and I'll call Mr. Reeves with our answer tomorrow afternoon, as agreed. Okay?"

"Okay," she agrees. "I don't want to hold everything up 'n' I haven't forgot whose ranch it is, it's just, umm, I been homeless before."

I study her worried face and any anger or frustration I feel toward her melts. I know Stu wants to go ahead with it at least as much as I do, so I'm sure they'll talk it over and I'm hopeful he can bring her around.

"So," he says after a bit, "you gals notice his missin' finger?"

"Yeah," I reply. "A lot of that going around. Wonder what it means."

"Don't mean nuthin' I don't s'pose," Stu opines. "Jerry. Jake. And now this Reeves guy. Just an odd coincidence. With cowboys, ropers anyhow, it's usually thumbs they're missin'. Or the ring finger 'cause the ring got caught on somethin'. I never seen so many guys with the tip of their pointin' fingers missin.'"

Except for the sound of the gears I imagine grinding away in her head, Red remains silent the rest of the way home. I'm sure she's not thinking about missing fingers. She's mulling over the whole store building/loan issues. I've known her for a decade and we're so close I think of her as a sister, but I didn't know she'd been homeless. When I think back, though, I should have realized it. When I met her in the summer of my Nick, she never spoke of home as the rest of us did. It wasn't just a summer away from her real life, bouncing from one rodeo to another. It was her usual transient life. She was homeless. I never thought she might worry about not having a place to live or that she and her family might have to leave Wacasko-Wâti someday. I never thought about the fact they're tenants and like all tenants, they're at the mercy of the whims and financial circumstances of their landlord. I never thought, period.

Red and Stu have put down roots, poured blood, sweat and tears into the ranch, paid for improvements, and before I moved here, the property taxes. With all that sweat equity it's as much theirs as mine except for ink on paper. I wonder if I can put the home quarter on a separate title, naming the three of us as owners. It would be the fair thing to do and would give them security. I make a mental note to look into it. I must be smiling, because Red gives me a strange look.

It amazes me that a person of reasonable intelligence and with a degree in business administration can be so slow to think of such obvious things. Proof book learning doesn't make a person smart.

"WHY WOULD WE AGREE to taking cattle as collateral? Anything can happen to them and we're left with nothing. I can't believe you'd even consider it, Nick."

"Think about it—"

"I don't have to think about it!"

"It's okay, Tommy," the dark-haired man says. He scratches at his five o'clock shadow, his ruby ring catching the last stray beams of sunlight from the window at his side. "Let him finish."

"Okay," Nick begins, "I told them it could only be a six-month term. They'll have the store going by then but it won't turn a profit for at least a year, probably longer. We nix that item she wrote in about a renewal option. She won't notice it and if she does, oops, sorry, good you caught it and so on. And we go back at it from another angle. Think about this: they won't be able to pay the loan off after six months, so they'll be banking on a renewal. We offer renewal then, don't seize the cattle, but insist on a mortgage. Maybe dangle something, a few more bucks or lower interest rate, to sweeten the deal. Then as soon as they can't make a payment, call the loan. Bingo!

The ranch and all the cattle are ours. Maybe we're big-hearted and let them stay on to do the work."

"We'd have to give them a shitload of money to bring the loan anywhere near the forced sale value of that ranch. That little bridging loan you're talking about would be a drop in the bucket."

"We got our own appraisers, don't forget. And the valuation also takes into account the business end of it. A few more cattle disappear, customers shun the store when we circulate rumours of people getting sick from the stuff they sell, the business fails, all their loans including what they have with the bank fall into arrears, and they're done. We pick it up for a song when it's foreclosed on." Nick lifts the bottle of Crown Royal and tops up the three shot glasses on the table. The men shoot their whiskey. Nick fills the glasses again but just sips his and says nothing, giving the other two time to think over his proposal.

"This isn't how we do it," Tommy says.

"No. But joining the congregation? They didn't bite on that so there's no way they'll sign the ranch over to the Children voluntarily. Even if they did join, you know how long it takes to get the True Believers to sign their property over. Do we really want to wait until they, er, *decide* to leave it to us in their wills and then how many more years before they die?"

"You know it doesn't take long for them to die once we're in their will."

"How would you explain the death of three people, one who's not even thirty?" Tommy asks. "House fire? They don't even live in the same house. And there's a couple of kids. That's a line too far."

"Never mind," Nick says, dismissing the idea with a wave. "We don't have that much time. The highway upgrade is going to be announced next spring and when the new road goes in, we need to get rolling on our resort."

"Goddamn those councillors all to hell anyway. I have half a mind to turn them in. A word in the right ear. Have the auditors look at their bank accounts. If they'd nixed the planners changing the route, we wouldn't have this problem. Now those two properties where the road was supposed to go are worth fuck all."

"Not completely worthless. We've found another use for them, don't forget. And we might need those guys right where they are again. What I'm suggesting here is a work-around, and it's legal. There no other way that I can see and we're not going to give up, are we?"

"No. But our guy. Maybe we chose the wrong one. I wonder if he's up for it for the job. Damn near had to dangle him out a window to get him to go back at it. How come he planted his feet like that? All he has to do is fuck her once a week. Jerry said she's good looking. How is that a big deal?"

"Yeah, she's hot," Nick says. "I got a chubby when the little minx pressed her thigh up against mine. I'd fuck her in a heartbeat. Maybe he's fallen for her and had an attack of conscience."

"He thinks he's in love? So soon after he takes the mark he forgets his covenant? Pfft!" Tommy says, and exhales sharply.

"You're right," the other man says. "He needs to get tough mentally and get this done or he's out, he pays us back or loses his ranch and he gave away a finger for nothing. Remind him he does what we tell him. The fish is hooked. Give them the money and let's get on with it."

Tommy drains his whiskey, slams the glass down on the table with a thump, and turns to Nick. "So she's hot and you'd fuck her, eh, Reeves?"

The dark-haired man says, "In that case, we should have her in the congregation."

"You fantasizing about new talent sucking your dick, Gabe?" Nick asks. "I'd expect it from Tommy, but you? Is that what it takes for you to get it up these days?"

"Jesus, I'm sorry I nominated you for the Triad. You young pups, just because a stiff breeze gives you a boner you think it'll always be like that. You'll find out. And anyhow, don't see you turning down any of the perks of being an Elder. Don't tell me you didn't think of it."

"Sure I did. Maybe she'll come around and join the congregation in time. But for right now, this is the only way."

"Okay then. Let's make it happen."

Twenty-Three

THINGS ARE SPINNING right along. Mr. Reeves sent a gopher to the bank with the loan documents. I scanned them under Irene's watchful eye, and signed. I got her to witness my signature. (She acted like it was a big imposition but I'm pretty sure she was flattered.) The gopher gave me a certified cheque in exchange for the signed agreement, and left. I deposited the cheque the second he was out the door. The next day Stu went to SunGlo with our order.

The store went up quick since it's "rustic" with only a small part of the interior drywalled and painted, for now. We had a good crew and it was just a matter of putting walls and a roof on top of the basement that was ready and waiting. Red and I put up the insulation and vapour barrier in the kitchen and bathrooms, ready for the drywallers who showed up the next morning. Arnie pulled a crew off another job to put ours at the head of the queue so the plumbing was done while Pete and a helper installed the electrical. Arnie also has his gasfitter ticket so he got the propane range and ovens hooked up.

The Grand Opening is today. We've done everything we can think of to insure a good turn-out. Red put up posters at the Coop, the Legion, the feed store—anywhere there's a public bulletin board—as well as stapling them to utility posts all along Maple Street and outside the Jasper and the Goodwill. We put ads in the Maple Creek News and dropped off brochures at the new Tourist Information Centre up on the Trans Canada Highway as well as the Chamber of Commerce in town.

We even bought a ten-second ad on CJOS All Country All Day Radio. I feel a glow of satisfaction when I hear it every morning on my drive to work. Ten seconds means everything important has to be conveyed in twenty-five words. We came up with: "Wacasko-Wâti Ranch Farm Store Grand Opening! Grass-fed beef. Pies baked fresh daily. Award-winning wines and jams. Everything locally sourced. Saturday ten to five, Cypress Hills Road."

I never thought it could be so challenging to write twenty-five words. I'd like to have said more, telling people about the free samples and something like "bring your friends" or "pony rides for the kids", but it's over the limit as is and a jump to a fifteen-second spot wasn't worth the added cost. The ad man okayed it with no added charge for the extra word. With such constraints, I didn't bother to explain the awards won were at the Maple Creek Fall Fair. We're aiming for bigger things, but for now, that's it. Although I've proven to be a proficient liar, at least this isn't completely untrue.

We think we've done all we can. We're serving coffee, giving away slivers of pie, and Red got Tony of Maple Creek Italian Foods to order in tiny baking cups for her so she's baked about a thousand two-bite sample muffins. Stu has set up a bar in the corner and he's ready to pour samples of his rhubarb and saskatoon wines. Marcy is at a table in the opposite corner where she'll serve jam on saltines. Red and I man the bakery counter and cash register.

The produce bunk has lettuce, rhubarb, corn and the little potatoes from our garden, and cartons of the wild saskatoons we buy from local pickers. Not much of anything, either, since we have no idea how much or even if it will sell.

There's no fresh meat, but we moved the freezer from Red and Stu's porch and it's full of beef steaks, roasts and what the butcher calls mince and we call hamburger—everything you get from one whole steer including soup bones.

We blew through our bridge financing and dipped into our line of credit besides. Now we need to generate cash flow back into the business and all we can do is wait and see if the store will be a success or if we're complete idiots. Me, actually, wait and see if I'm a complete idiot. I dragged Stu and Red into this kicking and screaming. Go big or go home, I said. If it's not a success it's all on me and I'll be working at the bank until I'm a hundred.

The boys are excited. They have shirts that are clean and stain-free because this is the first time they've been allowed to wear them, and they are the official greeters. They've also got a photo album of the rescue horses set out at the end of the counter and have been practicing their sales pitch. That was Stu's idea, and it seems like a good one because as he pointed out, while people are standing around sampling wine, pie and jam, they're a captive audience. And who wouldn't want to see pictures of horses two handsome young cowboys offer to show them? On top of that, Felix and his buddy Joe are here. There's a row of our quietest horses, including Nick's old horse Petey of course, saddled and waiting at the hitching post beside the barn. Felix and Joe, plus our boys if need be, will lead them for any small riders that turn up. One of the boys will hop on their own horse and lead the way around the corrals if there are older riders who don't need to be on the lead line.

We have a sandwich board out on the road with a couple of helium balloons tied to it, as if balloons are needed to draw attention to the only thing besides gophers on twenty miles of dusty gravel road.

The first car to turn in is Mom and Wiggles. I go to greet them. "Hey, you guys are early! You must've been on the road at six!"

"Yeah, just grabbed a coffee and headed out," Wiggles says. "Hope to git another coffee 'n' a couple of Red's rhubarb muffins pretty quick."

"I don't know if the coffee's done perking yet. I can't leave here just now, but why don't you go to my house and cook up a proper breakfast?"

"It's okay, honey," Mom says. "We can wait."

The boys scurry over to say hello and while Mom has Charlie and Johnny trapped in a hug, pointing out as she always does that they're growing up so fast they'll soon be taller than she is, the first actual customer of the day pulls in. And it's even someone we don't know.

If we were worried no one would show up, that worry was for nothing. The day goes by in a blur. There are a couple of lulls in traffic when we wonder if that's it, but then more people come. Arnie and Anita show up with her teen-aged girls and the look on Charlie's face when he clamps eyes on Kaylie, just two years older than he is and with a glowing halo of blonde curls, reminds me that he's growing up in more ways than just height. He seems undeterred by the fact she's several inches taller than he is. Johnny couldn't care less, but he tags along when Charlie takes the girls out to show them the horses. I have a feeling those girls may get a ride that's longer than just once around the outside of the corrals.

In the early afternoon, I'm just helping myself to coffee when Dan Baxter and a handsome older man come into the store. Stu beckons them and pulls out a couple of the full-size plastic glasses reserved for people he knows and pour three fingers of the light gold rhubarb wine in each. I head over to say hello.

"Hi, Lindy," Dan says when I come up beside him. "Place looks great! How ya doin'?"

"Good, thanks. Great, actually. You?"

"Yup, all good."

"Happy with the new tractor?"

"Very. Hey, this is my dad."

"Pleased to meet you, Mr. Baxter," I say, and reach out to shake his hand.

"Norm," he says as he takes my hand and just holds it. "Pleased to meet *you*. Danny said you were pretty. He sold you short."

"Well, thanks, Norm." I drop his hand and feel my face growing warm. I come back with, "I see where Dan gets his good looks."

"If he don't get off his butt and ask you out, I will."

"I'm, ahh..."

"The place looks great, Lindy," Dan says again. If his father was close enough, I think he would've rooted him with an elbow.

"Thanks," I say, glad to change the direction of that conversation. "Still work to do. No finish grading or lawn around the yard yet, as you probably noticed."

Jake materializes at my side and loops an arm around my waist, pulling me close. "Oh, hi, Jake," I say. "Do you know Dan—"

"I know 'em," Jake says.

Dan gives a quick nod but says nothing. Jake is frowning. Dan returns the frown. I'm reminded of two alpha dogs sizing each other up. Then Dan smiles at me and says, "Nice to see you, Lindy," and moves off with Norm right behind him.

When they're out of earshot I hiss, "What the hell, Jake?"

"You don't want to have nuthin' to do with them two," Jake hisses back.

"What?!? Why?"

"Because they're liars and thieves. It's a long story 'n' I ain't got time to talk about it now, but I mean it: keep away from them." He turns and strides away.

"Where are you going?" I call after him.

He shakes his head and marches out the side door.

I might go after him and insist he tell me more about the Baxters, or where he's going for that matter, but Red beckons me to help at the cashier counter. I paste a smile on my face and take over at the cash register.

I'm busy the rest of the afternoon, but even so, the scene with Jake replays over and over in my head. Is Jake jealous? Maybe it was a bit of a flirty exchange, but he has no reason not to trust me and he doesn't own me.

When it's nearing five o'clock and there are only a couple of customers in the store and two more at the picnic table out in front, a shiny new pickup pulls into the parking lot. A short, well-built cowboy comes through the door.

"Goddamn!" Stu exclaims. "Lookit what the cat drug in!" He hurries over to take the man's hand. They shake, slap each other on the back, and then Stu calls out, "Hey, Red! Come see who's here!"

Red comes out from the kitchen. "I'll be go to hell! Russ Benson! Thought you were dead!" she exclaims, and joins the two men.

"I'm a long ways from dead, little one, 'n' you are just as purdy as ever," Russ declares, and enfolds her in a bearhug, lifting her off her feet and kissing her soundly before setting her back down. Stu stands back, watching with an expression of genuine pleasure on his face, taking no offence at the man kissing his wife in what most would consider to be an inappropriate manner.

"Lindy," he calls out, "Come meet Russ!"

"Hey, Russ! Nice to meet you," I say.

"Nice to meet you, too. You know, I don't think as I ever met you but I seen you around back in the day. Yer Gobbler's daughter, right?"

"Now there's a nickname I haven't heard for a while," I say. "But yeah."

"I guess you quit the rodeo after that plane crash. Condolences, Lindy."

"Thank you." I bite my lower lip. It's astonishing, but even a decade later, a reminder of the sudden loss of both my fiancé and my father gives me a stab of grief.

"It was tough on all us rodeo bums," Russ says. He reaches out and gives my shoulder a rub.

I swallow and say, "it's the reason we're here. This was his place."

"Well I shore wouldn't of recognized it. 'Course the last time I was here was years ago, before I quit ridin' and started providin' stock fer rodeos."

"You guys must have a lot of catching up to do. Why don't you go over to the patio, get a drink, sit in the shade and visit?" I suggest. "Marcy and I'll put this all away. Stu, maybe get some steaks out for supper?"

"Already done," Stu says, "but I'll grab a extra one fer my ol' buddy 'n' I'm ready fer a beer. Right this way, buddy." The two men make their way out the door and across the yard to my patio.

We thought we would shut everything down at five but with customers still hanging around visiting at the picnic table outside the door, I go and hang the "CLOSED" sign on the sandwich board out at the road and let them stay as long as they want. I shoo Red out to join Stu and Russ while Marcy and I clean up the kitchen.

At last even Marcy has gone home and only our people and Russ are left. I tally the day's receipts before joining everyone on the patio in front of my house. Stu has steaks for the adults and wieners for the kids, plus foil-wrapped potatoes on the barbeque and there's a big bowl of green salad and buns for the hot dogs already on the table when I join them. Mom comes out of my house with a tray of condiments and sets it on the table in front of Wiggles.

"Where'd Jake go?" she asks.

"I don't know. I thought he might have told one of you guys."

"Nope," Wiggles says. "He went in yer house to make a phone call, then come out like his tail was on fire, heads over to the store, wasn't in there more'n two minutes then drives away without so much as a wave. He didn't say nuthin' to you?"

"No."

Red gets up from her seat next to Arnie and comes to stand with me. Pointing to the till tape I have folded up in my hand, she asks, "so?"

I hand her the tape. She scrolls down to the totals at the bottom, and says quietly, "Wacasko-Wâti farmgate store is on its way!"

Now it's a party.

"SHE SIGNED ON THE DOTTED line weeks ago. Why the fuck is he still bothering with her? I'm not so sure he isn't in love." Gabe leans back in the chair, tinkling his ring on his whiskey glass.

"He claims he isn't," Nick replies.

"Even if he is, I don't give a shit. He has to dump her before it's an issue with his new target." He takes a swallow of whiskey, then continues, "Besides, his wife is starting to make noises."

"Yeah, I know. She was bitching to me after the meeting on Sunday."

"She needs to be reminded it's none of her business. But maybe also remind him his primary relationship needs attention too. I read him the riot act when he called in this afternoon. He said they're starting patrols again and he can find out more about that. When are they going to quit those goddamn patrols? We haven't taken anything off the community pasture this year. Why'd they start patrolling again?"

"Who knows? On the plus side, when they're out patrolling, they're not at home," Nick replies.

"Well, there's that." He shoots the rest of his whiskey and sets the glass down. "But is that really worth it? I think he's too involved with her. You tell him to dump her. No excuses."

OUR FRIENDS ALL STAY overnight, with Arnie and Anita, Mom and Wiggles at my place. The boys gave up their beds to Anita's girls while they bunked in the camper with Felix and Joe. We convinced Russ to stay, and he took the couch in Red's living room.

I'm happy Russ didn't leave last night. The guys and Red had such a good time reminiscing about the good old days they could be heard laughing and talking long after everyone else had gone to bed, and none of them was sober enough to drive. Although I expected him back, Jake didn't return.

The plan was to congregate on my patio for breakfast. Anita must have gotten nicer since Christmas because she isn't bugging me now and I haven't called her Annette even once.

After a coffee and a quick bacon and egg bunwich, Red and I leave Mom and Anita to take care of the men and kids whenever they might make an appearance, and head to the store to get everything ready to open. The grand opening is officially over and we have no idea if we'll get any customers at all today, but we optimistically fire up the sixty-cup coffee percolator and set out the last of the little muffins for anyone who does show up.

While Red is looking after putting the sales area to rights, I take on the job of mopping the floors and I'm working my way out to the main customer area with the rolling bucket when Stu and Russ come in.

"Good morning, guys!" I sing out. "Anyone need an Alka-Selzer?"

"Hell, no," Russ says. "A beer 'n' a aspirin's all I needed, 'n' I already had that, thanks."

"Well, yer all set then," Red says.

"Ay-yuh, I'm all set too," Stu says, "if anyone gives a shit."

"I give a shit," I assure him.

"I do too," Red says. "You need to count yer empties so we can figure out how much product we gave away yesterday. Lindy needs it fer the books."

"Never git married, Russ," Stu says. "See what happens? Yer nuthin' but a slave. I swear, if the day ever comes I can't do all the work around here no more, she'll put me on the meat truck with the culls."

"Might not wait till then," Red says.

"Well, in that case, I better take a gander at that bull while yer still around to show him to me," Rus says.

"What's this 'bout a bull?" Red asks.

"Domino. I guess you wasn't in on that conversation last night, darlin'," Stu says. "Russ is a rough stock contractor."

"Yeah. So?"

"Well, I told him 'bout the old Brahman I picked up at auction last summer 'n' he wants to see him. So we're headin' over to the other place now."

"Why? You said he's no good as a buckin' bull or he wouldn't of been at the auction."

"Never know," Russ says. "He might of been retired 'n' somehow lost his way. He might be no good fer buckin' no more, but maybe he's good breedin' stock."

"Well, he's definitely virile," I chip in. "We never planned on breeding him but we have a number of beige humpy-back calves on the ground and we've got no idea how he managed that. Other than he's an escape artist. Thought he was never on the lam long enough but obviously we were wrong."

"Virility's a damn good thing, in a breeding bull," Russ says.

"Sure, if you got better fences than what we got," Stu says. "See you later." He and Russ head out toward Stu's truck. In minutes the quiet of the morning is shattered by the big diesel engine clattering to life and a plume of dust rises from the parking lot as they speed away.

"So now we breed buckin' bulls? Don't know as I care fer that," Red says.

"I know I don't. Maybe Russ'll take Domino and then we won't have to worry about the boys riding him."

"Not to mention havin' the bother of keepin' him over at Clark's."

"Well, it's not that bad. And it's only until we get better fences on the bull paddock. Now that the store's built, the crew can work on that next."

"More money out the door 'cause Stu couldn't let a sad-eyed bull go on the meat truck."

The sound of a vehicle on the road draws my attention. Jake? I look out the open doorway and see it's a car and rather than turning in, it's just sitting idling at the end of our driveway. I realize the closed sign is still on the sandwich board. I trot outside and up to the road, smile at the driver, and wave her in. I turn the sign to read "OPEN" and go back to the store.

Still no sign of Jake. I'm puzzled at his absence. He's often moody and aloof but he's never left in a huff like that before. I wonder if I should call him, but at the moment, the customer needs assistance at the meat freezer.

I dig through the frozen roasts to get to the steaks which for some reason are all on the bottom, and pull out half a dozen. This customer appears less than enthusiastic about the butcher paper-wrapped steaks so I unwrap one of the T-bones to let her have a look at it. She says, "I didn't think they'd be frozen. I guess they'll thaw by this afternoon."

"For sure," Red tells her, "but my hubby is the barbeque-er 'n' he swears by cookin' 'em while they're still at least partly froze. Says that way you git nice colour on the outside without gittin' 'em too well done. Put cornstarch on 'em 'n' you'll git a nice steakhouse crust."

"Cornstarch? Really?"

"Really."

"Oh great! Thanks!" She leaves with a bottle of rhubarb wine, a saskatoon pie, four steaks and a happy smile. As she's going out the door she says, "All I need now is ice cream for the pie!"

What goes better with pie than ice cream? Why didn't we think of it? All it would take would be a small investment in another freezer! I make a mental note to suggest it when my partners and I discuss what day we should be closed.

"Partner meeting later," I tell Red. "When Stu comes back, let him know."

"What does that mean, partner meetin'?" she asks. "You mean like when us three're sittin' drinkin' wine?"

"Um, sure."

"So now every night's a partner meetin'."

"Well, um..."

"I like it, partner!" She heads back into the kitchen.

Who thought it didn't make sense to offer meat and baked goods when people would be coming for the wine? Stu, that's who. I wonder how he'll react to the ice cream suggestion. Well, the cost is so little and it will be easy to get set up. Just another freezer and a call to Palm Dairies and it's done. I'm going to give it a try.

There's some truth to Red's claim my middle name must be Brutus. Brutus was Arnie's big, talented rope horse who had only one vice, but it was a bad one: when he took the bit in his teeth he just ran until he decided it was time to quit. You could turn his head to stop him but if you didn't catch him on the first couple of strides, the risk of putting him off balance and causing a dangerous fall meant it was usually better to just let him run. I'm not sure it's a good thing to be compared to Brutus. But he was a beautiful horse, talented and valuable, and Arnie sold him for big bucks when he quit the rodeo. I take it as a compliment.

Twenty-Four

N O ANSWER WHEN I called Jake Sunday night. I'm at my
desk Monday morning and still haven't heard from him, a fact
that isn't making me kindly disposed toward him. In fact, I'm starting to think of him as "that asshole", as in "that asshole" owes me an
apology. Usually followed by a bout of sadness when I wonder if it
means we're splitting up. It seems a small thing to break up over. I
never would have taken him to be the jealous type and he has nothing to be jealous about no matter how long I may have feasted my
eyes on Mr. Daniel Baxter.

I'm typing the third draft of the Bar O R loan application, a two-
page, single-spaced essay I've spent hours on. Everett reviewed my
draft of the thing, suggested improvements, I made the changes and
gave it to him to review again. Now we're satisfied with it. It has to
go with the courier today so there's no use asking Irene to type it and
Maureen is busy trying to do most everything else as it is. Honestly,
I don't know how Irene manages to look busy all the time since she
doesn't seem to produce anything. Must take a lot of time to count
all those pencils and make sure the inventory of scratch pads, typewriter ribbons and Liquid Paper is always up to snuff. Of course she
has to make up the monthly stationery order and it's also left to her
to check the waste baskets to ensure no one is throwing away carbon
papers before they're worn to tatters. No wonder she can't do my typing.

My mind wanders. Why does Jake think the Baxters are liars
and thieves? That's a harsh, nasty thing to say. They can't possibly be

that bad. I force my attention back on the Bar O R application, get Everett's signature on it and stick it in the bag for the courier, then pull the Baxter file. A quick review tells me nothing I didn't already know. I decide to order a credit report so we'll have all the info we need ahead of his upcoming review.

When I've got the order for the credit report sent off, I dump the file on the ever-growing stack waiting for Irene to put away. She'll have to do some filing sooner or later and she can't do Everett's and ignore mine. The look on the face of the Stationery Cop when she sees me add that file to the stack makes me feel a little better. Yes, I'm not proud of it but I'm that petty. Deny me a red pen, will you?

ANOTHER MONDAY AND the Baxter file is open in front of me again. I'm studying the TRW Credit Report for about the tenth time. Everett isn't worried about the recent FCC loan affecting renewal of the Baxter line of credit since the little half sheet memo from Regional Office confirming they were okay with it when I asked is securely fastened in the file. So everything is fine. Daniel Baxter, at least as far as we can determine, is neither a criminal nor even slightly sketchy and will get his renewal in the increased amount as requested.

There is one entry in the credit report that jumps out at me, though: a loan from Prairie Equity and Wealth Management. Not recent. Taken out about the time he had to pay out his wife's share of the ranch and retired not long after with a drawdown from his line of credit with us as soon as it was approved. He's making payments on time, appears to be living within his means and managing fine.

Prairie Equity showing up on Dan's credit report reminds me it was on Jake's too. Is that how they know each other? That doesn't make sense. More likely they've done business.

Jake showed up as usual on Saturday night. After a chilly, half-hearted reconciliation there was a lovemaking session that was so perfunctory I wondered if he even knew I was there. I wanted him to tell me more about the Baxters but beyond reiterating that I should keep away from them, he wouldn't say more. He said he was too tired for jibber-jabber and I should take his word for it. He's been working so hard, doesn't even get Sundays off, which I should know by now. After that snarky comment I wasn't sorry to see his skinny butt going out the door.

I can't remember the last time he stayed the night and I'm beginning to have serious doubts it's hay delivery that keeps him away. Martine and that episode at Billie's keeps popping into my mind. At the time I thought it didn't seem like she was an ex. Should I pay attention to these niggling doubts? But suspicion is toxic in a relationship. Then I tell myself that trusting makes it possible for him to lie to me. Am I making a fool of myself?

I close the Baxter file, get up, and put it in the basket on top of the file cabinet. Irene doesn't look up from her typewriter but I know she's aware of it. We've never been on good terms; I don't take it personally because she doesn't like anyone except Everett, but she's been downright hostile since I quit doing my own filing. Why? Because I'm a jumped-up steno and after decades at the bank she's still pounding a typewriter. I guess I can understand her resentment, misplaced though it is. I'm starting to feel a little sympathy for her when Everett's phone rings. He's gone out for lunch, which Irene very well knows, but she pretends not to hear it. It finally rings long enough I realize she is not going to answer it; I punch the button for his line and pick up the receiver. I look her way as I say, "Mr. Carey's office. How may I help you?"

When I've written down the phone message for Everett, I call Felix. His mother answers and says he was away at a rodeo over the weekend but she expects him back later in the afternoon. I leave a message for him to call me. I happen to glance at Irene. Her expression is plain mean and vindictive, like she stuck it to me by interrupting my train of thought by making me answer the phone and then I spoiled her enjoyment by making a personal call. She pulls out her little notebook, opens it, and writes something down. When she looks my way again, she looks smug. I'm pretty sure I just got another demerit.

I'll ask her to get me a purple pen on her next stationery order, just to see if her head explodes.

Twenty-Five

WHEN HE SURPRISES me by showing up on my doorstep at supper time Wednesday, Jake is more like his old self. Missed me so bad, he's going to get Jonesy to do some of the trucking so he doesn't have to be away from me so much, and so on.

He gets out of bed, pulling his jeans on as he stands.

"You don't have to leave," I say.

He turns and climbs back onto the bed, hovering over me for a kiss. "Much as I hate to leave a beautiful naked girl to go to my own cold bed, it's only fair. I have to git away real early tomorrow 'n' I know it always wakes you when I leave. Fact, I might not go to bed at all. You understand, baby?"

"Yeah, that's very thoughtful. Thank you." I hear the sarcasm in my voice but if Jake does, there's no sign.

He gets up again, picks up his shirt and shoves his arms into the sleeves, then looks around the floor until he finds his socks. He sits on the edge of the bed to pull them on.

"I'm surprised you still have so many orders," I say. "Didn't you tell me that after the first rush you usually have to store it until after second cut? Until dealers want more in the fall? Isn't that why you built that big new hay barn?"

"Yeah. It's different this year," he says. He turns his head to glance at me, then gets to his feet and goes to the door. At the doorway, he looks back and says, "heavy crop this year. I finally got on top of the irrigation thing. Second cut's nearly ready to take off 'n' I think I'll even git a third cut."

"Oh yeah? That's great."

"Yeah. Great. Love you," he says. He doesn't wait for my reply, just leaves the bedroom. I hear his keys jingle, then the front door slams. I get up, pull on my robe and watch his taillights from my bedroom window as he drives away.

"Where are you going, Jake?" I mutter. "I mean, where are you *really* going?

My stomach growls and I realize I had nothing but a peanut butter sandwich after work, no real supper, and I'm hungry. I go to the kitchen and get a bowl of Cheerios. As I munch I think back over the evening, wondering why Jake came by mid-week, something that hasn't happened in months. What was different about this week that made him "miss me so bad" when most weeks go by without so much as a phone call?

What did we talk about? He told me about a near miss he had on the highway when a car pulled into the road ahead of him and he had to brake hard to avoid hitting it. I was surprised, because he never shares anything. He even asked a few questions about how my week was going and asked if I was still riding with the patrols. When I said I was, he said since we don't even have cattle out there this year, I should quit. I told him that besides the importance of protecting everyone's cattle, it's a nice social thing. I pointed out that although months ago he said he'd join the patrols, that hasn't happened. He said he thought there were enough riders from the other ranches that he wasn't needed, and with all I have on my plate, I don't need to patrol, either. Just thinking of me, he said. Very thoughtful of him.

Are things between us normalizing? I can hope.

RED AND I ARE ON THE deck outside Red's door enjoying a cold glass of rhubarb wine before supper, well into what we now call our partner meeting. She's telling me about one of the afternoon's customers, the mother of a kid she knew in her school bus driving days. She's happy to learn he is getting extra help with his reading over the summer. I have a sense that despite all the work, she's loving the store because of interactions like this.

"I think you're enjoying your new career as a store owner," I say.

"You know, I really am. At first I couldn't imagine it like you done, Lindy. I know I was cranky 'bout it, spendin' all that money, goin' into debt. Now I know the Creator set you on my Path fer a reason. Imagine! Me, ownin' property 'n' even a business. Áátowa'pistotoyiiwáyi. I bless the day we met."

"Aww, Red!" I don't know what to say. I don't believe in the Creator and blessings and all that, but she does, so it is heartfelt. I can't begin to pronounce the word she just used but I know it's a Cree blessing, so I say, "Thank you! I bless the day we met, too."

Stu drives in and parks at his usual spot next to the shop. There's a bounce in his step to match the big grin on his face as he nearly trots across the yard and up the steps to where we sit. "Am I late fer the partner meetin'?" he asks.

"Yeah, you are. 'Spected you home an hour ago," Red replies. "What's with you? Ain't seen you move that quick since you were late fer supper 'n' you thought someone else was about to git the last pork chop. That gal at the Legion stick her boobs in yer face again?"

"Better'n that," he says. He goes into the house, comes out with a cold bottle of beer, and slouches onto the chair next to Red.

"I can't believe you'd think there was somethin' better'n flirtin' with Dora," Red says. "But you bin drinkin' all afternoon 'n' the first thing you do when you git home is go fer another beer? You know how many calories there is in beer? Maybe you should have a coffee instead."

"Oh shit, darlin', you know Dora flirts with everyone. I ain't stupid enough to think I'm special 'n' I sure as hell ain't stupid enough to ruin a twenty dollar beer buzz on a cuppa five-hour-old coffee. But wait'll you hear what I have to tell ya." He twists the cap off the bottle and takes a long swallow. "Ahhh!"

"So tell us, already," I prod.

"So you know I was meetin' Russ at the Legion?"

"Yeah?"

"Well, he's leasin' the old Johnson place over toward Elkwater. Buildings are the shits but there's lotsa land."

"So that's big news?"

"No, it's what Russ found out about Domino. He traced his brand. Made some calls. Turns out he ain't a Brahman. He's what they call a Plummer. Half Brahman, half Texas Longhorn come up from the States. 'N' he was a pretty good bucker in his day till he took a fall 'n' got hurt, so no good fer rodeo no more. They sold him, thinkin' he might do as a herd bull. Couple years ago one of his sons made a name fer himself in the big show 'n' they thought to git him back 'n' use him fer breedin' themselves, but by then they lost track of him. How he wound up in the kill pen at the auction in Weyburn where I got him, I guess we'll never know."

"Well, I believe the Creator set him in yer Path fer a reason," Red says.

I study Red's face but if she realizes this is the second time in minutes she's talked about the Creator and the Path, she gives no sign. She may be in the middle of one of her spiritual awakenings.

Stu doesn't comment, just shrugs and takes a swig of beer. I turn to him and ask, "How is this big news? We knew he was a bucking bull and we're not in the business of breeding bucking bulls," I point out.

"The big news is, turns out Russ thinks he's valuable since bull ridin's gittin' to be such a big money sport. He's got the right pedigree 'n' he's already got a son doin' good on the circuit. Me 'n' Russ're gonna go partners on him. He knows where we can take him to start collectin' semen. If things go the way we think they will, we can sell that stuff. Folks'll pay a thousand bucks fer a teaspoonful."

From the look on Red's face, I think she's as dumbstruck and skeptical as I am. Semen as a commodity? A thousand dollars for a teaspoonful?

"I think you 'n' Russ been visited by Wīsahkēcāhk," Red scowls.

"No visit from the Trickster, darlin'. It's a fact, they collect semen 'n' freeze it in what they call straws. Lasts fer years. And, he's already drummed up some interest."

"Umm," I say when my head finally clears, "Sounds too good to be true, but say Russ is right, he's your bull, why do you need a partner just to collect semen? Why doesn't he just tell you where to take him?"

"Russ is gonna find the right cows 'cause he's in the business 'n' knows what pedigrees 'n' so on to look fer 'n' he's out 'n' about, can pick up cows from rough stock breeders when he finds 'em at a good price. He's got the connections. We'll start breedin' our own bulls instead of buyin' prospects which as you can prob'ly guess is a crap shoot."

"And breeding them isn't?"

"Well, least they ain't expensive 'n' can be sold if they don't come to nuthin'. Russ'll buy the cows, fer starters anyhow. The calves will be ours, fifty-fifty, our share bein' the breedin'. Bulls like Domino don't come along every day, you know. We're gonna git our own brand registered PDQ 'n' git started right away. Don't need to collect semen fer our own cows, just live cover fer now, 'n' we'll have calves on the ground next spring."

"Oh, great," I say. "So these calves, they're going to be on whose ground? Not sure I'm comfortable with so many bulls eating hay and tearing out fences."

"Well, they ain't all like Domino that way. But anyhow, this is gonna all be at Russ's place," Stu explains. "We're thinkin' to move them pairs with the beige humpy-back calves over there to be bred back to him, too. Not the greatest 'cause a course they're Herefords but there's always a chance they'll throw more to him 'n' if not, then we'll have half Plummer heifers to A.I. with semen from another good bucker. 'N' there's the start of our herd. We're takin' the long view."

"So now you're in the bucking bull business."

"Now *we're* in the buckin' bull business, Princess." He drains his beer and asks, "What's fer supper, darlin'?"

"Leftover chicken 'n' potato salad. Kids're out pickin' beans."

"Ahh! Life is good," Stu says, and heads inside to get another beer.

Even though I still have niggling doubts about the "new old" Jake, the store is a long way from being profitable and there's that big loan hovering over us, we have the cash flow to make this month's payments and sitting in the shade drinking ice cold wine with my partners, I have to agree.

Twenty-Six

STU MADE A run to the Hutterite commune a few weeks ago and bought a couple of roasting chickens. We wanted to try them to see if we should negotiate a standing order for the Hutterites to supply us with chickens for resale. The chicken is flavourful and juicy and one of the big birds is enough for everyone in our family plus cousin Felix to have as much as they want. No small accomplishment with two growing boys and two always-hungry men.

We decide to get a dozen for starters, and to convince customers, we'll barbeque a couple and sell them in pieces, like halves and quarters. Stu moves the barbeque so it's right outside the store and we'll start Saturday to see how it goes. Since customers seem to like hanging around and now we need a place for the barbeque, we decide against putting in lawn right up to the building, opting instead for a patio. For now it's gravel, and when we have the cash, we'll pour concrete and build a roof over it. For every dollar coming in, there's five ways to spend it.

Our hay is being baled today so the haying crew is coming and going, picking up bales in the field and getting them stacked in the loft. It's hot, dirty work. Red has a nice thank you ready for them when they're finished stowing the final load: gallons of cold lemonade and home made pizza. Turns out the new commercial ovens are good for pizza too. The helpers are friends of Felix's, hard workers, and their appetites are as big as his.

"I should of made more," Red says as she observes the pizza disappearing.

"It's okay," I tell her. "No one else feeds them. They consider themselves lucky to get paid on the spot, and a feast like this on top of it? They'll love you for this."

"Don't care if they love me or not, so long's they come back next time we need 'em."

It's true, it's not easy getting help when you need it, especially at this time of the year when everyone is haying.

When Jake comes back Saturday afternoon, he's in a foul mood. I'm disappointed that Wednesday's good mood didn't last, and so intimidated by his scowl I don't ask what's wrong. When there's just the two of us and we're doing night feed, I do, however, ask him if he'll be around tomorrow.

"Why would I be around tomorrow? It's Sunday. I'll be on the road. As usual."

I exhale so abruptly it's almost a snort.

"Tell you what. I'll make up an itinerary for you so you'll know where I am every day 'n' you won't have to nag at me to find out. Would that make you happy?" He's got such a black look on his face I'm speechless and turn away. I'm relieved when he humps a bale into a wheelbarrow and runs it down the alleyway, tossing hay into each paddock.

When he's tossed the last of the hay and comes back in the barn where I'm filling buckets with grain for the riding horses' morning feed, his frown is gone and when I go up to the house, he follows.

He says he's sorry for snarling at me but he's so tired, burning the candle at both ends, won't take it out on me again. We have sex in the shower. Maybe it's make-up sex, although we didn't really have a fight, but in any event, sweet Jake is back. In bed after, he makes no move to leave. I snuggle into his armpit, loving the contact comfort and enjoying the scent of Old Spice soap on a rope. I'm asleep in seconds.

When I wake up, I'm surprised to see it's nearly seven. I don't know when Jake left because I was sleeping so soundly I didn't hear him leave. I can't remember the last time I slept this late.

There's vehicle traffic outside. I get up and look out the window to see two horse trailers parked by the corrals. It's the Sunday patrols getting ready to head out. Stu's beat up straw hat with its ridiculous turkey feather jutting skyward is in a group of half a dozen wranglers and I realize they're already deciding which quadrant everyone will be responsible to patrol to this morning.

I wonder if Red and Marcy can manage the store without me for a while so I can join them. I hurriedly pull on jeans and a shirt, trot across the yard and into the store. I can already smell muffins and the big percolator is gurgling away.

"Good morning," I sing out.

Red and Marcy both look up from their tasks and return the greeting.

"Do you think I could jam out of helping you guys here this morning and join a patrol, Red?" I ask. "I hardly get a chance to ride anymore."

"Hmm, er, I guess so," Red says. "We've got things pretty much under control here. Still. Never know if we'll get busy or not."

"How be if I head back in early, so I can be here all afternoon, just in case?"

"That works," Red agrees.

I grab a muffin out of the day-old-specials bin, then turn and leave the store, trotting over to where the men are still in earnest discussion. "Hey, Stu! I'd like to go on patrol this morning," I tell him. "Can you wait a few minutes until I get saddled up?"

"Sure thing. But these guys can start now 'n' you can go with the next group."

"Okay! Could you get the boys or Felix to get my horse ready while I grab a quick bite?"

"Red's got the boys doin' somethin' 'n' Felix ain't here," Stu says.

"Oh? Is he rodeoing today?"

"Nope. Said he had somethin' to do fer you. But I'll git Chica fer you."

"Thanks," I say. It takes me a second to remember what I'd asked Felix to do. Since the news Jake is getting Jonesy to do some of his deliveries Felix's task may no longer be necessary, but with no way for me to stop him, it'll just have to play out.

A crew cab carrying four cowboys, the guys that ride rescue horses instead of bringing their own, pulls up beside us. We greet them as they spill out. They pull their saddles out of the truck box and lug them into the barn before following Stu down the lane along the back of the corrals to get their mounts for the day.

I head to my house to get ready. When I've bolted down my muffin and brushed my teeth, I fill my canteen and go to the barn where Chica is tied to the rail with the rescue horses that are being saddled. I give her a quick once-over with a dandy brush, pick her feet, then tack up and lead her out, only a little behind the guys. As we round the rigs and head for the staging area, I spot two new arrivals. The Baxters! They're already on their horses. I hope I'm assigned to the same quadrant they are.

Turns out because he sent the first group south, Stu has us all going north, with instructions to pair up, make sure there's someone with a rifle in each pair, and fan out to cover the area between the fence next to the correction line road and the Track. I tell him I have to be back by noon to help in the store.

"Sure, Princess, stick with Dan 'n' Norm, then. Just head on back when you have to."

I agree, and mount my horse.

We all head out together until we're on the community pasture, when we split up to cover our assigned territory. I stay close to Dan. The way we keep looking and grinning at each other makes me doubt we'd notice rustlers before we rode right into them. I hope Norm is paying more attention. He's the one with the rifle, after all.

When we head over a ridge and spot the fence and the road, Norm calls out, "You two follow the ravine. I'll go up here along the fence but I'll stay within a few hundred yards of you. Give a yell if you see something." He lopes off, leaving us to follow the cow path down into the gully. Am I imagining things, or did he just deliberately put his son and me alone together? Deliberate or not, I'll take it.

When the path widens enough to allow it, Dan drops back to ride beside me. "Is he a Paint?" I ask, indicating his horse with a lift of my chin.

"Dunno. Got him at an auction."

"Well, he's pretty typey. I bet he is."

"I agree. But I didn't pay the price of a purebred Paint and he's a good horse which is all that matters." He moves closer. Chica pins her ears and snakes her head.

"I guess she needs a little more space," he says.

"That's mares for you," I reply. "She likes the guys to stay about ten feet away."

"Like some gals I know," he says; then grins, and nudges his horse ahead.

We don't come across the herd, only old sign, but we do find a couple of steers in a stand of aspen. We haze them along so they can be reunited with the herd. Fortunately they stay on the cow path ahead of us until we see another group to the south, then they break and crash through the bush down into the dry creek bed.

The creek bed is more pleasant than the open trail, filled with birdsong and shaded by the stands of willow and aspen and saskatoon bushes that flank it, so we follow. This is where I'd rather be anyway, even though we can't see anything outside of the narrow ravine and we may be too far from Norm for him to hear us if we yell. There's been no rustler activity here for so long I'm not worried.

Although I'm a little disgusted with myself for being attracted to Dan given I'm in a relationship, he's so pleasant and easy to talk to, so unlike Jake these days, I'd be happy to spend the rest of the day riding with him. He drops back to ride beside me now and then when the path is wide enough and if Chica will allow it.

Much too soon it's noon; we meet up with Norm and two other riders, and it's time for me to head home. I take my leave. The trail we call the Track that divides the community pasture roughly in half is the quickest, most direct route back to Wacasko-Wâti and is so exposed no rustlers in their right minds would do anything anywhere near it, so I head in that direction.

My solo ride home is uneventful except for a little spook and snort from Chica when a meadowlark flies up just a few feet ahead of us and then goes on to flap around on the ground as if injured, in hopes of leading us away from its nest. It gives me time to examine my situation with Jake. As odd as it seems that there should be deliveries Sunday at all let alone every Sunday, Jake claims feed stores are open and weekend farmers can't get their hay any other time. That may be true, but why don't the feed stores get enough hay laid in during the week? They do, but even with Jonesy helping, there aren't enough days in the week for him to get to everyone. Not everyone has banker's hours, if I hadn't noticed. His tone was so sharp I felt like I'd been slapped. That reaction is frequent now, and proves the cliché 'familiarity breeds contempt'. No wonder I don't miss him when he's not around. That, and the fact my life is pretty much the same whether he's here or not. Except for the sex of course. Is that enough?

I love him, but he seems to have changed into a different person. If I think about marriage or even living together, I realize unless things improve I don't want either. And if things did change, could I trust it to last? No. Now that I've made that admission, is there any path forward?

THE STORE IS BUSY ALL afternoon. Stu sells all his barbequed chickens and bemoans the fact he didn't do more. We run out of both chickens and steaks in the freezer. The boys picked corn first thing in the morning, and we run out of that by mid afternoon. Our corn patch is just about finished so we'll definitely have to plant more next year. For this year, as long as it's in season we'll see about buying it from neighbours. There is a definite learning curve to stock management.

By five, the riders have all packed up and gone home. I thought I might invite Dan and his dad to stay and have a beer after the store closed but when they came in to pick up a pie and the barbequed chicken they reserved earlier, I was busy in the kitchen and didn't get a chance to talk to them. It's just as well, because soon after, I notice Jake sitting on my patio having a beer with Stu. When the cash register is rung off, Marcy, Red and I join them.

"Didn't expect you back today," I say by way of greeting Jake. "You're full of surprises this week."

"Missed you too, baby," he says. He swirls what's left of his beer and adds, "I got done early 'n' thought I'd swing by. Didn't think you'd have a problem with it."

"I don't have a problem with it."

"Hey, Princess," Stu says, "how was yer ride this mornin'?" He gives me a look that suggests his reason for butting in was my rather cool tone. I take a breath. Maybe I was kind of sharp. I give Jake a quick kiss and sit on the bench beside him.

"I was really glad to have a few hours in the saddle," I tell everyone. "It's been a while. Chica was perfect, just one little spook when a meadowlark flapped around." I get to my feet and announce, "I'm going for a glass of wine. Anyone else?"

"Bring the bottle," Red says.

I come back to the patio, holding a cold bottle in one hand and three glasses by their stems in the other, just as Felix drives in. He parks, gets out of the truck, and although everyone greets him he doesn't make a move to sit down. "You want a beer?" I ask.

"I guess, yeah, thanks. Um, you got somethin' other than Bud?"

"When did you git so damn fussy?" Red asks.

Felix shrugs and shuffles his feet.

"I have Blue," I tell him. "I'll get you one."

"Missed you today, Felix," Stu says. "S'pose you got snagged by some young lady."

"I, er..."

"No need to explain. Have fun while you can, boy," Stu says, "before you git a ball 'n' chain 'n' can't have fun no more."

"As I recall you were pretty anxious to get your ball 'n' chain," I say, and set the wine and glasses on the picnic table.

"Ay-yuh. What was it Arnie said? By then I'd been happy long enough."

Felix barks a laugh, then follows me into the house. I open the fridge, grab a Labatt's Blue and hand it to him.

"Thanks," he says. "Say, about this morning..."

Jake appears in the doorway behind us and asks, "Got one of them fer me?"

"Thought you liked Bud," I say as I turn to face him.

"Well, you know what they say, variety is the spice of life."

I shrug, get another Blue and hand it to him.

"Thanks." He takes the can and pops it open, then frowns and looks from me to Felix and back to me. "Did I interrupt something here?"

"What do you mean?" I ask.

"Looked like you were gittin' yer heads together. Secrets?"

"Secrets?"

Jake shrugs then turns and goes to the door, opens it and stands waiting for us to follow. "Coming?" he asks.

We follow Jake to rejoin the others on the patio.

Felix drains his beer in short order and says, "Thanks fer the beer, Lindy."

"You leavin' already?" Red asks.

"Yeah. Gotta see a man about a dog." He gives us a smile and a wave, tosses his empty beer can in the bin, gets in his truck and drives off.

Charlie comes out of the house in time to wave goodbye. "Why ain't he stayin' fer supper, Mom?"

"Didn't say," Red replies.

"Maybe his mom's expecting him," I suggest, but I wonder, too. I think his reason for coming was to talk to me, and whatever he had to say was something he didn't want Jake to hear. I don't have time to ponder it, though, because as Felix is leaving, an RCMP cruiser turns in and stops in the middle of the yard.

"It's Dwight," Stu observes, and goes to talk to him. It's a long enough conversation we're all starting to get antsy waiting to find out why he's here. Dwight often stops by when he's in the area just to say hello. Usually he'll have a coffee and a muffin and use the john, but today although he gets out of the car he makes no move to join us, just leans on the open door and talks to Stu.

When Stu steps away from the cruiser, Dwight looks our way. He calls out, "have a good evening, folks," and nods before climbing back inside and driving off.

Stu comes back to the patio shaking his head, his forehead creased in a frown.

"What's up, hon?" Red asks.

"He was lookin' fer Gary Meyers. Missed him, of course."

"Why'd he want Gary? Something happen?"

"Ay-yuh. While he was out patrollin' this mornin'," Stu replies, "rustlers hit his place. Reckon they got thirty head. The missus was away at church. All quiet when she left at nine, nothing goin' on when she got back at noon. Took 'em right outta the damn yard. Quick 'n' dirty 'n' none of the neighbours seen nuthin.'"

We all sit in stunned silence. The implications are undeniable. Whoever these rustlers are, they knew Meyers would be on patrol and that his wife never misses a Sunday service.

"Has to be someone we know," Stu says with a long exhale. "Them goddamn rustlers is people we know."

"Who?" Red asks the question on all of our minds. "Who? I can't believe it's one of our friends."

We're all quiet. Lost in our own thoughts.

Finally Red says, "I didn't think Meyers had all that many cows."

"Ay-yuh," Stu says. "They never had any on the community pasture, only joined the patrols 'cause he wanted to help. Thirty head could be all they had. Hope the hell they can survive on their canola and lentils."

"Think I'll swing by there," Jake says. "They must be worried. Maybe I can help 'em out by buyin' any hay they got that they won't be needin' now." He gets up and heads for his truck.

Nice idea, helping them out like that. But the Meyers farm isn't near Jake's place so he's not going to just "swing by" on his way home. I wonder why he wouldn't phone and ask if they wanted to sell their hay.

Worse, I wonder if I mentioned that Gary Meyers was one of the patrollers when Jake and I talked about it on Wednesday.

Twenty-Seven

WHEN I DRIVE into the yard after work Monday, Felix's truck is parked in its usual spot next to the barn. After the mysterious way he acted yesterday I'm anxious to talk to him so I don't go to my house to change, but instead search him out and find him scrubbing a fermenting tank in the wine shed.

"Hey, Felix," I say, "you're working late."

"Yeah. New must going in tomorrow. Have to git these tanks cleaned out 'n' ready."

"And the cycle begins again."

"Yeah."

"You wanted to talk to me?"

"I do." He gets down off the ladder and removes his rubber gloves.

"I don't mean to interrupt. You could keep working while we talk."

"Naw, yer timing's good. I'm done."

"Oh. Okay. So—what?"

He tosses the gloves onto the shelf and runs a hand through his hair to brush it off his forehead. "So," he begins, "I followed Jake when he left his house yesterday morning, like you said. I thought he was making a big hay delivery," he says. "That right?"

"Right."

"Well, he left in his pickup 'n' he didn't have hay."

I draw a sharp breath. "No hay?"

191

"No hay," he reiterates. "I followed him to a place out north east of here. Nice place. Rich lookin'. Even a statue of a bull at the gate. I waited fer half an hour or so but he never come back out. Seems like a pretty popular place. There was a dozen other vehicles parked where I could see 'em. No way of knowin' how long he was gonna be so I decided to come home. Then I thought, that's funny, when I was watchin' Jake's place I never seen his semi. Wonder where it got to. Maybe someone else was deliverin' hay?"

"Jonesy is, I guess. But I'm pretty sure he was riding patrol yesterday."

"So he couldn't of took it. I thought maybe Jake's rig was on the other side of his hay barns 'n' I was curious. So I went back to his place. Still couldn't see it. I was about to drive away when I thought, maybe it's loaded 'n' ready to go as soon as he gits home. Didn't make sense but maybe it's inside the barn. Might as well have a look. 'Bout what you'd expect, no trailer, but lots of hay in the first two barns. Pretty well full, in fact. I was just walkin' through between them two headin' fer the big one a ways back when Leo come racin' over on a ATV lookin' fit to be tied 'n' ast me what the, er, what I was doin'."

"Leo? Didn't think he still lived there."

"Well, I dunno if he lives there or not but he acted like he owns the place, anyhow. I said I was lookin' fer Jake, wantin' to talk to him about gittin' some work. More likely lookin' to steal somethin', Leo says. Called me a chug and told me to git back on the Rez before he called the cops 'n' I could explain to them what I was doin' sneakin' around their place 'n' where I got my truck. He was goin' fer the rifle on his ATV so I didn't hang around."

"Oh my god, Felix! I'm sorry." Imagine Leo speaking to Felix like that! They've known each other since kindergarten. It's hard for me as a white person growing up with every advantage to imagine what it's like living in a brown skin. I rub his arm and shake my head. "Jake was worried the rustlers might decide they need hay and try to steal it. Maybe that's why Leo's back, so there's always someone on the place. Doesn't excuse him being so obnoxious, though."

"It ain't the first time."

"That's sad, Felix. Sometimes I'm ashamed of my, er, my people."

"Not yer fault." He shrugs. "Anyhow, I never had a chance to git a look inside and wasn't till I was drivin' out I noticed the red Camaro on the far side of the house. Jake's old truck was parked there, too. Maybe he gave it to Leo? I shoulda noticed sooner but didn't expect vehicles to be parked behind the house what with all that parking space between the house 'n' the other buildings. I thought no one was home or I wouldn't of gone pokin' around. Can't blame folks fer not likin' that."

"No, I suppose not," I agree.

My mind is abuzz. The place Felix described has to be Hazel and Jerry's ranch. Has he joined their church? Why wouldn't he tell me he has? And if Jake gave his truck to Leo, why didn't he say so? Why the lie about trading it in? Was Leo in Pillerton? Or was it really Jake, and he didn't get the new truck before Christmas as he claimed? What would Jake be doing in Pillerton? But if he was in Pillerton then, what about losing his finger that day? Of course, that story about how he lost his finger still doesn't make sense either. And his hay barns are full? How can that be, if he's on the road seven days a week making deliveries? I'm so lost in thought I barely realize we're out of the wine shed.

Felix breaks into my thoughts by asking, "You ever wondered why he built that big new building way over where he did?"

"What? Oh. Jake's new hay barn. I haven't been to his place since last fall so I never saw where he was building it, but he did say it was away from the main yard so the semis don't have to go through the barnyard."

"Yeah, that could be," he allows, "although you'd of thought he'd of put it closer to the road in that case. Can't even see it from the road. Have to be in their yard to see it. That's a lot of driveway to plow come winter."

"That's right. I'll ask him about it," I say. "You staying for supper?"

"Is that an invitation?"

"Absolutely. But while I go change, check with your cousin. She's the cook in this outfit and maybe she'll feed both of us."

SHE DOES INDEED WELCOME both of us to the supper table. Being Monday and not a baking day after a busy week, I thought Red might have taken advantage of her day off to kick back, maybe read one of her favourite Louis L'Amour paperbacks, or even just doze in the lounger on the deck. But no, she harvested vegetables and now she's on a mission to get them in the freezer.

After supper of cold roast beef leftovers, garden salad and new potatoes in their jackets, Felix heads home. The boys, Stu and I pitch in to get the five-gallon pails of peas shelled while Red scrubs and slices carrots. The kids hear everything even if they seem to be totally engrossed in whatever else they're doing and Red's busy so when the peas are all shelled, I don't bother her about the Jake deception, just say good night and head to my house.

As I'm getting ready for bed, I mull over Felix's news. No hay delivery, a visit with Hazel and Jerry instead. Leo has the truck Jake told me he traded off. He shows up here on a Sunday, late in the afternoon. Why? Because Leo caught Felix at his farm? Was he wondering if Felix saw something he doesn't want anyone to see and he wanted to make sure Felix couldn't talk to me? If so, it was pointless because he couldn't hope to stop Felix from talking to me indefinitely. It's puzzling. As sweet as he was on Wednesday, that visit was unusual too. And why the sudden interest in the patrols? I don't like what I'm thinking.

Should I have called Jake tonight? Is it too late to call him now? But I can't quite figure out what to say. In the end, I decide it's better to leave things as close to normal as possible until he shows up again.

AS IT TURNS OUT HE doesn't come all week. That's normal. But when there's no sign of him Saturday afternoon as usual, when the store is closed I call him. After half a dozen rings, he answers.

"Jake?"

"Yeah. Hi, Lindy."

"What's going on?" I ask. "I expected you today."

"I never said I'd come today."

"No, you didn't, but usually on Saturday—"

"We need to talk."

"Yes, we do. I have a lot of questions. Are you coming over tonight?"

"No. What I have to say won't take long."

I feel a tightening in my chest because I don't want to continue this conversation, while at the same time I know I have to. "Sounds ominous," I manage to say.

"Yeah, uh, well, no use sugar-coatin' it. We're quits, Lindy."

I say nothing, just listen to him breathing while I swallow around the lump in my throat.

"Lindy?"

"I heard you," I manage to squeak out.

"It ain't good no more."

I nod, realizing he can't see me but unable to find my voice to agree. I'm not even sure I do agree. Despite my misgivings I thought we were getting back to normal. After a moment, I hang up.

He's right. It's no good. I tell myself I'm glad he did what we both knew had to be done. But my questions haven't gone away. Now how will I get answers?

It's too early to go to bed and I wouldn't be able to sleep anyway. I get a glass of wine and turn on the television, scroll through the channels and find a movie, but can't focus on it. I finally fall asleep on the couch sometime after two.

I RIDE WITH THE PATROL all day Sunday. I try not to think about Jake, but "he dumped me" pops into my mind frequently and as emotionally tough as I pride myself on being, I'm hurt. I had questions he needed to answer, and I guess some part of me hoped there were reasonable explanations. Maybe he didn't want to tell me he joined that church, knowing my thoughts on religion. Maybe he didn't want me to know he'd given Leo the truck because we'd talked about how if you give kids stuff they don't work for, they don't value it. Maybe he really didn't know Leo was in Pillerton at the same time as Martine. Maybe I misremembered and he didn't ask who was on patrol and I brought it up, mentioning Gary Meyers because it was unusual for him to come. Or maybe I didn't mention Gary at all. Maybe, maybe, maybe.

Being dumped is more painful than I expected.

Both Baxters are patrolling this morning too, but I went out with the first bunch when it was still barely light out, so we're not together. I wouldn't even have realized they were here except mid-afternoon I hear a sharp whistle, look across the valley and see Dan on his black and white pinto. We exchange a wave. Their rig is still in the yard when I come in but I spend extra time in the barn, clean my tack, and take the long way around to get to my house to avoid them and everyone else. That I avoided Dan surprises me given how pleasant his company has been. I guess I'm just not ready to admit to the world what a fool I've been.

I haven't even told Red yet. I suppose I should go to help close up the store but instead I open a bottle of wine and sit drinking it by myself. If she needed help, Red would send one of the boys to see why I was holed up in my house when there was work to do. I tell myself she and Marcy can manage.

When she shows up after supper, Red makes straight for the cupboard with the wine glasses, gets one, and joins me in the living room. I'm already more than halfway through the family-size bottle. When she picks it up to fill her glass she gives me a look, but doesn't comment.

"How was the store today?" I ask.

"Not busy. Crazy thing happened, though. One of the customers asked Stu where the chicken come from 'n' if it was cooked long enough because he heard someone got sick from it."

"What? How's that possible?"

"Dunno. We've et it 'n' never got sick, 'n' Stu told him that. The guy didn't believe him 'n' was talkin' loud so everyone in the store heard about it. Lucky Dan Baxter was there 'n' told the guy he gits these chickens every week 'n' there's never been a problem."

"What do we do about talk like that going around?"

"Nuthin' much we can do, I s'pose, just hope that's the end of it. You know how good them cooked birds sell. We don't wanna hafta quit that!" She takes a deep breath and sips her wine before asking, "Good ride today?"

"Yeah," I reply as I study the hangnail on my thumb before chewing it off. Damn! Now it's bleeding.

"What's goin' on, Lindy?"

"Jake dumped me," I blurt out, and catch my bottom lip in my teeth to stop it from quivering. Admitting it to Red, I'm more emotional than when Jake actually gave me the news.

"Oh! I never seen him drive in."

"He did it over the phone."

"The damn coward!"

"It's better that way." I realize the truth of that as I say it.

"Sorry," she says. She's quiet for a minute or two, then continues, "It kinda looked like you weren't as crazy fer each other like at first, when you couldn't keep yer hands off each other," Red says. "Usually takes a couple years fer that to stop."

"You and Stu still can't keep your hands off each other," I say, picturing Stu reaching for her hand whenever she's close.

"Ain't nearly like it was at first, when he would drive all day fer a date with me," she says. She takes a breath and closes her eyes for a heartbeat as if she's taking a trip down memory lane. After a moment, she asks, "Are you okay?"

"Well, yeah. When I think about it, ever since he was suddenly unavailable for Christmas and then seeing his truck in Pillerton on Boxing Day I've had doubts. He said he bought his new truck before Christmas? I never told you this, but the inception date of the loan was after Boxing Day. So it was probably still his truck when we saw it in Pillerton. Next to Martine's." I guzzle the rest of the wine in my glass and fill it again. "There are other lies. I don't think I even know how many others yet. I think he only showed up here on Wednesday to find out who would be patrolling and I think I mentioned Gary Meyers. And I had Felix follow him last Sunday. I was right. No hay delivery. He was at Hazel and Jerry's. Why wouldn't he tell me about that?"

"You had Felix follow him?"

"Yeah."

"Hmm." She sips her wine and I wonder what she thinks of me getting Felix to do that. But apparently it's okay because she continues, "That's funny. Not another woman, but a church service? Why would he keep it a secret?"

"I can't figure that out myself. Maybe she meets him there? You know what they say, suspicion torments the heart."

"That's what Elvis says, anyway," Red agrees. "Ain't seen much of him lately but when he did come around he seemed he was pissed off a lot. I thought you guys had been fighting."

"That's just it, we didn't fight. Not really. I'd ask him something, he'd get mad, end of conversation."

"You know, I didn't like the way he's been treatin' you fer a while now. Downright mean sometimes. It's just as well it's over. Right?"

I nod.

Red drains her glass and passes it back and forth from one hand to the other as if she's going to say something else, but when I lift the bottle and reach out to refill it, she says, "Um, no thanks, I got things to do. But if you want—should I stay?"

"It's okay, Red. I'm okay. You go ahead. I'm really tired so I won't be up much longer."

"Okay. Maybe we should smudge the house."

To get rid of malevolent spirits and every last trace of Jake? I don't believe in it but she does, and who knows? Maybe there's something to it. It can't hurt. "Yeah, maybe we should."

"Tomorrow?"

"Tomorrow," I agree.

"See you then." She gives my shoulder a pat as she passes my chair.

When I stumble to bed it's so early it's still light out and I can hear Charlie outside, yelling something to Johnny. Despite my emotions running wild, I fall asleep right away. Maybe because of the wine.

I wake up when the clock reads 2:37. I get up and go to the bathroom, then come back to bed and try to fall sleep again. At 4:49. I realize I'm staring at the ceiling. I can see it now because the room is becoming lighter in the pre-dawn. I'm not going to be able to get back to sleep so I get up, pull on my robe and make a pot of coffee.

There's plenty of time before I have to get ready for work so I take a mug out onto the patio and watch the sunrise. Another hot day is on the way but now it's just warm, quiet and beautiful. Somewhere nearby a meadowlark sings. Down in the chicken yard the rooster crows. Far off, cattle moo. There's the occasional whinny from the horse herd. Grasshoppers begin waking up, wings rattling as they fly off. The beginning of a new day at Wacasko-Wâti.

I'm used to Jake being part of my life even if only in small doses and now that he's gone there's a void. I tell myself I should never have gone out with him. I wanted a ride home with Stu and Red because I didn't want things to go too far after the dance. Turns out I should've been concerned about the months after, not just that night. But then I would have missed a lot of nice times, too. Time to discard the unpleasant memories, pack the good ones away, and get on with my life as a single woman. I don't need a man. Maybe Red was right and I wasn't okay on my own. I'll give myself a year to work on that.

Twenty-Eight

J AKE IS IN my past. Leave him there and get on with life. Sure, good idea, and I would do that except for the suspicions I can't quite banish. I don't care about the church meeting thing or him/his truck being in Pillerton, not really. There's more than just him cheating that worries me. He could find out which community pasture Ernie was working any given day without raising eyebrows. There was that unusual Wednesday visit when he asked about the patrols. And the timing of the break-up, coinciding with Felix being caught snooping (no other word for it).

Something else Felix said piques my interest: the new hay building. If the reason for having it away from the other buildings is just so semis don't have to go through the cramped area in the barnyard, why not just build a new road access so rigs could come in from the back?

Adding to my suspicions is the strange fact that in nearly nine months I've been to his place once, and then only briefly. There's always some reason for him to come here instead. Why?

When you learn about one lie, it's natural to wonder if there are others. I should call the RCMP and tell them what I think. I start to make that call, but hang up when I realize I would sound like an idiot. You think your ex-boyfriend is a rustler because he built a new barn too far away from the old one? Sure, lady, we'll look into it.

Felix didn't say how far the new building is from the other barns, but it must be a fair distance if it can't be seen from the road. I seem to remember his driveway is quite long, but the house and barns are easily visible from the road. Maybe it's not all that strange, but I can't put it out of my mind. By the weekend, I realize the only way to stop these crazy thoughts from bouncing around in my head is to go and see for myself.

Sunday morning when he should be away at his "hay delivery" meeting, I drive to his place. It's taking a chance because if he's around, he'll recognize my truck, think I'm stalking him, and I'll have no excuse if he confronts me and calls me on it. I ask myself if I care, and realize I don't.

A sporty red car appears in my rear-view mirror and despite the dust, pulls right up close behind me. I'm going slower than is reasonable and think about speeding up but decide against it. Let the asshole pass! In a minute, he does. A few minutes later I come to the Jordan's Hay Farm sign. Jake's place. I slow even more and gawk, looking for who knows what. I see no signs life. Jake is supposed to be gone so that's as it should be.

Not much farther on there's a rise, then a dip, with a little clump of aspen in the ditch. I make a u-turn so I'm facing back the way I came and pull off, tucking the truck in beside the trees. My plan is to go into the field and hike back to Jake's place. If Felix is right about the location of the new barn, I should come to it without getting near the main yard. If no one's around, I'll check it out. I have my Kodak Ektralite with four more shots before the film is finished. I'm set.

Assuming this road's like ours is or at least was before we opened our store, that red sedan is likely the only traffic there will be for hours, so I'm not worried about someone coming by and stopping to see what I'm doing.

I haven't gone far into the hay field before a dually with clearance lights comes over the hill. I race back to where the aspens are, climb through the fence and duck into the tall grass as the truck slows and stops. As I get back up on the road I fuss with tucking my shirt in.

I walk up to the truck, embarrassed to recognize the driver as Norm Baxter.

"Got a problem, Lindy?" he asks, grinning like a Cheshire Cat. I imagine he's enjoying having caught me peeing at the side of the road.

"Hey, Norm," I reply, "not anymore."

He laughs, then asks, "what're you doin' out here, anyhow?"

He knows I was dating Jake—has he already learned that we've split up? Then I realize I'm past Jake's place, so even if Jake and I were still together, it would be odd for me to be here. Obviously I didn't come here to pee in the ditch.

"I was, um, hoping this road lead to the historical site. You know, the Cypress Hills Massacre site? But I thought it was closer so when I got this far I figured it was the wrong road, and turned around." I wave my hands and add, "and then I, er..."

"Well, the road to the massacre site is the next one to the west. Comin' from yer place you would of drove past the sign pointin' the way."

"Oh? I wonder how I missed it."

"It ain't that big," he says. "Wish they'd put up a bigger one. Lots of folks, even tour buses, miss it. When they realize they've gone too far 'n' wanna turn around, them big buses got a problem on this narrow road. Half the time they come into our yard to turn around. So anyhow, you can't git to the monument on this road, but you can git to our place. About a mile further on. White farmhouse. Red barn. Anytime yer out this way, stop in. Even if it's just to use the biffy."

I chuckle and I can feel my face getting warm. "Well, now you tell me!"

"What did you wanna see the massacre site fer, anyhow? Nuthin' there but a plaque on a pile of rocks."

"I dunno. It just seemed like a good thing to do on a Sunday. The Regina Leader Post had an article about it a while ago. And I've seen the tours advertised. I figured, hey, if it's so famous I should check it out. Did you know it's the reason the Northwest Mounted Police first came this far west?"

"That so?"

"Yeah. You know, I lived in Calgary my whole life until a few years ago, so close and yet I've never been there, so..." I shrug as my words trail off, hoping my face isn't too noticeably red.

"I imagine it's Fort Walsh the tourists wanna see but the road to it takes you past the monument. You should go to the Fort instead of just the monument if yer interested in that kinda stuff."

"Thanks! I will!"

"Okay. Well, I got groceries includin' ice cream so I'd better git. Nice seein' you," he says.

"You too," I reply.

He puts his truck in gear and drives off.

I walk back to my truck, past it and into the scrub aspen on my way to the field again when another truck comes along. It slows. I wave to the driver to let him know I don't need help. It seems there's more traffic on this road than on ours, and I've already been seen by three people. I need to figure out a way to get in there without the dead giveaway of leaving my truck parked on the road. For today, mission aborted.

I go back to my truck, get in and drive, slowing as I come to Jake's place. This time I notice the ATV parked at the first hay barn. I don't have a clear view owing to the shelterbelt of caragana bushes that surrounds the yard but I get a glimpse of someone in a ball cap beside it. I can't make out who it is and naturally I can't stop for a better look. Coming from this direction I do, however, have a view of the yard at the far side of the house that I couldn't see passing the other way. There's a red car next to the stoop. I think it could be the car that passed me earlier. A dark-haired woman with a grocery bag is just closing the trunk.

I think I'm looking at the real reason Jake dumped me. How is it she's comfortable enough in the relationship to bring groceries to a house I've only been in once in nine months? How often has he gone from my bed to hers? He hates to leave me to go to his cold, lonely bed, my ass!

Now I'm pissed.

ON WEDNESDAY, I RETURN home from work, park in the garage, and after changing out of my office clothes, head over to Red's for our daily partner meeting. Red and Stu are in deck chairs as usual, but neither looks happy and their greetings are unenthusiastic.

"What's with you two?" I ask. "You look like you just lost your last friend."

"Worse," Red says.

"We been shut down, Lindy," Stu says.

"What do you mean, shut down?"

"A govermint guy come by 'n' served us with a notice. We can't do no more bakin' or sellin' nuthin' except fer the wine 'til they do a full check of our stuff. Check our equipment to see how clean it is 'n' so on. They got a report of people bein' sick."

"As if we don't clean everything proper!" Red says with a snort. "We et all the chicken that didn't get sold 'n' never got sick. There can't be nuthin' wrong with our stuff. I think someone got sick 'n' thought it was from our stuff even though it wasn't."

"I think it was some guy who didn't wanna admit where he actually got it from, like a titty bar," Stu suggests. "Don't worry. We'll pass inspection with flying colours 'n' be up 'n' runnin' again right away." He picks up the wine bottle, fills a glass and hands it to me.

I sink to a chair beside Red, take a long sip, and then ask, "When is this inspection going to happen?"

"Dunno. He said he has to schedule it 'n' will let us know."

"That's ridiculous! I'll call the guy tomorrow. Did he give you a card?"

"No," Red says. "I never caught his name when he said who he was, but he was wearin' a suit 'n' had a briefcase."

"His car looked real," Stu says, "like a pool car. Logo on the door and numbers on the back."

"Did he give you something? Do we have an official paper, like a notice?"

"Yeah, he stapled it up beside the door."

I get up and trot across to the store. There's a legal-size paper on the door jamb. No phone number, but the Canada Food Inspection Agency logo is at the top.

I feel sick.

Twenty-Nine

WHAT WITH SPENDING so much mental energy, not to mention personal time (lunch hour and coffee breaks) trying to get someone at the Canada Food Inspection Agency on the phone and accomplishing nothing except running up demerits in Irene's little book, I don't give my lie about being interested in the Cypress Hills Massacre site another thought until the next evening when my phone rings.

I reluctantly get up off the couch and go to the phone table in the hall. "Hello?"

"Oh, uhh, hi, Lindy. It's Dan. Dan Baxter. Red gave me your number."

"Oh, she did? Hi. How're things?"

"Good. How're things with you?"

"Oh, you know, same shit, different pile."

"Here too."

After a brief pause, he says, "They say it'll rain tomorrow but be nice again on the week-end."

"I hope it does rain. Land could really use it."

"Yeah. It would be good for the land." Another pause. Then he says, "Hey, Lindy, I was wondering if you might have a few hours off from the store sometime over the weekend. Dad said he was talking to you and you said you were interested in the Cypress Hills Massacre so I thought maybe we could go to Fort Walsh together."

"Well, as it happens, I have more than a few hours off."

"Oh? How's that?"

"Long story. The Reader's Digest version is, we got shut down."

"Oh no! Why?"

"Remember that guy complaining about being sick and asking Stu about the chicken? And you told him you've had them and never had a problem?"

"Yeah. He got you shut down? How?"

"I don't know. I guess he reported it to someone. I don't even know how he'd find out who to report it to. So far I've had no luck finding out anything."

"What are you going to do?"

"Well, there'll be an official inspection but I haven't been able to get a hold of anyone who can tell me when."

"Meantime, you're shut down."

"Yup." I take a deep breath. "Anyway, until it's solved, I have weekends off."

"Well, if there's an upside, that's it, I guess."

It turns out he's never been to Fort Walsh either, even though it's barely a half-hour's drive from where he lives and—surprise!—he's been wanting to go for ages.

Of course I say no, given I'd just made up my mind to be celibate for at least a year and also that I don't need or want a man in my life.

It's Saturday and I'm on my way to his place now.

Red didn't exactly jump up and down with joy when I told her. Not that she has anything against the man, it's just that she thinks it's too soon after my split with Jake, and him not coming to get me is disrespectful on his part plus I'm making it too obvious I'm after him by letting him get away with that, on my part.

"I'm not after him," I declared.

"Well it's sure gonna look like you are, 'n' I'm sure he's thinking it."

"It's just better that way."

"Well, I s'pose it's a good thing to take yer mind off the store business," she said. "Wisht I had something to take mine off it."

"Maybe you want to come along?"

"Don't be crazy. I guess I'll scrub down the store kitchen again. We clean so good, I don't git it. Where can them listerine germs hide? Maybe I need to smudge the place again."

It was on the tip of my tongue to tell her for about the tenth time it's listeria and Listerine is mouthwash, but instead just said, "Why not?" Maybe sage smoke will actually help. At the very least, it might make her feel better. I didn't tell her he wanted to pick me up but I declined, because Dan coming here would mean I wouldn't have an excuse to drive by Jake's place. Not just there and back, but there and back twice. I let her draw her own conclusions, namely that like when I went to meet Jake at the dance, I want to avoid a long ride with him if things don't go well.

I haven't told Red I want to sneak a look at Jake's new hay barn. Maybe I should, but since my aborted attempt I haven't been back so it's not like I'm keeping much of anything from her. I'm entitled to secrets after all and besides, with the store problems it hasn't been front of mind.

Now I slow to barely more than a crawl as I pass Jake's yard but see nothing of interest, even when I stop the truck at a spot offering a view of the yard on the far side of the house. Empty.

I drive on and when I come to another access, stop again. I can't see a building, but the wide dirt lane through the hayfield must lead to it. It's muddy now not just because of the rain, but because the sprinklers are over-spraying it. It's surprising they're running the sprinklers today after that rain yesterday. They must have a really good well. Other than the sprinklers, nothing to see here.

A half mile or so farther on, the hayfield ends and pasture begins. Soon I come to a big red barn and an old-style two-storey white farmhouse. The Baxter place. If that pasture I just drove by is his, it adjoins Jake's hayfield. When I was wondering how Jake and Dan knew each other, I didn't think about them being neighbours and their addresses, being post office boxes, didn't tip me off.

I turn into the driveway and a couple of dogs, border collie types like ours, come running. Norm is in a chair on the verandah and Dan, who is lounging on the rail nearby, straightens, stubs a cigarette out in an ashtray on the railing, and comes down off the verandah to meet me.

"Hey," he says as I slide out of the driver's seat and close the door behind me. "Any trouble finding the place?"

"Nope. I was almost here when I met your dad on the road last week."

"Hi, Lindy," Norm calls from his seat in the shade. "I see Danny finally smartened up 'n' got you out on a date."

"I think you may have had something to do with it."

"Guilty," he admits. "So, yer headed over to Fort Walsh?"

"That's the plan," Dan replies.

"Well, why don't you head into town after 'n' git a nice supper somewhere. Don't hurry home."

"Sure thing, Dad. You got any other dating advice?"

Norm snorts and dismisses us with a wave.

Dan leads the way to his truck. As he opens the passenger door for me he says, "I thought only old women were matchmakers. Hope he didn't embarrass you."

"Not at all," I assure him. "You didn't ask me to come with you today just because he, er, he—"

"Because he nagged me into it? No."

I climb in and when he's gone around to the driver's side and settled behind the wheel, he turns to face me and says, "He told me about seeing you up on the road there, and your conversation, though, and it gave me an idea, or an excuse to ask you out. That's all." He looks away for a second and then faces me again and says, "I'm glad he did."

I study his deep blue eyes. Is the attraction still there? As Stu would say, ay-yuh. Double ay-yuh. I feel my face growing warm. Thankfully, before I turn bright red he turns his attention to putting the key in the ignition.

"You really want to go to Fort Walsh?" I ask.

"Don't you?"

"Um, sure, sometime. But unless you're really keen, I would just as soon have a tour of your ranch."

"Okay, well," he points across the yard, "There's the barn. There's the corrals. Those critters in the corrals are cattle, bet you've seen those before. The house there. This is about the only flat spot on the property, like your place and every other place bordering the Badlands: yucca grass and scrub brush, practically desert. And that's about it." He frowns and cocks his head, then continues: "But if you want, how about we take a ride into town, pick up some McDonalds and some drinks, and then come back here? One thing we do have that you might not is a little sandy beach where the creek makes a dog's leg. Under water when the creek's high but it's been lower than usual this year and that rain yesterday wasn't enough to do much, so it'll be a nice spot for a picnic."

"Maybe I'm a cheap date, but I think a picnic would be perfect."

So that's what we do, more or less. We nixed McDonalds and opted for sandwiches from the Italian Deli, stopped at the Liquor Barn to get a six pack of beer, and by three we're through the gate, heading along a rough track through the pasture. Dan was right, it's pretty much the same as at our place: a flat section for the first bit after leaving the road, then rolling hills that become progressively steeper as we get closer to the actual Badlands. There are stands of scrub aspen and hawthorn with the odd maple, a few lodgepole pines and silver buffalo berry bushes thrown in, broken up by wide swaths of native prairie grasses.

When we come to a rocky outcropping Dan says, "Have to hoof it from here." He turns off the engine and we get out. I take the blanket he digs out from the back seat, he carries the food and beer, and we start along a cow path that leads into a ravine.

"Check this out," he says, and stops up beside the rock.

My first impression was wrong: It's not an outcropping, but rather a granite boulder the size of a single car garage surrounded by a ditch or rut. It's totally out of place in the nearly featureless grassland.

"It's a buffalo rub," Dan explains. "Some government guys—archaeologists, historians, geologists—have been coming around. We put in that gate we came through so they can drive across the pasture and don't keep driving us crazy going back and forth through our yard. Anyway, they call it a glacial erratic, carried here by glaciers and left behind when the Laurentide Ice Shield melted. You know Cypress Hills was a suture zone[1] between the Laurentide[2] and Cordilleran[3] ice sheets[4]?" He looks at me as if for agreement.

"No. I guess I was absent the day the economics prof lectured on that."

"Economics?" He chuckles and says, "Oh! Sorry! I guess I think everyone's as interested in rocks and ice ages and other stupid shit like that as I am."

"I *am* interested. In fact, I want to know."

"Okay," he says with a sharp nod, and continues, "So, for thousands of years, bison rubbed on it to help shed out their winter coats.

---

1.   https://en.wikipedia.org/wiki/Suture_(geology)

2.   https://en.wikipedia.org/wiki/Laurentide_Ice_Sheet

3.   https://en.wikipedia.org/wiki/Cordilleran_Ice_Sheet

4.   https://en.wikipedia.org/wiki/Ice_sheet

That's why it's so shiny. The last bison was killed over a hundred years ago but our cows use it now."

"Speaking of cows, why aren't there any out here? You don't always keep them in those corrals where you have to feed them, surely."

"No, but over winter when the creek flooded, the fence that crossed it got ripped out. Now the fence stops a ways away and the cattle can get into the neighbour's land. You know my neighbour, right? He takes a dim view of my cows coming in, marauding through his hayfield, even when he has his own turned out on it. Of course it's okay when it's his cows coming into my pasture. It's not a hayfield, after all, so what difference does a few cows make?"

It's on the tip of my tongue to say something like 'that asshole', but resist the urge. Jake is in my past and I don't want to talk about him. But now I know why Jake and the Baxters aren't fond of each other. Good fences make good neighbours, as the saying goes. "Why don't you fix the fence?"

"I did, last year. No help from the neighbour, by the way. This is the second time it's been ripped out. When the water's high the fence is far enough into the creek the cattle can't get around it. I expect it'll be back to normal next year but if not, why bother? We have enough summer grazing in the south pasture. Or will, if we put some cows out on the community pasture. When the creek comes up again in the fall, this will be our winter pasture."

"Makes sense," I agree. I run my palms over the rock's smooth surface, and my mind is flooded with images of the great walls of ice melting away in time lapse photography, to be replaced by vast grassland filled first with woolly mammoths, then bison—bulls, cows and calves—peacefully grazing, coming here to scratch that itch. It's awesome in the fullest sense of the word and I'm humbled by my own smallness and unimportance in the universe. "This needs to be protected," I say quietly.

"Yeah. Early homesteaders used it as a landmark. You can still see the grooves from their wagon wheels." He points to ridges in the sod. "They're talking about designating it a provincial historic site. A big feature, point of interest to stop and admire en route to Cypress Hills Interprovincial Park and of course, Fort Walsh. Don't know how I feel about that. It would mean giving up all the land from here to the road, and having flocks of tourists coming through. Bad enough having to give up the land they want for widening the road."

"They pay you for it, though," I offer.

"Sure, and maybe even enough to pay a good chunk off my mortgage. But a swath cut right across the middle of our pasture? A nuisance. Don't think they could pay us enough to make it worth it. But there's nothing we can do to stop them if they decide to expropriate," he says. With a resigned shake of his head, he leads the way along the cow path down into the ravine.

He's right, it's a pretty spot: a finger of sand with the creek gurgling along on three sides. I spread the blanket and Dan puts the food bag on it before going to stick the beer in the creek. I'm beside him next to the water when he opens the box, takes out a bottle and twists the lid off before handing it to me. When he has his own he says, "Cheers!" We clink bottles and I take a good long drink.

I go back to the blanket and settle on it, then pull a sandwich out of the bag. He sits and digs out his own. My mouth waters and I realize I'm actually hungry. I take a bite and grin at Dan as I chew.

I ask him how long he's lived here, where he went to school, things about himself that aren't too personal even though I'd really like to know the reason for his divorce. He's well spoken and after that mini-lecture about the rubbing rock I'm not surprised to learn he has a Bachelor of Science degree.

"Did you want to be a doctor?"

"Not a g.p. Research, I thought. But then an unplanned pregnancy. Forgot about education, spent a few years selling cars before I decided city life wasn't for me. The country's a better place to raise a family, or so I thought. I bulldozed my wife into going along with it. Figured she'd grow to love it. Didn't happen. My daughter hated it too," he says. "Little girls are supposed to love horses, right? She didn't."

"I'm sorry." And I really am. I pick up a pebble and lob it into the creek. "Didn't know you could make enough selling cars to buy a ranch, though. You must have been really good at it."

"I was. But this crap land that takes 10 acres to support one pair unless you have irrigation isn't expensive at the best of times, and there was that downturn in the economy, so..." He shrugs as his thoughts trail off.

He asks me enough questions to make me think he's interested in me, too. I tell him I went to Queen's University and got a business degree. I don't tell him about Nick or the plane crash, I just explain my father was a rodeo rider and I met his friends Red and Stu in my lost summer following the rodeo. When my father died I inherited the ranch. I tell him I was married for a few years, we split amicably and I moved to Wacasko-Wâti then. It's mostly accurate.

It's a hot afternoon. We take our boots off, roll up our jeans, and wade into the creek. He says, "we could easily walk across here. Until last summer, we'd be chin deep standing where we are."

"No sandy beach?"

"No. We swam here though, because the drop-off wasn't steep and the bottom was sandy instead of muddy. Hope it gets back to that."

I fish out the last two bottles of beer and pass one to him. As he takes it, we lock eyes and he leans in for a gentle kiss. As sweet as it is, I'm not ready for more. I escape back to the blanket to dry my feet and put my boots back on.

He joins me to do likewise, and asks, "Was I out of line?"

I shake my head. "No. I wanted to kiss you. It's just—I don't want to go too fast. I'm sorry."

"No, don't be sorry. Fast or slow, as long as we're heading in the right direction I'm happy. Are we? Heading in the right direction I mean? Or is it too soon to know?"

I shake my head. "No. Not too soon."

"We're good then?"

"We're good."

He digs his cigarette pack out of his shirt pocket, opens it and offers it to me. I shake my head. He takes one, lights it, and as he blows smoke out, loops an arm around my waist and pulls me closer. "Thanks for coming today," he says.

"Thanks for inviting me."

It's peaceful, sitting so near this gorgeous man, the sun warm on our faces, the creek meandering along next to us. A clutch of Mallards floats by. A small yellow bird appears in a bush on the other side of the creek. "Look! A canary!" I whisper.

"Common Yellowthroat," he corrects me. It sings for a couple of minutes then flies off, disappearing into the bush again.

After a bit he says, "Next time, we should take horses into the Badlands. Make a day of it."

"Don't take this wrong, but I hope I can't make it."

"Oh yeah, your shutdown. For your sake, I hope so too," he says.

Much too soon I notice the shadow of the bushes and the far bank of the ravine is lengthening as the sun dips lower in the sky. "I hate to cut this short, but it's getting late," I say. "Reality calls."

"Yeah." He butts his smoke in the sand, stands and takes my hand to help me to my feet. We gather our things, head back up the trail and get into the truck. On the short ride back to his house, we keep glancing at each other and grinning. Yes, I'd say we're heading in the right direction.

When I'm back in my own truck on my way home, I slow as I get to where I think we turned off the road to get to the rubbing rock. There isn't an actual approach, just a place in the ditch shallow enough to drive through. The gate is the improvised kind: a few fence posts that don't go into the ground. No chain or lock. Bright orange surveyor's tape marks it. I won't have a problem finding it again.

I cast my mind back on the afternoon with Dan: our pleasant conversation, his impressive knowledge on many subjects, that sweet kiss. And the history of this area! If he hadn't pointed them out I wouldn't even have noticed those ridges in the prairie sod made by wagon wheels all those decades ago.

They head straight for Jake's hay field.

Thirty

"I SHOULD'VE TOLD you sooner," I admit. It's our partners meeting, although since we don't have much other than ranch business to discuss now, maybe it's just Red, Stu and me drowning our sorrows at the end of the work day.

"Well, I don't like you goin' there snoopin' around. What if yer right 'n' there's somethin' shady goin' on? It could be dangerous. Felix said Leo come after him with a gun, right?"

"Well, I don't know if 'came after him' is exactly how it went. He had a rifle, yes. But we took rifles with us on patrol, too, Red. And anyway, it's probably nothing. I'll probably find nothing but hay in that big new barn."

"I agree with Red," Stu chimes in. "It's a bad idea. If yer determined to find out, I'll go, up front 'n' honest, tell Jake we need hay 'n' I want to have a look at it before I buy."

"That your idea of up front and honest? Lying about buying hay? Anyway, he'd show you the hay in the old barns."

"I'd insist on seeing the other hay, over in the other barn."

"He'd just say it's all gone and the hay in the old barns is all there is. And then you'll do what? Buy hay we don't need? Tell him you don't want it because it's not good enough? Good luck. He gets big money for his horse hay but it's not good enough for our horses?"

"Well, maybe I say I'm interested in his new building, there. Wanna admire it. Hell, I don't know, Princess, but it ain't right, sneakin' around. If they catch you at it how're you gonna explain it?"

"If Jake's in with the rustlers like you think, you'd be damn lucky if he even asked you to explain yerself. They already kilt one person, remember?" Red says. "Goddammit! Why don't them govermint guys get on with their inspection so we can start the store up again? You wouldn't have time to run off on such craziness then!"

Stu blows out a long breath. "I know you, Lindy, yer gonna go. Don't matter what we say, yer gonna go. But at least don't go alone."

"You want to go with me?"

"Hell no! You ever seen me run anywhere?"

"Well, who else am I going to take with me? Anyway, I'm not going to run. I'll just go when there's no one around, take a peek inside, and leave."

"Best laid plans," Stu says.

"Goddamnit girl, you got a head like a rock! If you got half a brain you'll come to yer senses by Sunday but if not, I'm gonna git Felix to go with you," Red says. She jumps up and goes inside, slamming the door behind her.

"That's harsh," I say.

"She don't like the idea no more'n I do," Stu points out. "Think about it, Lindy. Please?"

"I will," I agree. "See you tomorrow." I get up and head for my house. Of course I'll think about it, but it's unlikely I'll change my mind. I've already been thinking about it for days, after all. I'm not afraid. Jake and I aren't together anymore and he lied to me about a lot of things, but I still believe those moments of tenderness were real. He wouldn't hurt me. But if Felix going with me makes Red happy, I'm okay with that.

The other thing I've been thinking about for days and that I haven't told my partners, is my phone conversation with Nick. We're close to the end of the term on the bridging financing and I called him ask if there were papers to sign ahead of renewal. He said there was no agreement to renew, not without more collateral. *What?*

I said I'm certain there was. He said he's certain there wasn't, but he'd discuss it with his partners to see if they're willing to renew as is. Like he's a nice guy and he'd do it for us but he doesn't make the decisions. I dug out the paperwork and found the clause dealing with renewal. It talks about a further six month renewal and six months after that. But instead of saying *will be offered*, it says *will not be offered*. I signed the damn thing without realizing they'd added a word. It's a ridiculous clause, awkwardly worded and an obvious trap. They were counting on me not noticing that one added word. That's why they were so accommodating, delivering the documents to me at the bank instead of to my house on the weekend. Waving that certified cheque under my nose like a carrot in front of a mule so I could practically smell the money. Without close inspection the agreement looked exactly like the draft. Nick was right. There is no option to renew.

If I held off telling Stu and Red about spying on Jake because I didn't want to worry them, this problem with the loan renewal is a hundred times worse and I have no idea how to raise the subject. There's some turds you just can't shine up.

FELIX TROTS BACK TO the passenger door of my truck after closing the wire gate behind us, jumps in, and we speed away. Well, speed is a relative term. Bouncing across the prairie while dodging stands of buffalo berry shrubs and being mindful of rocks and dips, it's more like we lurch away. I worry about being seen and I'm eager to get out of view of the road, but I haven't even shifted out of low gear. Once we drop over a slight hill on the downslope to the gully where the creek runs, I breathe a sigh of relief. The buffalo rubbing rock is visible in the distance and I head for it.

I don't stop there, of course, just turn north and follow the old wagon trail. Now I shift into second but it's still pretty rough going so we're not gaining much speed. I lose the track for a time, pick it up

again, and before long we're at the barbwire fence separating Dan's
pasture from Jake's hay field. I stop the truck and we get out.

Felix pulls his thirty aught six out from behind the seat and once
we've climbed through the fence, slings it over his shoulder.

When he showed up this morning with his rifle I was against
him bringing it, but he insisted. "We might see deer," he explained
when I called him on it. "Mom needs meat."

"If you fire that thing, someone's bound to hear and come to see
who's hunting out of season. And how would you explain me being
with you? I came along instead of one of your buddies to help carry
it back to the truck?"

He barked a laugh and said, "hell no, woman! You have to skin
'n' butcher it 'n' then pack it out, while I sit in the shade and smoke.
Better bring yer skinnin' knife."

I gave him the middle finger salute. I don't have a skinning knife,
I don't think he skins them in the field, and I had serious doubts
about the rifle being for deer. But I didn't argue. He's the one who
had a confrontation with Leo, after all. I showed him the Swiss Army
knife I always have in my pocket.

"Dunno what good that little gadget will be, but no worries. I'll
loan you this," he told me, and patted the ten-inch knife in its sheath
on his belt.

Felix is status Cree so it's legal for him to hunt all year anywhere,
not just on the Nekaneet Reserve. This whole area is their ancestral
land. He keeps his mother in meat and always shares a kill with other
elders who have no hunters in their family. It's not just being a good
bronc rider that makes Felix Bear Robe so well respected. Leo Jordan
should be half as decent.

Now we're making our way through the hayfield.

"Hey," I say as we walk through the timothy-brome-alfalfa, "I
think we should head over that way more." I point to the western
edge of the field where the cultivation stops at the edge of the ravine.

"If we're going to go with the hunting story, we should at least be where we'd be more likely to find deer."

Felix nods, so we head over into the ravine. I hear running water. Not much farther downstream is where Dan and I had our picnic. The bank isn't too steep here. A few dozen yards on there's a game trail and we follow that.

I worry we might go too far and pass the barn. As if reading my thoughts, Felix asks, "how will you know when we're where you want to go?"

"Umm." I shrug. "I guess I'll have to go back up to the hayfield and take a look. But we're not quite there yet, I don't think."

We continue along the path. The sound of running water grows in intensity. "It sounds like there's a waterfall," I say.

"Rapids, at least."

The ravine makes a sweeping right turn and once we round the corner, we discover the reason for the sound of rushing water. The creek is dammed and water cascades out what looks like a floodgate, dropping about six feet to the creek bed. There's a small lake behind the dam and on the edge of that, a wooden platform housing a pump. The motor isn't running now but it's connected to a pipe in the pond on one side and another leading up the bank.

"This must be the source of water for Jake's irrigation system," I say.

We follow the pipe up the bank and drop to our knees to peer up over the edge. I draw a sharp breath at what we see: a series of corrals, several loading chutes and what looks like a squeeze chute adjoining the "hay barn". The whole back of the building is open. Not doors open, just *open*, as in a three-walled structure. The corrals are empty but there's the distinct smell of cattle. The pipe we followed up from the creek heads out to the hayfield but branches off to the corrals, likely to serve water troughs. There are no people or vehicles in sight. No hay either.

"He won't be keeping hay in that barn, open like that," I say.

"He could," Felix says, "but hay don't usually need a corral or water."

Just then we hear a motor and see someone on an ATV come around the far corner of the barn and head our way. We scramble back down to the path and jog along it until we can duck into the bushes, then turn to watch our back trail. "If he's not coming down into the ravine, we'll go back up and see what he's doing," I whisper.

The ATV stops at the top of the ravine. When its rider comes down the bank carrying a gas can, Felix whispers, "Leo."

Leo pours gas out of the can into the tank by the pump, then starts the motor, adjusts the speed, and when satisfied, turns to go back up to the bank. He stops for a moment as if studying the ground, then looks our way. I now know what writers mean when they say someone's heart was in their mouth or their guts clench or turn to liquid. When Leo turns and carries on up the bank I let out the breath I didn't realize I was holding.

When we hear the vehicle leave, Felix starts back. I stop him by grabbing his arm. "Hold on," I hiss.

"Don't you wanna see what he's doing?"

"Yeah, but now I don't think it's a good idea. He saw our tracks, even if he didn't come to check it out. He might be watching for us. He might have gone back to get his rifle. Although we have that hunting story, he wouldn't take kindly to someone with a rifle with the range of yours hunting so close to their yard. And do we really trust him not to shoot us and say he thought we were, er, cougars?"

Felix frowns as he considers it, then nods agreement.

A short distance along our back trail, Felix stops me with a hand on my arm, and points. Just coming out of the willows on the opposite bank and heading down to the creek is a majestic buck. At the creek, he drinks. "Six points," Felix whispers. He pulls his rifle off his back and lifts it to his shoulder.

"Felix! No!" I exclaim.

The deer's head snaps up; suddenly on high alert, he looks around and in a split second spins and bounds up the bank to disappear in the bush. Felix gives me a sideways look and clicks his tongue as he slings his rifle over his shoulder again.

"I don't want to risk a confrontation with Leo, Felix. Okay?"

After a moment, he gives a sharp nod of agreement and we continue, but instead of crossing the hayfield where we might be seen, we stay in the ravine until we reach the fence. Dan is right, it stops below the high water mark so it does the job when the creek is high enough but now thanks to Jake's dam, it's nowhere near the water. We go around it and climb up onto Dan's pasture, following the fence back to my truck. It isn't until we're back on the road heading for home I finally dare to take a deep breath.

"If they're filling the trough, they must be expecting to need it," Felix points out. "What're you gonna do?"

I shrug. "I guess I'll tell Stu and Red first, and we should call Dwight. Haven't thought beyond that."

"No? You haven't thought about lunch?"

I look at him, smile, and give his arm a fake punch. "Didn't your cousin give us both a big breakfast?"

"Yeah, but that was hours ago."

My stomach is still in knots after our near miss so I can't even think of food. But Felix is like Charlie and Johnny—always hungry. "I'm sure we can scare up something."

As we pass Jake's driveway I notice someone standing in the middle of the yard looking our way. Jake? Does he recognize my truck? I tell myself it doesn't matter if he does.

STU AND DWIGHT ARE on stools at my island and I'm just topping up their coffee mugs when Red comes in with a basket of her two-bite meat pies. She got the idea from Tony at Maple Creek Italian Deli, who makes something similar he calls calzones. They're quite a bit bigger and are more like a pizza that's been folded in half. Red's are made from the trimmings of pie crust. It's a recipe she's been experimenting with since the kitchen's been shut down, optimistic they'll be great to add to the pastry counter when we open again.

I fill a mug for her and set about making a second pot. "Eat 'em while they're warm," she says as she sets the basket in front of the men, then sits and picks up her mug.

"Those look good. What are they?" Dwight asks.

"Mini-meat pies," Red tells him.

"I call 'em rat turds," Stu says. "Seems appropriate, bein' as this is Wacasko-Wâti."

"Like anyone's gonna buy 'em if we call 'em rat turds!" Red clicks her tongue and pushes the basket closer to Dwight.

"She's not amused," Stu points out needlessly.

"Can't blame her," Dwight says.

"No rat turds involved, Dwight," Red assures him. "Lemme know what you think."

He takes one and bites off half. After a few chews, he says, "Delicious!" He finishes it off before turning to me to say, "You know, Lindy, having a corral and a run-in shed for cattle isn't illegal. Telling you it was a hay barn when it isn't, also not illegal."

"But with the rustling going on, and Jake knowing where the community pasture manager would be, as well as who was patrolling..."

"I agree it's suspicious. But there's no probable cause. There's no way I'd get a warrant. You know any judge is going to ask..."

"I know. Hell hath no fury like a woman scorned."

"I was going to say, they'd like to be sure it was a credible report. But yeah, I'd never be able to get a warrant based on what you just told me."

"Can't you even go and look? You know Jake, maybe just say you were passing by or something?"

"Yeah, I know Jake, but that would be suspicious, being the first time I ever just dropped in. I could go and tell him there had been a report of illegal activity at that new barn, and see if he'll show it to me voluntarily." He takes a sip of coffee and says, "I know what you're going to say, that he won't show it to me if there's anything not on the up and up and there's no way I could force it. So I don't really know what good that would do other than to put them on their guard if they are, er, running stolen cattle."

"How can we get around that, then?" Stu asks.

I press my lips together trying not to smile. He just said *we*, an indication he believes me. Red does too, I think, but she hasn't signed on to what she calls my sneaking around.

"Well, I don't think there is a way to get around it, Stu," Dwight says. "Maybe it'll take catching them with stolen cattle. How could we do that? And we'd still have to have probable cause to look for them in a corral that's not in plain view."

I throw up my hands and lean back against the counter. "If we knew someone had cattle stolen, then snuck in and saw them there?"

"It would still be an illegal search, any evidence found wouldn't be admissible and Crown Counsel wouldn't authorize charges."

"Not if it wasn't a cop who did it and then that person reported it. That would give you probable cause, right?"

"Lindy, fer chrissake!" Red says. "Dwight, tell her, it ain't safe. They already kilt someone."

"Red's right, Lindy."

"Well, what other option is there? Do we have to get someone on the inside to blow the whistle on them? Like, to go under cover?"

"That would be good."

"But that could take years! Meanwhile, hundreds of thousands of dollars worth of cattle vanish. People's livelihoods are destroyed."

"Well, it sure isn't safe for you or Red's cousin to go in there, even if you think they'd buy that story about hunting if they caught you." He helps himself to another mini-meat pie.

"What about that dam, though. It's not legal, is it?"

"It might be. If he had permission."

"Can you find out? If he had permission, I mean?"

"I guess so, Lindy. But then how do I explain knowing about it?"

I shake my head slowly. "Maybe Baxters complain about the creek being so low?"

"Sure. Or..." he shuts his eyes and tilts his head back as if deep in thought, then opens his eyes again and looks around. "Maybe Fish and Wildlife, maybe responding to a report of poachers. It's in their purview, so that works."

"That would be perfect!" I exclaim.

"Don't get excited. It'll take a while to check for permits. Tell you what, though. Maybe it would be a good thing to make them nervous. I'll pick Jake up and take him to the station for an interview. I won't call him a suspect, just a person of interest who may have important information."

"Or maybe Leo. He might be easier to get a confession out of."

"Maybe, but don't get your hopes up. The best we might hope for is that he'll report it up the command chain. Maybe we round up a few of his friends for interviews and see if anything shakes loose. We just might identify the weak link and get a break."

"Well, it's something. And if it's the best you can do—"

"It is."

"Well I'll take it. Coffee's done," I observe. "Fresh cup, anyone?"

"Not for me, thanks," Dwight says. He puts the last of his mini-meat pie in his mouth, picks his hat off the counter at his elbow and gets to his feet. "I'm keeping you folks from your supper. Thanks for coffee. And call them what you want, these little doo-dads are delicious, Red. I'll look for them when your store is back up and running," he promises. "You folks keep in touch, eh?"

"You, too," Stu says. He gets up and accompanies Dwight out the door.

When Red and I are alone, she says, "I don't like that look on yer face, Lindy."

"What look?"

"The one that says yer plannin' somethin'."

"What's to plan? You're right, Dwight even agreed, it's too dangerous for Felix and me to even think about going back there. I haven't forgotten that they killed that rancher over in Fort Qu'Appelle." I fix what I hope is a sincere expression on my face and meet Red's gaze. It must be working, because her frown relaxes and she finishes her coffee.

"I'll be goin', then," she says. "I have one of them poisonous chickens in the oven. You wanna come fer supper?"

"Um, as delicious as that sounds, no thanks. If you leave me the meat pies I'll polish those off, have a soak in the tub, and get to bed early. It's been a while since I hiked as far as I did today and I'm pretty well done in."

"Okay. If yer sure."

"I'm sure."

I really am tired. Besides, I have phone calls to make and I have to practice what I'm going to say.

Thirty-One

I ARRANGED TO meet Nick at the Tourist Information Centre on the Trans-Canada Highway on my lunch hour. I didn't tell Red and Stu about it this meeting and I chose a spot well away from town to avoid being seen by anyone I know.

On arrival I go into the little building, check the racks to make sure there are still Wacasko-Wâti Winery brochures there, get a Dr. Pepper from the pop machine, then go outside and sit at a picnic table in the grove of sapling poplars to wait.

A gleaming silver sedan pulls into the lot and drives up to park next to my truck. The driver gets out and opens a rear door to let an older man out, then closes it and stands with his back against the car, hands folded at his waist. Nick climbs out of the opposite rear door carrying a briefcase, joins the older man, and the two of them come across the grassy verge bordering the parking lot to where I sit.

Nick says, "Hi, Lindy. This is Mr. Richardson."

"Hello, Lindy," Mr. Richardson says. "Thank you for meeting us here today."

"Least I could do," I say. Nick's shit-eating grin makes me want to puke. I'm puzzled at him bringing someone else along and decide Richardson must be the boss or at least the decision-maker. He's obviously someone of importance, given the fancy car and a driver who looks like a Secret Service wannabe. So hopefully it's an indication there's room to negotiate, and we can get a deal done today.

The two of them sit on the bench across the table from me. Nick digs a file out of his briefcase, puts it on the table and asks, "Did you review the contract after our last conversation?"

I nod and take a sip of pop.

"So you agree there is no commitment to renew?"

"Yes." I'd like to call him a sneaky underhanded sonofabitch because that wasn't what we talked about, but I should have read the thing more carefully before signing it, so that part of it is my fault. "So does that mean you aren't going to renew it?"

"That's right, we're not, at least not the way it is," Nick replies. "But we do have a solution. We understand you've run into problems with your new farm store and that's the reason you can't retire the loan."

"We knew from the start we wouldn't be able to retire the loan this soon, Nick. *You* knew from the start. We did think we'd be able to make a substantial payment and that's how the deal was supposed to be written up—"

"But that's now how it's written up, is it." He's obviously savouring his *gotcha!* moment. I wish there was something I could say or do to wipe the smirk off his face..

"I know it's not!" I snap. "And I know it's my fault for not realizing you added that one little word. My fault for trusting you. Anyway, we can't retire the loan now, so all we want is for you to accept what we can pay now, and give us more time for the rest."

"What's going to change? What's going to be different six months down the road? Will you be able to retire the loan then?"

"You know we won't. But we will be able to make a payment. Calves will be weaned soon so we can sell them and pay it down by a good chunk. We'll have the farm store up and running again and make another payment in six months."

"So you sell off some of our collateral to make a payment?."

"You lose the calves but get the money."

"You could sell them and keep the money."

"Yeah, but we wouldn't. We're actually honest."

The insult isn't lost on either of the two fancy-dressed men across the table from me. I don't miss the split-second flash of irritation that crosses Nick's face before his neutral expression returns. At least that grin is gone. Red wasn't fooled by this creep. I need to start listening to her more.

"You didn't put cows out on the community pasture so you'll run out of grazing pretty quick," Nick says evenly. "How are you going to pay us and buy feed too?"

He knows we don't have cattle on the community pasture? "We'll be fine," I say.

"If you've got money to buy feed, maybe you should give it to us along with the calves."

"Then how would we buy feed?"

"Yeah, you're in a tough spot," Nick agrees, and shakes his head in mock sympathy. "Obviously we don't want the cattle to starve. They're our collateral, after all. And we still have confidence in your venture, Lindy. Instead of calling the loan, we're offering to let you keep the money from the sale of calves. That'll give you working capital to get you through to next year. The loan amount will be increased by the amount of sale proceeds, plus interest, of course."

"Of course," I respond.

"Of course. But before we do that, we need collateral that can't walk off or get sick and die," Mr. Richardson says. "I believe Nick said a mortgage on your ranch was discussed when he met with you. We'll pay out the existing mortgage and give you a new one, to include the bridging loan amount, so you still have just the one mortgage. Hand me the new documents, would you, Nick?"

He takes the papers from Nick and smooths them on the table. Nick hands him a pen and as he's holding it, poised to sign, I notice his index finger is missing to the first knuckle. Nick. Jake. Jerry. And now this guy? Those soft white hands sporting that cabochon ruby ring don't belong to a rancher. This can't be a coincidence.

"Yes, we discussed it with Nick," I say. "We didn't agree to it then and I'm not going to agree to it now."

"Agree or not, your position is different now," Mr. Richardson says. "Mortgage, or we seize the herd. Your choice." He marks an X where I'm supposed to sign and pushes the pen and papers across to me. I scan the pages, not really seeing anything

"We can manage, you know. As soon as we get the all clear from the Food Inspection Agency and open the store again. You know we made good money—"

"You don't really think that, er, *issue* with the Food Inspection Agency is going to be solved any time soon, do you? Or that it's the worst thing that can happen?" Mr. Richardson asks. "What would you do if your land was expropriated to be taken into Cypress Hills Park?"

"That won't happen."

"Don't be so sure. You must know the new Grasslands National Park is taking up more and more land every day. I heard they want it to join up with the Cypress Hills Park. And those kangaroo rats that live nowhere else in the world? And those endangered burrowing owls? A word in the right ear about your operations damaging their habitat—"

"We don't damage their habitat."

"So many ways to make it look like you do. But enough talk," Mr. Richardson says, his tone hardening. "Give us the mortgage and none of that happens. We'll pay the fees to get the lien registered."

There's a bolus of heat in my gut and it seems to be spreading. I guess it's what writers mean when they say their blood boiled. I seldom lose my temper but I'm about to. How could I have been taken in by Jake? I thought I was so clever and I walked right into this trap. And there's nothing I can do about it. I think I might cry.

I won't give them the satisfaction of seeing me dissolve into a puddle of tears. I stand up, awkwardly climb out from the picnic table and toss my pop can into the bin as I pass it on the way to my truck.

"We're going to call that loan, Lindy!" Nick calls after me. "You can say goodbye to your entire herd!"

"You'll have to find it first!" I shout back, and break into a trot.

I RACE BACK TO TOWN, my thoughts in turmoil. It's dishonest to hide the collateral, but they deserve it. It's not like we're never going to repay their loan but if their collateral disappears, maybe they'll think again about the renewal. Whose position would be different then?

We need to move our herd to Russ's place, and the sooner the better. The bank is closer than home, so I need to get there as soon as possible and phone Stu. My truck is barely controllable on the sharp curves at this speed. *Take it easy,* I tell myself, *it'll take them a few days at least to actually seize the cattle. We have time.* I force myself to ease off on the gas pedal.

I pull into the parking lot behind the branch and take the nearest available spot, then hurry inside. By the time I'm at my desk, I've calmed a bit and at least have an idea of how I'm going to tell my partners about our current situation. I don't even sit down before I pick up the phone and call Red. Stu answers.

"Hello?"

"Hey, Stu—"

"Lindy! You're finally back! I bin tryin' to reach you. All hell just broke loose."

"Wha—?"

"It's bad. Real bad! The bailiff is here. A couple of 'em, actually. And a bunch of wranglers showed up with horses. Jake's with 'em.

They're unloadin' now. 'N' a cattle hauler just drove in. There's a bunch more up on the road, waitin' to come in."

"Oh my god," I breathe. I close my eyes collapse into my chair. How is this happening? How could they possibly organize this so quickly?

"What should we do?" Stu asks.

"Nothing we can do," I tell him, sinking to my chair. "I'll come home."

IT'S A SUBDUED PARTNERS meeting as we sit on the patio watching the last cattle hauler head down the road. The bailiffs are gone and the wranglers are loading their horses. Jake and Leo are the last to leave. As they drive past, Leo, in the passenger seat, looks our way and gives us the middle finger salute. Jake looks straight ahead.

"Pfft! As if goddamn Jake don't know we're sittin' here," Red says. "Whatever went wrong between the two of you, you'd think he'd have the decency to come 'n' tell Stu 'n' me hello or he's sorry."

"Well, he's feelin' guilty. 'N' you see that smirk of Leo's? I'd like to slap it right off the little rat bastard's face," Stu growls.

"I hope he feels guilty, but maybe he's proud of how easily he screwed us over," I say. "Those people he set us up with have their fingers in everything."

"You sure this is legal, what they done, though?" Stu asks for the tenth time.

"Yeah, it's legal." I heave a sigh and shake my head. "What I can't figure out is how they got this all rolling so fast. Only thing I can think of is that they must've had it ready to go in case I didn't sign the mortgage. But how did they set it in motion?"

"There's a pay phone at that tourist place, right?" Red asks. "They phoned someone. Someone here."

"Yeah, maybe someone waiting by the phone at the Husky. No one would think twice about a bunch of bull haulers parked there. Jake! Goddamn Jake!" I feel like screaming but content myself with a growl. "*Grrr!* I'm sorry, guys. Both that I didn't tell you what was going on and that I pushed you into it to start with. All totally my fault."

"Remember my outlook on life, Princess?" Stu asks. "No use blaming blame, it don't change nuthin'. Let's talk about where we go from here."

Felix comes out of the wine shed and crosses the yard to join us. "That's the last of them?" he asks. "Bastards're gone? They took everything?"

"Everything but the horses," I reply. "Guess they didn't want a bunch of rag tag rescues."

"Hey!" Stu exclaims. "They're gonna hear you. They may be rescues but they still got feelin's."

Ordinarily, I'd chuckle at that. Today I just take a breath. "Truth is, the horses weren't valuable as collateral because anyone with a grain of sense knows they're a liability, not an asset. Result is, now we've got nothing to sell and bills still coming in."

"Well, at least we won't have the expense of buyin' feed now that we got no cattle to speak of."

"Yeah, hay lasts so much longer when you've got no animals to feed. Maybe we can sell it to Jake." Tears fill my eyes; I wipe them away, biting my lip to stop myself from sobbing.

"We still got the horses. And, we no longer got that loan hangin' over our heads, right?"

"Well, yeah—"

"'N' whaddaya mean we got nuthin' to sell? We still got wine 'n' a few folks interested in horses. A definite maybe on the mule. And Domino—"

"Oh, yeah, Domino. I forgot about him," I snort.

"Don't go makin' small of Domino, Lindy. Like I said, we got no cattle *to speak of.* There's Domino 'n' half a dozen pairs with him."

"Oh, that's right! The ones with the beige calves!" Red exclaims.

"That's something," I agree. "I guess it's a good thing I never told Jake we moved them over to Russ's place."

"Yup, the way it's lookin', that's a *damn* good thing," Stu agrees, and hisses something under his breath. I think he might have said '*motherfucker*', except I've never heard him use the word. "Wonder how Jake missed him. Some semen was sold, too, don't fergit. Might still git a few more buyers fer that. So havin' that horny ol' bull is turnin' out good." He reaches for Red's hand and traps it under his on his thigh. "We'll be all right, darlin'. Don't worry."

"You know, the big boss said something that makes me think they're involved with us being shut down somehow. Wonder if that's possible. And what about the land expropriation?" I ask. "If they've got the connections to get the store shut down, do you think they can, er, do something to make the expropriation happen too?"

"He's just blowin' smoke," Stu replies. "But tell you what. We'll go to the municipal office next week 'n' see what we can find out. 'N' if you can find out where the food inspection office is—likely in Regina?—we might take a trip there, too."

"Even if he's right, about the expropriation I mean, it would take years."

"Yup. Years. 'N' it wouldn't be the end of us. We'd have the money to buy somewheres else. Maybe it would have to be somethin' smaller. Might not be nice. But worse case? We move. So long's no one dies, that's all that matters."

"You're right, of course. But I haven't given up and I'm sure as *hell* not going to let Jake get away with this."

"What're you gonna do to stop them? They got our herd. 'N' as far as Jake goes, you can't do nuthin'," Red says.

"Don't be so sure."

Thirty-Two

S O MUCH HAS happened since my picnic with Dan it's hard to believe it was only a week ago. Exactly a week. Making Jake pay at least in a small way begins today.

I'm at Dan's place and we're saddling horses for our trail ride. I said I'd bring Chica and Norm could ride out with us, but Norm didn't want to come along, or at least that's what Dan claims, so I left Chica at home and I'm going to use Norm's horse, Smarty. Dan went along with my suggestion that rather than heading south to the power lines and into the badlands, we ride up to the beach where we had our picnic. I made sandwiches and have them in my saddlebags. Dan has beer in his.

He's standing on my right as I finish the tightening the cinch, and slides a couple of fingers under it as if checking to see that it's not too loose.

"Is it okay?" I ask.

"Yeah," he replies. "Not checking up on you. Just something I do without thinking. I came to adjust the stirrups for you after you mount."

"Thanks," I say. I gather the reins in my left hand and reach up to grasp the horn. He stops me from mounting with a hand on my arm. I'm suddenly very conscious of how close he is. He leans in and we kiss.

"Thanks for coming today, Lindy," he says quietly.

"Oh! No, thank *you* for inviting me." I laugh, take his hand and give it a quick squeeze. "Not that you had a choice. Don't tell Red I called you. She'd think it was, umm, too forward of me."

"I'm glad you did! Hell, I was trying to work up the nerve to call you but since last week when I suggested taking a day to ride out into the Badlands and it didn't sound like you thought it was a good idea, I was afraid you'd turn me down. I figured the prettiest girl around would have, well, er, lots of guys."

"Thanks, but nope. No guys." The smell of him, aftershave mingled with horse and smoky-minty breath, is masculine and pleasant. He gives my arm a rub and sensing my interest, pulls me in close for another kiss, this one lingering. Finally I pull away and smile. "Can't stay here all day," I tease.

"Suppose not," he agrees. He steps back as I put my left foot in the stirrup and swing up into the saddle.

Although Norm and I are close to the same height, his stirrups are too short for me. I move my legs back out of the way as Dan lets first one then the other down a couple of holes, then mounts his horse and we head through the gate into the north pasture.

"Should we follow the creek, or is it too steep? Is there a better trail?" I ask.

"Not steep here like it is farther upstream, but there's too much bush, so best to follow the cow path, for a ways, anyhow." He nudges his horse into a walk. I give Smarty a little nudge with my heel and fall in beside him. Once through the gate there's a pronounced path and we follow that. Dan reins his horse off the path to let me come up beside him, and we ride side by side, chatting.

I ask, "so, what's your week been like?"

"Fine," he replies. "I'm a little worried about one of the cows, though. That's the only thing out of the ordinary."

"Oh? What's up?"

"Well, she's never been quite right. Falls down if one of the other cows bumps her. And she's been kind of wobbly for a while. It's gotten bad the past few days so I've got her quarantined. Vet's coming tomorrow."

"Any idea what's wrong with her?"

"Well, our pasture's decent enough, I think, and the water's fine so I don't think it's polioencephalomalacia."

"Polio?"

"Not poliomyelitis, if that's what you're thinking. Polioencephalomalacia is caused by excessive grain, which definitely isn't the case, or too much sulphur in the feed or water. With only one animal symptomatic, I don't think sulphur's the problem either but I've taken samples in to be checked."

"Is it fatal?"

"Not usually, or at least it's treatable. The other possibility I'm thinking of is bacterial or viral encephalitis or even lead toxicity."

"Is it contagious?"

"I'm not sure. Hopefully the vet will be able to give me some answers. Most likely he'll just want to do some tests." He blows out a long breath, then turns to me and grins. "What about you? How's your week been?"

"Well, um. The shits, really."

"The shits? Why—"

"I guess you haven't heard the news. I would've thought the whole town would be buzzing about it by now."

"I, er—"

"We had our herd seized."

He pulls his horse to a halt and faces me. "The bank did that?"

"Not the bank. They wouldn't give us the money to build the store so we got it elsewhere."

"Well, you're not kidding, it's the shits. Are you going to be okay?"

I shrug. "Guess so. Not the end of the world. Looking at a few options." I catch my bottom lip in my teeth to stop its trembling and shake my head. "Soon as we get the store up and running again, we'll pick up a few head of cows maybe. See what goes through the sales. Not the end of the world."

"Lindy, I'm sorry."

"Thanks, Dan. I just wanted you to know. Now I don't want to talk about it for a bit. Okay?"

"I get it," he says. "No more ranch problems. Just a beautiful day for a ride with a beautiful girl. Okay."

"Perfect."

We reach the rubbing rock and turn the horses onto the path that leads down the ravine. When we get to the sandy beach, Dan dismounts and lights a cigarette while we let the horses drink.

"Too soon to stop for lunch, don't you think?" I ask.

"Oh? You up for more miles in the saddle?"

"I am."

"I, uh, okay sure," he agrees with a shrug. When the horses have finished drinking and Dan is back in the saddle, I nudge Smarty along the bank. When we come to a stand of bush that blocks our way, I rein him into the creek to get around it, pleased when he goes forward without objection. "You really are a smarty," I tell him, and scratch his withers. Stu is right, you can't beat these ranch-rode horses.

We reach the fence and Dan calls, "End of my property, Lindy! Let's turn back."

"Oh no, not yet! The creek doesn't belong to Jake, you know."

Dan comes up beside me, his expression perplexed. I guess he's wondering if my reason for today's ride is to get back at Jake by having him see me with his adversary. I don't know how to let him know that's not the case, so I smile and nudge Smarty past the fence, ending any possible objections. When the bank becomes too steep, I push

Smarty up as if heading out of the ravine. About half way up, we come to the game trail Felix and I followed to get to Jake's dam and I turn Smarty onto it. When it's wide enough, Dan comes up beside me again.

"How far do you plan on going before we turn around?" he asks. "Horses had a drink, now I'm getting thirsty. Wish I'd put the beer in the creek back there."

"Listen! Sounds like there's a waterfall. Is there one?"

"I don't know, I've never been up here before."

"Well, wouldn't it be nice if there was! Maybe we'll discover another nice spot for a picnic." I hope it sounds believable. Damn, I'm getting good at subterfuge. I experience a twinge of guilt.

"Yeah, maybe," Dan agrees. "Tell you what, though. If there's a swimming hole, you're going to get wet!"

"You have to catch me first!" I challenge, and give Shorty the canter aid. He leaps from walk to lope and I'm once again impressed with how responsive and well trained the little Quarter Horse is.

We lope along the trail for a bit, slowing to a jog when we come to the dogleg in the creek where the ravine curves to the right. Once around the bend, the dam is in clear view. I halt and Dan pulls up beside me.

"I'll be damned! *Fuckin'* asshole!" he exclaims. "No wonder we barely have water down at our place."

YES! Exactly the reaction I hoped for and although spending time with a handsome, articulate man and riding a good horse on a beautiful day is hard to beat, it's the reason for this outing after all.

"You didn't know about this?" I'm all innocence. "Didn't he have to have your permission or anything?"

"I knew he had a water licence but that doesn't give him the right to block the creek. I figured with the creek so low, he must be using a well for his irrigation. And permission? No one notified us about it." He takes off his hat and rubs his forehead on his sleeve before setting the hat back on. He studies the dam for a few minutes, then says, "Lindy, I hope you don't mind, but I really want to talk to Dad about this. Maybe we can eat lunch when we're back at the house?"

I nod. "Of course."

We turn our horses and head back. We're in the yard in under an hour. Norm comes out of the barn to the hitching rail where we're unsaddling the horses, his face grim. Seeing his troubled expression, Dan asks, "Something wrong, Dad?"

"That cow that you got in the pen by herself? She's worse. Can't hardly stand. Got up once, staggered a few steps 'n' fell down again."

"Goddammit," Dan says. "She down now?"

"Ay-yuh. Think we need the damn vet today, never mind waitin' till tomorrow," Norm says.

"I'll call his office and see if they can get him here today. Meanwhile, let's check the rest," Dan says. He turns to me and says, "Sorry, Lindy—"

"It's okay, Dan."

"It's just—you know a down cow is a dead cow."

"Yeah. Can I help with checking? Maybe we should ride out?"

"Um, no, I think we're okay. But lunch—"

"Don't give it a second thought. I just hope it turns out to be, um, loco weed or something."

"Thanks, Lindy," he says, worry evident in his furrowed brow and the tension around his mouth. One down cow may not sound like much when you've got so many, but I'm sure he's worried it's just the beginning and there are more to come. He starts to turn away, then hesitates for a moment and says, "I'll call you."

"SO THERE AIN'T GONNA be an inspection?"

"No. They don't know anything about it. They want me to mail them the notice and they'll look into it. I won't hold my breath." I look up to see Everett watching me from his office door. A jerk of his head lets me know he wants to see me. "Listen, Red, I have to go. But it's great news. Gear up for the week-end! Phone everyone you know and ask them to phone everyone they know. And I'll be home at the usual time." I hang up the phone and go to Everett's office.

I smile and ask, "What's up?"

"Close the door," he says. There's no answering smile on his face.

I comply, then sit in the chair directly across the desk from him. I experience a twinge of concern at his expression.

"There's been a complaint, Lindy," he tells me.

"A complaint?" I ask, and wonder what Irene has been up to now. "What about? Too many personal calls?"

"Personal calls? Um, no. There's an allegation of, er, *irregularities* in your files."

"Irregularities? What irregularities? What file?"

"I don't know how to say it, Lindy. The, um, complainant says you've, er, taken money from his account and only put part of it against his loan."

"What? But that's crazy! I couldn't do that. I *wouldn't* do that!"

"I know, Lindy, but the fact is, the withdrawals from his current account don't match the payments on his loan."

"But that can't be!"

"There's more. Something about inflating the value of your assets, I mean, Wacasko-Wâti's assets, in order to get your operating credit loan. Tax fraud. Bank fraud."

"But Everett! You know me—"

"Yeah, I do. And I'm sure it'll work out all right. Regional Office is sending examiners out to look through everything. They'll start Monday. Meanwhile, you're suspended. Effective right now."

"Suspended?"

"Think of it as a vacation."

"Vacation?"

"Yeah. We'll call it that. Irene and I are the only ones who know it isn't."

I cover my face with my hands and take a few deep breaths. "This can't be. It just doesn't make sense," I mumble into my hands.

When I look at Everett again, he says, "I'm sorry. I'm sure it'll blow over."

Unable to say more, I'm suddenly very anxious to leave. I shake my head, stand up and hurry out of his office, avoiding eye contact with everyone. I get my purse out of my desk drawer and when I straighten up, I'm surprised to see Irene right in front of me.

"I'll have your key, Lindy," she says, and holds out her hand. There's a smirk on her face. It's the happiest I've seen her look since I started working here.

Thirty-Three

MY BOYFRIEND, WHO only a few weeks ago said he loved me, dumped me. Worse, he's part of a plot that took our cattle and I suspect he and his "bad people" are behind the complaint that got me suspended from my job as well as the bogus shutdown by the Food Inspection Agency. My mistake was trusting him. Telling him I increased the valuation of the ranch. Talking about who was riding patrols. Things I thought were everyday subjects between two people in a relationship. But his love words were lies to suck me in and I was so gullible I fell for it.

We can get the store up and running again but it's lost its momentum and will take time and advertising dollars to get back to where it was. Even then, cattle are our mainstay. Without them and without my wages, how will we make the balloon payment coming due on our bank loan? What about the embezzlement allegation? And now they're going to say I inflated the value of the ranch to get that loan? I still think it's reasonable, but what if they don't agree and I get charged? Jail time at worst, suspended sentence and a criminal record at best. No chance of a job at the bank with that on my resume and there aren't many places to work in Maple Creek. Fewer still that would hire a felon.

I'm in such a funk it's an effort to get out of bed in the morning. As a result, it's after noon and I'm still in my bathrobe drinking my first coffee of the day when there's a tap on my door and Red comes in.

"Good morning," she says. "It's like a damn cave in here. Why don't you open the curtains? 'N' have you even brushed yer hair? You look like hell."

"Thanks," I mumble. "Need me for something?"

"Nope. I had a little trouble gettin' the oven to light but Stu done it fer me."

"What, then?" I hear the near-snarl in my tone, look up and muster a smile. "Grab a mug."

"Naw, no time. But Louise called lookin' fer Felix. You seen him?"

"No."

"I mean yesterday. You see him yesterday?"

"No." Now I straighten up. "You mean, she hasn't seen him since yesterday? It's not that unusual, is it?'

"No, but he was supposed to work here yesterday 'n' he no-showed. Which you'd know if you so much as stuck yer head out the door. Louise says he went huntin' Wednesday mornin' 'n' ain't been seen or heard from since.

I'm in no mood for a scold, but I ignore it. The news about Felix is a surprise. "He went hunting alone?"

"Yeah, that ain't all that unusual neither. She wasn't worried, thought he'd crashed here, but he usually lets her know. When he didn't come home yesterday neither, 'n' didn't call, that's when she started to worry. Him not callin', that's unusual. His buddies went 'n' checked where he usually hunts but no sign."

The memory of that six-point whitetail buck we saw at the creek when we were leaving Jake's place flashes to the front of my mind. I'm suddenly wide awake and jump to my feet. "I think I know where he might have gone."

"Where?"

"Out behind Jake's. We saw a deer when we were there. A good-sized buck. He wanted to shoot it then but I wouldn't let him. I bet he's gone back to see if he can find it again." I head around the island for the back hall.

"You ain't goin' to Jake's alone!"

I turn to face her. "No, I'm not going to Jake's at all, I'm going up the ravine at the back of his property, same as Felix and I did. And I'll get Dan to go with me. Meanwhile, let Louise know and it's time to report him to the cops as missing."

I shudder, thinking of what might have happened. Did he fall, maybe slide down one of the steep parts and break a leg? Maybe fall when he was crossing the creek, hit his head and drown? Did he wound the deer and have it turn on him? Unusual, but not unheard of. Or worse: did he run afoul of Leo?

I hurry to my room, grab my jeans off the floor, and as I'm pulling them on, hear Red on the phone. When I'm dressed and come back to the kitchen, she holds the phone away and says to me, "Louise says thanks, and she's going to let Joe and his other friends know. They'll want to go with you."

"Okay," I agree, "but I don't want to wait for them. Tell them to go to Baxter's and check in with Norm. He can direct them. Maybe they start searching the along the creek behind their property, and work north. They should eventually meet up with us."

When she's conveyed the message and hung up, I take the phone and dial Dan. I give him a brief explanation. He agrees to go with me. I tell him I'll get there as soon as I can.

I'M WITH DAN IN HIS truck driving along the trail we rode horses up, was it just six days ago? Is it really less than two weeks since our first date? I had to tell him about Felix and me seeing that deer during our reconnaissance of Jake's so-called hay barn and of course I then had to admit I knew about the dam when I insisted we ride farther up the ravine. He gave me a narrow-eyed scold-type look. First

Red and now Dan. She'll let it pass but Dan has said very little since my confession. I doubt there will be other picnics in our future. I don't know if there are any other eligible bachelors in the area so my promise to myself to be celibate for a year may be an easy one to keep, but at least he's going with me today.

We pass the rubbing rock, carry on up toward the property line and spot Felix's truck at the fence.

"That must be his truck," Dan says. He drives up beside it and puts the truck in neutral. I start to get out.

"Hold on," Dan says, and I stop, half in and half out the door.

"What?"

"So now we know he's in this area. Let's go back and get the horses. We can cover more territory that way and we can easily cross the creek if we need to."

"But what if he's right near here, just fallen and broken a leg, or something?"

"Give a shout. If he answers, he's close. If not, we go and get the horses."

I nod and get out, then trot along the fence to the edge of the ravine. Cupping my hands around my mouth, I yell, "Felix! Felix!" No response.

Dan comes up beside me and shouts his name, too, and when there's likewise no answer, says, "Now we go get the horses."

"That'll take too long. You go ahead. You can pony Smarty for me and I'll meet you down on that game trail. I'm going down to where we saw the deer..."

"You'll get lost too."

"Don't be silly! I'll stay by the creek. I can't get lost there." I turn and start off.

"Damn it, girl!" he exclaims, and follows me.

"You're coming?" I ask as he trots up beside me.

"I'm not letting you go alone," he explains, "just in case."

"In case of what?"

"In case you need help."

When we reach the creek, we go around the last fence post, then up the bank to the game trail. The trail has numerous deer tracks interspersed with paw prints of various smaller animals, maybe skunks, coyotes, badgers, and Dan points out what he thinks are cougar prints.

"See? It's dangerous. What will you do if you come face to face with this cat?"

"I'll yell and wave my arms around."

"You don't really think that'll stop it, do you?"

I refuse to be drawn into a *what if* conversation so I ignore the question and hurry along the trail. I worry Felix's tracks have been obliterated by animal traffic but only a little farther on there are human footprints. It's been dry and windy, so the tracks are filling with blown dust, but there are still a few clear boot prints. I'm confident we're on the right track. I call his name as I go.

"I don't know if he'll even be able to hear me," I wail.

"They can probably hear you at Fort Walsh," Dan says.

Not much farther along, the trail turns from sandy to gravelly glacial till and we lose the boot prints completely.

"He probably went down across the creek and into the bush," Dan says. "We need the horses."

"He wouldn't cross the creek here, I don't think. It's too deep and fast here. Besides, the place we saw the deer is farther on."

"Easy to cross the creek there?"

"I don't know."

"It's shallow where we had our picnic. We should go back and cross there."

"I hate to think we have to backtrack that far. There must be a place closer where it's narrower. Or at least not as deep. And he might still be on this side, too." I call his name a bunch more times, and when there's no answer, turn to Dan and suggest, "Before we go back, let's go farther along the trail and see if we can pick up more tracks, or see a place where he went down into the creek."

"I dunno, Lindy. I think we're almost at the dam."

"Just a little father. If we get to the dam and there's no sign, we'll turn back." I don't wait for him to agree, and set off north along the game trail again.

"Lindy, come back! He probably crossed the creek where we lost track..."

I ignore him and break into a jog, remembering my father saying he might not always be right, but he was never wrong. I guess I think that way, too. I come by it honestly. That, coupled with the Brutus in me, I imagine Red's right and I have a head like a rock. Realizing that now doesn't stop me, though. I hear Dan's footfalls behind me. I didn't think he would let me get too far without him.

I round the bend in the ravine where I have a clear view of the dam, and slow to a walk, studying the ground. I spot a boot print, and call back to Dan, "Here!" I strike off at a jog again, only stopping when I'm at the dam, right where Felix and I climbed up and peered over the bank. I wait until Dan is beside me and say, "I bet he went up there. Look at all the tracks!"

"Lindy, of course there's tracks here. You said Leo came here to put gas in the pump—"

"Did I?" Funny, but I don't remember telling him that. Or even that we saw Leo. I thought I only told him about seeing the deer and that I knew about the dam when I lured him here.

"You did," he continues. "Why would Felix go up there? He's not going to find that buck in the corrals. Let's go back and cross the creek, so we at least have a chance of finding him."

"What...? Listen!"

It's not easy to hear much other than the water falling from the opening in the dam, but I'm sure I just heard a cow bellowing, and men's voices, although not clearly enough to make out any words.

"Something's going on up there," I say, and start up the bank.

Dan grabs my arm and pulls me back down beside him. "They're just doing something with their cattle. They have cattle, you know."

"I know. But I need to tell them about Felix being missing. Maybe they've seen him. Or they'll help us search."

"Lindy, they're not going to help. And they're not going to like you sticking your nose in..."

"What? Sticking my nose in what?"

He frowns and doesn't say more. Now he's starting to annoy me. I wrench my arm out of his grasp and scramble up the bank before he can stop me again. When I'm far enough up I stop and peer over the edge. There are a couple dozen steers in the corral. Jake and Leo are there, and there's another man I don't recognize They've got a fire going and a steer in the squeeze chute. A cloud of smoke rises from the animal in the chute. Animals this size would have been branded a year or more ago.

"My god, Dan! They're overbranding!" I hiss. I turn to face Dan and my heart sinks. He doesn't look surprised. In fact, he looks angry.

"Goddamn, Lindy, why d'you have to be so stubborn?" Before I can process what's happening, he has my arm and twists it up behind my back. "Now you're going to get a good close look," he snarls. "Don't say I didn't try to stop you." He pushes me ahead of him up over the edge and toward the corrals. I see Jake at the corral fence. He comes to meet us.

"You were supposed to keep her away from here," Jake says.

"You know her better than I do. Do you think you can stop her from doing anything?"

Jake shrugs and says, "short of hog tying her, no."

"You're hurting me," I hiss. "Let go of me!"

Dan relaxes his grip on my arm but doesn't release me.

"What are you going to do with her?" Jake asks.

Dan clicks his tongue and exhales audibly. "I don't know. Put her in the pen with her friend for now. I'll let Nick know we've got her, too. Let the Triad decide what to do with them."

"They're looking for us," I tell them. "There's a whole bunch of people looking for us. You won't get away with this!"

"Well, they're not going to look in Jake's hay barn, are they." It's not a question. "If they had anything on him, they wouldn't have let him go. Thanks for fingering him, by the way."

"I, er—"

"We wondered why they picked him up for questioning. Now we know. I imagine you'll have to do some penance for that clever little trick."

"So they know where I am."

"So they still have no probable cause for a search warrant. They'll question Jake again. He'll say he didn't see either of you. But they'll come to me first because you said I was going with you and your truck is at my place. I'll say I told you to wait until we could come back with the horses but you wouldn't listen. You wanted to go ahead while I went back to get the horses. I saw you cross the creek at the sandbar but when I came back on horseback I couldn't find you. I figured you must have met up with Felix and walked out, probably to wherever he left his truck. And his truck will never be found. Take her arm, Jake."

Jake takes my wrist in a vise-like grip, and Dan lets my arm down from behind my back but keeps a grip on it. Together they propel me along the corral fence toward the barn.

Leo and the other man stop what they're doing to watch. "Help me!" I yell. "Stop them! Don't let them take me!" Leo's face contorts into a smirk; the other man turns away to open the squeeze chute and let the cow out.

I was right. I now know who the rustlers are.

Who said knowledge is power? This knowledge might be a death sentence.

Thirty-Four

I 'M PROPELLED DEEP inside the building and thrown into a corral-type stall, barely getting my hands out in front of me in time to avoid a faceplant. When I'm on hands and knees, Jake squats beside me, grabs my arm and turns me to face him. Only now do I see Felix, apparently unconscious, slumped in the opposite corner. His face is so battered I don't know if he could see if he opened his eyes. His arms are behind him and I realize he's tied to the wall. Just as I'm about to be.

"What did you do to Felix?" I demand. "Jake, why are you doing this? You were like family. The boys...Red and Stu...they all love you. And all those nights we spent together—"

"Shut up!" he hisses.

"But you said you loved me! I know you meant it, at least at first—"

"I said, shut up!"

"He always tells them he loves them, don't you, Jake?" Dan says. "I bet he didn't wait longer than your second date to confess his love for you."

I think back. Yes, it was too early in our relationship, and at the time, I brushed it off.

"I'm sorry, Lindy," Dan continues, "this is my fault. I wouldn't have gotten involved, but when Norm saw you going into Jake's field that day, we thought you were spying on him. Stalking him because you couldn't accept being dumped. We couldn't take a chance on you stumbling on our, er, well, *this*. The Triad thought if you got involved with me you'd forget about him. My mistake was taking you to the creek. In my defence, I thought I'd get more than that one measly kiss. Besides, we didn't realize you weren't stalking Jake, you were actually looking for this. But, ahh, well! You're full of surprises."

"Let us go," I plead, trying to maintain eye contact with Jake. "Jake! We won't tell anyone. Felix fell and got hurt when he was hunting. I found him. End of story."

"Jesus, Lindy, do you think we're as gullible as you are?" Dan asks with a snort.

"What about Norm? He's going to wonder—"

"He's an Elder, fer chrissake," Dan says.

An Elder? Like in Hazel and Jerry's religion? What does that have to do with anything? I shake my head and force my thoughts on my immediate predicament. "Joe Little Child... And a bunch of Felix's friends are looking for us. They're good trackers and they're not stupid. Red told them I was suspicious of this place and she knows this is where I was coming to look for Felix. I don't think you're going to want to take them on." It's only partly true. They would be searching the ravine and wouldn't have a reason to come into Jake's yard looking for a deer hunter.

"Don't hold your breath, Lindy. Norm will have sent them south instead of north," Dan says. "They won't be coming this way."

"The cops will, though. I told them where I was going, too. They'll come, and with a search warrant this time!"

"You won't be here long enough."

Despite my kicking and flailing, Jake catches my wrist and tightens a rope around it, then reaches across behind me for my other arm. I struggle but he holds me easily and quickly has both wrists together. "A wrap 'n' a hooey, just like tie-down ropin'," he says, then chuckles. He fusses with another rope, feeding it through the stall boards, and loops it through between my wrists. He gets to his feet, joins Dan, and they leave the stall. The door swings shut and I hear the clunk of the bolt being thrown.

"I have to pee!" I call after them.

"I guess you'll have wet pants, then," Dan calls back. They laugh like it's the funniest thing they've heard in their lives.

Their laughter fades as they move away. I hear a diesel engine and the hiss of jake brakes. Someone yells, "Bull hauler's ready." After that, just whistling and dogs barking and steers bellowing, the usual sounds of cattle being loaded.

I squirm my arms, flip around, growl in frustration. Then I lean back against the rails and sob.

"Lindy," Felix says quietly.

"Oh, Felix! You're awake!"

"Yeah. Have been fer a while."

"How'd they get you?"

"Leo." He chuckles wryly. "He's tougher than he looks."

"You shouldn't have come up here."

"Didn't. I took a shot at that deer but the bullet must of hit a branch 'n' deflected. I was looking fer a way to cross the creek without getting completely soaked 'n' I guess Leo heard the shot. He come looking fer me. I hadda put the rifle down or he'd of shot me but when I did, he used his rifle butt on my face. If not fer that, I think I could of taken him." Another chuckle.

"It's not funny, Felix!

"It sure ain't," he agrees.

"You've been tied up in here since Wednesday?"

"Yeah."

"But..."

"They give me a drink once in a while. Untie my hands so I can eat a can of beans. And two of 'em take me to the outhouse. So if you can hold on, you prob'ly won't have to pee yer pants."

"Good to know," I agree, "but not my biggest concern at the moment."

"Yeah. Well, just so you know, if you try anything when they're takin' you fer a piss, they'll lay a beatin' on you."

"Oh. That's why you were out cold when they brought me in."

"Yeah."

"Bastards! I can't believe Jake would go along with it! He knows you. You've worked together."

"It's his kid. Leo's out of control, like a pyscho... um..."

"Psychopath."

"Yeah. It's like he enjoys it."

"Sadist."

"Yeah. You know he was in Juvie?"

"No. Jake never mentioned it. What did he do?"

"Dunno, but when he got out 'n' was back at school, you'd of thought he was a rock star. Had a following. Nasty bunch. Everyone was afraid of them."

"Seems like he hasn't improved." I close my eyes and mentally run through what happened to get me—us—here, and realize I'm totally to blame for Felix being so badly beaten. "I'm sorry," I say after a bit, and sigh.

"Not yer fault."

"Of course it is! Don't you dare let me off the hook like that! You know why your cousin says my middle name is Brutus? It's because that was the name of Arnie's rope horse. He was known to take the bit in his teeth and bolt and nothing would stop him. I always thought it was a compliment. I'm beginning to see it wasn't."

"I didn't have to come here, right into Leo's back yard, lookin' fer that buck."

"Anyway. I guess there's no use blaming blame. We're here. The question is, what can we do about it. There must be something."

When he doesn't reply I wonder if he's lost consciousness again. In the gloom of the stall, it's impossible to tell if his eyes are open.

Then he asks, "Did I hear him say somethin' 'bout tie-down ropin'?"

"Um, yeah. Like I'm no different than a calf."

"I wonder..." Felix says, and then is quiet again.

I think about it, then tell him, "I think his exact words were: *A wrap and a hooey, just like tie-down roping.*"

"A wrap 'n' a hooey? He didn't tie me like that! Not even two wraps? That's just about nuthin', Auntie! You can work yer hands outta that! Keep tryin'."

"It feels pretty tight," I tell him, pulling at the ropes as best I can.

"You been to rodeos, you seen how many calves get loose on their own? They only gotta stay tied fer six seconds. 'N' he'd only use a single wrap on a calf he didn't think was very strong. Just relax, then jiggle. Relax, 'n' jiggle. It might come loose."

"He wouldn't tie me up with a knot that could come loose that easily."

"He would, if he didn't want you to stay tied."

"Like, he wanted to give me a chance to get away?"

"Maybe. What I don't get is why he would say how he tied you, with the other guy right there."

"Hmm. Well, Dan isn't a cowboy, not really. Just a city slicker who bought a ranch. He might've said it thinking I'd know but Dan wouldn't. Although with all that's going on, I doubt he's that decent. Grrrr!" I growl and keep squirming, trying to pull first one wrist and then the other out of the rope.

"We all liked him, remember. He must of liked us, too. You especially."

"With friends like that, who needs enemies, right?"

I squirm with renewed vigor. It seems to be working. I relax and discover it's definitely working. The next pull and I realize my wrists aren't tight against each other any more. Another few minutes of twisting and squirming my arms and the rope holding my wrists comes loose. It takes me a second to realize I'm free.

"I'm loose!" I exclaim.

"Ssshhh!" Felix says. "They could be close."

I take a deep breath and realize he's right. I crawl across the stall to him, and matching his low tone, say, "Let's get you untied."

He leans forward so I can access the rope holding him. He's right, it's a different knot. And it's tight. I start to work on it.

"You still got that little knife in yer pocket?" he asks.

"The knife?"

"Or—maybe you don't keep it on you."

I'd forgotten about my Swiss Army knife. When did I last empty the pockets to wash these jeans? Don't even know for sure when I last got dressed, much less when I washed them. I straighten up and shove my right hand into my pocket. I could practically cry when my fingers close around the knife. I pull it out and open it.

"This little gadget might be good for something after all." I slide the blade between Felix's skin and the rope and start to saw.

Just then I hear muffled voices, then make out Dan telling someone he's going to check on us before he goes to retrieve his truck. Through the planks of the stall front I see him silhouetted in the man door. He slams the door behind him. I have barely enough time to scurry to where I'm supposed to be before he crosses the open space and is at the stall door.

"We're fine," I assure him. "You go on and get your damn truck."

He swings the door open and stands, arms akimbo, grinning at me. "Your little buddy doesn't look fine."

"No thanks to your friends."

He comes into the stall and kneels beside me. "You know, you never gave me more than a couple of kisses. Even though you were just a job, I liked it. I should have gotten more out of it. I earned more." He takes my shirt front and pulls, popping the snaps open.

"Ahh," he says, and sighs. "Not much to see, is there? Anyhow, any more'n a mouthful's wasted." He reaches inside my bra.

"Bugger off," I squawk. It takes all my willpower to keep my hands behind me and stay still so he doesn't realize I'm no longer bound.

"Okay, sure," Dan says. "I'm really more interested in what's in your pants, anyway." He unzips my jeans and starts working them down.

"Stop it! Dan, for the love of god, don't do this!"

"You'll like it. Don't worry."

"No, I won't like it! You're going to go to jail for this! Quit before you do something you'll really regret."

"No one's going to jail. You're going to Pillerton to join the other Children of Noah wives, and believe me, I'll be the most desirable of all your new husbands."

"Gaaah! Get off me!" I screech, and squirm away from him. He cocks his head and frowns as he realizes I'm not tied.

His hands close around my throat and he growls, "Well now, how did you manage that? Doesn't matter. Maybe it's more fun this way anyhow." He's choking me with one hand while he works my jeans down with the other. He wrenches the waistband of my jeans with enough strength to lift me off the ground.

"Stop it! You're hurting me!" I'm trying to scream but he's pushing my neck back against the boards and squeezing my throat so hard I can barely breathe. It seems as if the light is fading and my vision is becoming blurred. I hear Felix yelling something. There's a sort of buzzing in my ears and everything seems far away. I have felt this way once before, when I fainted. I realize I have one chance before I pass out. I bring the knife up and ram it into his flank. Hot blood sprays over me. He makes a gurgling *gaah!* sound and collapses over me. I kick and squirm to roll him off.

I gasp for air, then collect myself and scurry to Felix. My hand and the knife slippery with blood, I manage to saw away at the ropes. It seems like it takes forever before they spring free.

"Are you okay, Felix? Can you walk okay?" I ask as I help him to his feet and fix my pants.

"Yeah. Might be slow but..."

"Here, let me help." I loop his arm over my shoulder and we start for the door.

Dan groans, squirms and rolls onto his back. He puts his hand over his wound and gasps. "Lindy! Don't leave me! I need a doctor!"

"Tell it to your friends."

"They're gone. They won't be back for hours."

I stop and look at him, lying there in the dirt, blood seeping through his fingers. He definitely needs a doctor, but the blade is less than three inches long so I'm sure that stab wound is survivable even if he doesn't get help for a while. Felix is looking at me, no doubt wondering if I'm really gullible enough to help my attacker and risk our own freedom.

I'm not.

"Good to know," I say, and turn away.

By now Felix can walk without my help, and we make our way to the open end of the building, holding up when we get to the end of the wall. Although Dan said the others were gone and wouldn't be back for hours, I peer around the corner. There's no activity.

"Do you believe him?" Felix asks. "Did they really all leave?"

I shake my head. "No way of knowing. Could've just said that so we'd relax our guard."

"That's what I was thinkin'."

"Best we go ahead on the assumption they're going to come after us," I conclude.

Felix gives a sharp nod of agreement; we head for the ravine, wondering if we'll get far enough away before we're discovered missing. I heave a sigh when we're over the bank, out of sight from anyone up in the yard.

Felix is lagging and I wonder how badly those beatings have injured him. I stop to give him a breather, and ask, "What time did they bring you that can of beans?"

"Uhh, I guess whenever they thought of it."

"So no way of knowing when to expect them, then," I conclude.

"Prob'ly soon, though."

Already the sun is dipping below the horizon and the shadows in the ravine are lengthening. "You okay to go on now?" I ask, even though there's no choice.

"Uhh, yeah."

We haven't gotten far when we hear excited voices coming from behind us.

"The bastard!" I mutter. "They won't be back for hours, my ass!"

I make out Jake's voice, now apparently in command, directing someone to get the ATV and go to where the trucks are parked. Does this mean they're going to wait for us there and give up chasing after us? I turn to look. No such luck. Leo and the other man are both coming down the bank. We're too slow.

"We have to cross the creek, Felix, and quick," I say. "Wait until we're around that dog's leg so they can't see us do it. Think you can manage?"

He nods. He's too pale. I hope he has enough strength to push through.

When we're a few meters around the bend, we leave the trail. The ground is the gravelly here, and the bank is steep enough we slip and slide as we make our way down to the creek. Here the water is running fast. I step off the bank to start across. Felix doesn't follow.

"Come on, Felix!"

"I can't swim, Auntie."

There's a complication I didn't expect. I reach up to take his hand and tell him, "It's not that deep. We can wade across. Together. Grab my belt." He steps down into the creek beside me. I latch on to the back of his jeans. When he's done likewise to me, we start across.

We're halfway across when the bottom falls out from under us and we both submerge. Felix loses his grip on my belt but I tighten my grip on his; we bob to the surface, to be swept along a few hundred meters. Soon the creek widens and flattens and we're able to touch bottom again.

The far bank is undercut by the rushing water and is about two feet above the level of the creek. We grab the overhanging willows and I manage to pull myself up. Felix is still struggling. I take his upper arm and pull. He scrambles up and crawls in under the bushes beside me.

I'm on all fours, pushing branches out of the way to crawl out, when I realize Felix has turned over onto his back and is still prone less than a couple of body lengths from the creek, eyes closed, his breathing laboured. I hunch down beside him and say, "We're pretty well concealed here, Felix. I think it's all right for us to rest, at least for a while. Are you hurting anywhere?" Stupid question. He's probably hurting everywhere. But I want him to talk. "Your face? Do you have a headache? How about your legs? Can you still walk okay?"

"My, uhh, shoulder."

Now I notice the lump near his shoulder that shouldn't be there. My god! He's either got a dislocated shoulder or a broken collar bone. Couple that with being tied to a wall for days and eating only a can of beans now and then, not to mention the probable concussion, and it's a wonder he managed to stay with me.

"You're really badly hurt! Why didn't you tell me?"

He sighs, or maybe it's a groan. He starts to shiver. "You go."

"I'm not leaving you," I tell him. In wet clothes on top of his serious injury then the pain he must have been going through to get this far, I worry he's going into shock.

"But maybe... Without me you can... get to my truck."

"Felix! It's not open for discussion." Get to his truck? He's obviously not thinking clearly. I don't want him to black out so I try to keep him talking. "We're not going downstream, or try to get to the truck. They'll be expecting that. In fact, they're probably already there. Right?"

"Ahhh...."

I continue: "We're going upstream, and then we'll strike out west, to the monument, and hopefully, flag someone down there." It looks like going anywhere might be beyond him at the moment, but I don't want him thinking he's putting us both at risk. "We can rest and gather our strength. We're safe here for now."

His breathing slows.

"Felix? Felix?" He doesn't respond. I'm not sure if he's out cold or just sleeping but there doesn't seem to be much I can do about it.

I lie down beside him and gather him into a hug as best I can without causing more pain, in an attempt to warm him. It'll be risky going over the rough terrain in the dark, but the twilight won't last much longer anyway and maybe it's wise to wait for moonrise.

I'll let him sleep for an hour.

Thirty-Five

I BECOME AWARE of the sound of running water. Insects are buzzing in the branches around us and somewhere not too far off, a meadowlark sings. I awake in a panic. It'll soon be sunrise. I hadn't meant to fall asleep at all, much less sleep through the night.

When I open my eyes I see Felix watching me, his face just inches from mine. His colour is better but still unhealthy, about like dirty wash water. I squirm to release him from what in other circumstances would be an inappropriate aunt embrace. "You're awake," I say, pointing out the obvious.

"Yeah," he says.

"How do you feel? Think we can make it to the monument?"

"Yeah. Best sleep I've had in days," he says, and grins. "Always wanted to sleep with an older woman."

"Don't you dare tell anyone we slept together," I scold.

"You know we're not actually related," he says.

"What?" I draw a quick breath. "Don't be an ass! No time for joking around. We have to get going. Right after I pee." I crawl out from under the low shrubs, stand and walk far enough that Felix can't see me, to take care of business. Then I go to the grassy area near the top of the ravine and scan the area for pursuers while I wait for him. He comes out of the bushes, spots me, and with his hand inside his shirt to stabilize his injured arm, comes up to join me. His colour has improved a bit more. Maybe it's just that he's already flushed with the exertion of the climb.

"Don't overdo it. If you need a rest, for god's sake tell me. I don't want you passing out."

He agrees. We climb up out of the ravine and strike out across the rolling prairie, keeping the rising sun on our backs. In what seems like all morning but is probably only a couple of hours, we come over a slight rise and see the road a few hundred meters off, just on the other side of a small band of horses. I'm flooded with relief.

No sooner do I let out a breath than I realize the horses are nervous, standing statue still, ears pricked. They aren't looking our way. I turn to see what they're watching so intently. Two riders. One on a pinto, the white in its coat gleaming in the morning sun.

Damn! They already figured out we crossed the creek, and it didn't take them long to spot us. I'm suddenly aware of how exposed we are. The quiet is shattered by the loud *crack!* of a rifle shot. The horses spook and gallop away, parting to go around us.

Felix is wearing his camouflage hunting clothes but I'm in my favourite red paisley shirt. For anyone with the intent, I'm an easy target out here on the sun-bleached grass of the open prairie. And apparently, they have the intent.

"They might hit a horse!" I exclaim. "Or us!"

"No at this distance," Felix says. "Dunno why he took a shot."

"Can you run?"

"Not faster than a horse," he says.

"If we can make it to the fence..."

We start running. Even wounded as he is, Felix keeps up and we get to the fence while the horses are still a good distance away. Felix can't stretch the wires apart one handed so I do it to let him climb through, then he holds the top wire up for me. My shirt snags on a barb but rather than taking the time to release it, I just throw my weight at it. The cloth rips but I'm through.

We dash through the ditch and up across the road. Our pursuers are close enough now we can hear the hoofbeats. We can go into the field across the road, but there's no cover there. We'd be sitting ducks until we could run far enough to be out of range again. And at the speed the horses are coming, we won't make it.

"Get down!" I hiss, and we dive to lie prone in the dirt and weeds, the roadway providing a barricade. "If they've got wire cutters, we're dead," I whisper. Why am I whispering? They know where we are.

The hoofbeats stop at the fence and Dan calls, "Come out, come out, wherever you are!" He laughs. A creak of wire alerts me to the fact one of them has dismounted and is climbing through the fence.

"Didn't need wire cutters," Felix says.

Of course they didn't. I was more worried about being shot than of being caught again. No escape now. They win. Question is, will they take us to wherever it was they planned to before we escaped, in my case to join the wives in Pillerton, or just shoot us where we are?

Felix looks ashen, and I realize although he started the morning quite strong, the trek has taken its toll, and that sprint to the road drained the last of his energy.

"I'm sorry, Felix. I'm so sorry I got you into this." I get to my feet without waiting for a reply and step up onto the road, where Dan comes to meet me. He left his rifle on his saddle but Jake is still on his horse, rifle pointing my way.

I gather my pride, stand tall and straight and say, "You look a little pale, Dan. Not feeling so good this morning?" I ask. I notice a red spot the size of a tennis ball on his shirt and point to it. "Thought you would've got that stitched up. Looks like you sprung a leak."

He presses his hand to the wound, then pulls it away to see it's bloodied. "That little jab didn't do me any good, Lindy, but I'm a god-fearing man and I'll forgive you."

"Yeah, well, don't bother. I'm just sorry I only gave you one little jab."

Felix comes out of the ditch to stand beside me, swaying slightly. I reach to steady him but Dan grabs my arm and jerks me away.

"Don't try anything if you don't want your face messed up more than it already is," Dan warns him, then says to me, "Glad the knife wasn't any bigger. If you'd used a pig sticker like the one we took off him, you might have really hurt me."

Of course if my knife was that big they wouldn't have let me keep it. I look at Felix again, worried he might be close to losing consciousness, when my attention is drawn to a cloud of dust on the road about half a mile away. A vehicle, coming this way! How long before it gets here? I force my attention on Jake. "Thanks for the poor job you did of tying me up, Jake," I call out. "I guess you wanted me to get away."

"Don't worry," Dan says, "The Triad are going to speak to him about that. I'm not pleased he took that shot when we were so far out of range, either. You'd almost think he wanted you to notice we were coming for you. You won't be the only one doing penance." He makes a sort of *tsk* sound, and shakes his head. "I should've been assigned to you in the first place. At least I'm not married. But he's the one who's still got a loan to work off."

"You're married, Jake? To Martine, I imagine?"

"If it's any consolation, he kept going back to you weeks after he was told to stand down. Martine's pissed at how much time he spent with you after you signed the loan document," Dan replies. "It has caused problems in his marriage."

"Oh, that's too bad," I gush. "Does this asshole speak for you, Jake?"

"He's a man of few words," Dan explains. "Let's get going." He takes my arm to frog march me along. I plant my feet but despite his injury, he's strong and pushes me hard enough I have to scramble to keep from falling.

"Hey, Dan! There's a, er, looks like there's a bus comin'," Jake calls, and slides his rifle into its scabbard.

Dan looks up the road in the direction Jake is pointing.

Felix collapses.

Dan exclaims, "Fuck!"

The approaching bus is like nothing I've seen before: tall, white with blacked out windows. There's what looks like Chinese lettering on the side. It stops a few yards away and the driver slides the window open.

I struggle to get out of Dan's grasp but he's strong enough to hold me. He can't force me to move, though, not with my feet planted. He'd have to drag me. And leaving Felix in a heap at the side of the road is bound to raise questions.

Dan comes to that conclusion about the same time I do. He releases my wrist, looping an arm around my shoulder and covering my mouth with his hand as he pushes me with enough force I can't stop myself from taking a few steps. Now the two of us are near enough to Felix it might look like we're rendering aid. He turns to put his body between us and the bus driver. I see the dimple in his cheek that forms when he smiles. How did I ever think that little dimple was sexy?

"Hello. I think miss sign. Is Cypress Hills Massacre on this road?" His English is heavily accented. Maybe not Chinese, but definitely oriental.

"Yeah, just about a mile further on," Dan says. "We'll get out of your way just as soon as we help our friend up."

I'm not going to let dozens of witnesses get away, and struggle so he has to use both arms to hold me. The instant his hand is off my mouth I scream. He recovers quickly, cutting my scream short by slapping his other hand over my mouth. Not completely over. I open my mouth, get a hold of some part of his hand and bite down as hard as I can. I taste blood.

"Agggh!" he exclaims, and jerks his hand away. Suddenly I'm free. "Help!" I yell.

I start crying and collapse next to Felix.

Thirty-Six

FELIX COMES IN the door and up to the bakery counter where I'm putting a new batch of saskatoon muffins into the display case.

"Hey," I say. "You look about one hundred percent! How's the ribs?"

"Ninety-nine percent, anyhow. Still a little sore. Least I don't have to sleep sittin' up no more. It's my shoulder that gives me the most grief. 'N' I've never had headaches like what I've been gittin.'"

"Yeah, from your concussion, I guess. And a dislocation with massive torn ligaments like that takes a while to heal." I slide the door closed and smile. Although the bruises on his face are fading and the swelling from his shattered orbital bone has gone down, and even though the bump from his nose being broken isn't huge, his face will never be as beautiful as before. It doesn't seem to bother him, though, and he still has flocks of girls after him.

"Where's your buckle bunnies today?" I tease.

"Guess they gave up. Hope so."

"Oh yeah? You're a one woman man now?"

"You know I am."

"I do," I agree, and nod. "Want something?"

"Just, uhh, a coffee 'n' a couple of them little rat turds."

I get a small paper plate and use tongs to get the two biggest mini-meat pies from the bin, hand the plate to him and say, "On the house. You know to help yourself to coffee. I'll see if Lucy can take a break and join you."

"That's great. Thanks," he says, and goes to the end of the counter where we have the self-serve coffee and tea things set out.

I go back into the kitchen where Lucy is taking another tray of muffins out of the oven. "Felix is here," I tell her. "Why don't you go on your break now? I can take care of the rest of this batch."

Lucy's face lights up and she says, "Thanks!" She wipes her hands on her apron and goes out to the customer area to join her new boyfriend.

When I have the current batch of muffins out of the oven and on a cooling rack, Marcy tells me she's putting pies in next and doesn't need either me or Red, so we leave the kitchen, get our own coffees, and join the young couple.

"Stu around?" Felix asks when we're settled. "I wanted to see him 'bout comin' back to work before Joe takes over my job in the wine room fer good. I think I can manage at least a short shift."

"Well, that's good news, but don't worry. There's enough work around here fer both of you. When Stu calls home, I'll tell him yer back. You know the process 'n' can teach Joe. Might give him an extra day or two before he has to come home," Red says.

"He's not home?"

"No. He and Russ're headed south for some big money bull riding thing," I tell him. "Imagine! Not a real rodeo, nothing but bull riding, the craziest damn event in rodeo! In Vegas, yet."

"Oh, the big show the Professional Bull Riders is puttin' on. I fergot about that. Drummin' up more buyers fer Domino's semen?"

"That's right. Goddamn stuff is like gold all of a sudden."

"Because that son of his got moved up in the PBR ratings, I guess. Great news," Felix says.

"Sure is. It'll help get us back on our feet."

"Well, I got news, too," Felix tells us. "You knew them crooked money guys took yer herd to Baxter's, right?"

I nod. It's the reason he didn't want me helping with that down cow or checking the rest of the herd for symptoms. Hearing his name provokes a slow but very intense burn. It must show on my face, because Felix says, "Don't worry, Auntie, yer gonna like this. I ran into Eric Boyko at the Husky just now."

"The president of the Cattleman's Association?"

"That's right. So, Baxters had a cow come down with mad cow disease. Hadda destroy the whole herd. Sonofabitch claimed it wasn't his cow, that it was Jordan's. I guess there was some mixing of their cows. So Jordan's herd hadda be destroyed, too, 'n' he had such a bunch goin' through his operation, they'll be busy tracing everything fer a while."

"Oh my god!" I hate to think of all those beautiful animals destroyed for nothing but at least the villains who gave us all that grief have paid a price. As for Jake, Leo and Dan, and Norm too of course, I hope they can't sleep, worrying about their upcoming court dates. They might still try for a plea deal, especially if they're tied to that murder, but they'd have to rat out Nick Reeves and Gabe Richardson and who knows how many others that rank above them. I doubt they'd do that, so they will probably take the fall.

"It's like they say, Felix," Red says, "the chickens have came home to roost. Did you know Lindy was back at work? 'N' they paid her for the whole time she was off? The gal who fixed the records to make it look like Lindy was up to no good is in trouble. They charged her with somethin'. It was them same damn money guys put her up to it."

"Yeah. A few unexplained deposits in her account. And she was fired on the spot," I say. "It's sad, though. She was so close to retirement. I don't know if she'll be okay."

"She was a burr under yer saddle the whole time you worked there, 'n' you feel sorry fer her?" Red asks.

I shrug. Do I feel sorry for her? There are moments when I do. I glance out the window and see the tall white bus with the Japanese logo on the road, slowing as it approaches our driveway. "Tour bus is here," I say.

"Well, back to work," Red announces. She gets to her feet and scurries off back into the kitchen.

I get up too, and tell Lucy, "You can take your break later, Lucy. We're going to need you on the floor now. Don't worry. With Felix getting back to work, he'll be around so much you'll be sick of him."

He looks at her as if she's the sun and the moon, and the way her eyes are glowing as he takes her hand and gives it a squeeze, I rather doubt it. It reminds me of how I felt when I was with Nick. I wonder if I'll ever have that feeling again. I realize it doesn't matter if I don't. I'm lucky to have had it once.

Oddly enough, the gut-wrenching angst and profound sadness I usually experience when I think of Nick doesn't come. The memory of him, his silly grin, his goofy tricks, his gentle loving, feels like a blessing.

Everyone says grief lasts a year. Maybe it never really ends, but instead, changes from a caterpillar eating away at your heart into a butterfly to brighten your unguarded memories.

I think now it'll be true when I tell Red I'm okay on my own.

www.ingramcontent.com/pod-product-compliance
Lightning Source LLC
Chambersburg PA
CBHW052021020726
47501CB00004B/1171